In 1813 the United States and Nathan Jeffries fight for their lives. Son of a dissolute naval hero and a Quaker beauty, Nathan has barely survived the first six months of the war.

Now the country and Nathan face terror and death on land and sea. Fighting both the wrathful British and the powerful, sadistic Michael Fredericks, Nathan finds himself hunter and hunted in a brutal world of betrayal. It will take superhuman effort and luck to even survive at this great turning point for Nathan and his country!

DEATH OF CAPTAIN LAWRENCE. "DON'T GIVE UP THE SHIP." PAINTED BY ALONZO CHAPPEL.
ENGRAVED BY H.B. HALL

For Shelley

Published by Capstan Communications, Annapolis MD

ISBN-13: 978-1493564293
ISBN-10: 1493564293

Printed in the United States

Cover image "The Battle of Lake Erie." Painted by Julian Oliver Davidson. Courtesy of thebluewhale.tumblr.com. Inside front page images from wikimedia commons.

1813: Reprisal

BERT J. HUBINGER

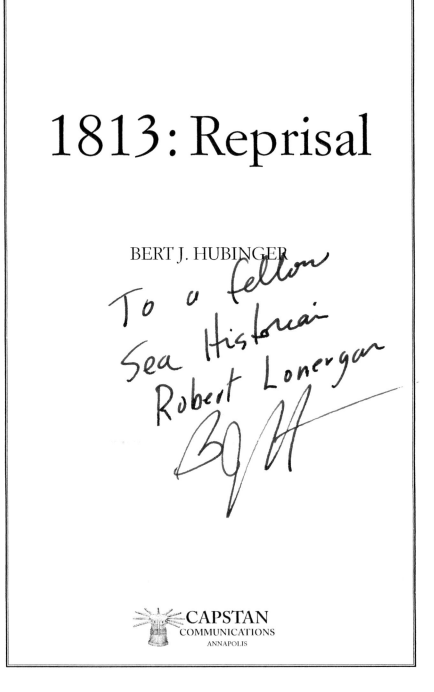

To a fellow
Sea Historian
Robert Lonergan

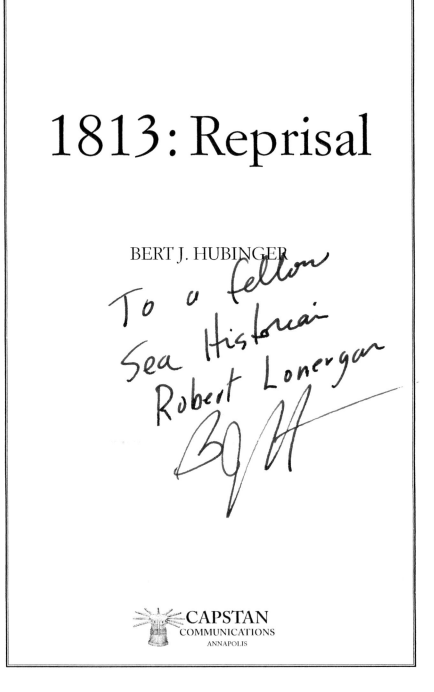

CAPSTAN
COMMUNICATIONS
ANNAPOLIS

Acknowledgments

To Carol Callahan, Susan Kosisky and Caroline Kosisky

ONE

Homeward bound to Baltimore - *January 23, 1813*

60 days so far on this cruise. Aboard approx. 100,000 pounds in specie and valuable cargo. Course NE by N. Sunrise clear, now partly cloudy. Wind freshening. Martinique still visible to the south, Dominica Channel 14 deg. 54 min. N 59 deg. 00 min. W.

N. Jeffries, master of privateer schooner Merlin

AT 5:30, NATHAN WAS on the quarterdeck again, pacing, growling, imperious, pompous. Dawn would be at about 6 AM, and he could already imagine the sky lightening, with the sails of the British *Medusa* to the southeast. That would spell their doom. Their captain would show no mercy now. Back up on the quarterdeck, the glittering sunrise scattered its silver and gold across the sea, expanding from the horizon. *100,000 pounds in the hold!* A fantastic sum, a sea of silver and gold, more than half of a million dollars, beckoning a new life (what was left of his life) in the Promised Land after so much loss: he was now 21 years of age. As captain his share would be at least 10,000 U.S. dollars—a lifetime of work in most occupations, in one cruise! By early spring he would see his father, and Catherine, and a few friends, with his share. A new life, at least, for those whom he must care for, a small and dwindling group. Nathan knew he would remain a pariah, continue to receive hateful looks, but at least he would be a wealthy pariah.

That was a word he had learned from Peter Hughes. Pariah. Peter was another bitter loss, now allied with the British. With a vast and life-altering sum from his first real cruise as captain, Nathan knew he should feel triumphant; but he could trust nothing after losing his father's beloved *Bucephalus* to the *Scourge* back in '11, then joining Turner and the brave friends in arms of the brig *Cormorant*, only be "pressed" aboard *Guerriere*, beaten in turn by Auster and Coxe, and then saved by "Old Ironsides." And then, *Cormorant* disappeared, presumably lost with all hands presumably, and Nathan survived without his friends, his faith, and finally his mother, Amy Jeffries, the blood, bone and sinew of his life. All gone.

All except the killer instinct once shown by his father, William, now a broken drunk. Nathan had also killed. He felt sickened by his actions, although he was proud that he had taken no civilian life, and inflicted few civilian injuries, from his attacks on enemy merchant ships and adventures in all those islands. The West Indies were a slave-owner's paradise, mostly run by British and French governors whose loyalty only extended as far as the beaches of their coral-shoaled islands. The reds and yellows of the reefs delighted him, but the greed of the slave-owners, the misery of their property—sickening and yet profitable. And of course, he reminded himself, there are still many days ahead and *Merlin* must remain prepared for any and all hazards.

But their fortune was homeward bound, possibly as soon as his mother's birthday in February. The real price was four of his men, dead and buried at sea, with the fate of his cartel ship, the *Elizabeth*, her own precious cargo and all the prisoners still unknown. A dozen bad wounds when they took the ship, three who would probably not recover, one who had lost his arm. Little Jason, son of Enoch Earleigh, William Jeffries' closest friend, would not lose his leg; the wound was clean and did not smell, just a big, healthy scar from the puncture. Jason and his other favorite crew including Jack Logan he sent home on the *Elizabeth*. Thanks to First Mate Thompson's fastidious attention to detail, not one serious case of yellow fever or scurvy was left. The amputation of Parkman's arm had probably saved his life; sometimes Thompson was right. But there was still much to do, treacherous reefs and currents to contend with. Nathan begrudged every further delay in a strange harbor and the risks of further infection on the long final crawl up the Chesapeake to reap substantial profits for 1813.

But now Nathan Jeffries, master and commander of the privateer *Merlin,* could hardly believe that he and his crew were about to break out into the Atlantic, free men—and rich. A vast fortune safely stowed, cargo consisting of an amazing assortment of goods, not counting more than 18,000 pounds in the gold and silver coin, notes on the Bank of London and Lloyd's—just six months after sister-ship *Rossie,* under Commodore Barney, returned with half a million pounds profit for the owners. By this time the British blockade ran in earnest from Chesapeake down to Trinidad. His "Letter of Marque and Reprisal for privateer Merlin, Master N. Jeffries and crew thereof," signed by President James Madison, certified that costs and risks were all his and the ship's owners. And that every man aboard was in their charge. Their adventures had led to a hold filled with enough doubloons, guineas, crowns and pieces of eight. They captured firearms including eight carronades, 1000 flints, lead, powder (mostly from Antigua), Dublin pistols (.65 caliber), four sets of Wogden dueling pistols, like the ones that killed Alexander Hamilton, two crates of British navy cutlasses with boarding axes, a gross of New Land Pattern .65 holster pistols, seven stand of well-used .75 Brown Bess muskets and revolutionary new Baker breech-loading rifles—even a dozen flintlock pistols from Belgium. And that was all without mentioning the seven pipes of Madeira, ten firkins of gin, bags and bottles inside barrels with sugar, pepper, molasses, indigo, nutmeg, cocoa, rum, cinnamon and ginger—exotic spices commanding prices by weight like gold at the quay.

When they had reached San Juan, outward bound, Nathan had decided, against First Mate Thompson's advice, to trade the entire remaining store of salt cod, timber and grain for the precious and sometimes illicit cargo available there. They had stood into Dominica, Guadeloupe, Grenada, Martinique, Santiago, for some additional cane. They had spoken, or hailed and conversed with a Dutch bark. And then *Merlin* cut a swathe of profitable destruction through the British merchant ships in the Caribbean, all the way down to Castillo de San Marcos. Sighting El

Morro in San Juan. Their cutting-out raid on Barbados was the single biggest haul, according to Mister Thompson, also an expert in specie and all supercargo matters.

Soon they would sink all land, and make for due north, giving the Antilles a wide berth. Maybe Amy could look down and, seeing his "success," forgive his many failures. Even the haughty Catherine would be impressed. Nathan felt only hate now for the British, especially the navy. The affable Captain Hull and his crew had saved him, but he had failed to avenge himself against Richard Auster—Barbara Steward had to do that for him.

"Cap'n," the bosun, Conor, barked, shaking him out of his reanimate misery. "Mister Thompson he say we should—"

Nathan turned and shouted. "Harris, ease that lift! Hoist the topsail and brace together! Tom, keep a better eye on those maintop men!"

"Aye, sir," shouted the bosun's mate with exaggerated patience.

"Cap'n, beggin' pardon, Sir!" Conor roared again relentlessly in his ear. "Mr. Thompson sent three more men from the foretop! He says we got to lower the topmasts for some bad Atlantic weather—those shoals are just a few miles under our lee."

"Mister Thompson!" Nathan yelled, storming forward. They knew the routine, the remaining crew aboard. This time giving Antigua a wide berth, they hope to reach the Atlantic and skirt the Bahamas, and if the weather held, find no friends of the British or Napoleon. After nine narrow escapes, the crew were in awe —Ol' Nate could do no wrong. Their faith in him terrified this young man who would constantly dream of disaster whenever he allowed himself a few hours' sleep.

Even life before '07 resonated with a vast, restless guilt: William Jeffries ranting about the navy's lost opportunities to make *guerre de course* work against the British in 1807—with the help of the privateers, of course. "Don't you touch her—you have disgraced the Friends!" Nathan would shout when William got violent. And Amy's love turned, too. "You have also disgraced the Quakers, my son," she would whisper. And then periodically of course the nightmare of drowning, under Archibald Coxe, sometimes Richard Auster himself, with nobody else aware that he was dying.

Nathan had never let his mind wander so on deck. Thompson now stood by the foremast pinrail. Nathan strode up to his first mate and said quietly, "Mister Thompson, I thought I had made it very clear in my cabin that you were not to change sail without my permission."

"Sir, the foretopmast is sprung!"

"The new one we just traded for extra hemp and Madeira?"

"Yes, sir—maybe they got the best of that one."

My God, thought Nathan, is that in mockery?

A voice from aloft shouted down, "Sir, we're ready to drop the topgallant."

"Belay that order!" Nathan bellowed.

But then Thompson made up for it, as he always did. "I am sorry I didn't talk to you first, Captain," said his second-in-command loudly, over the crew, blocks, rigging and whitecaps, setting up for some weather to test their stowing of the last casks and extra spars below.

"What I want you to do, Mister Thompson—"

"Meantime may I locate a possible replacement? Iron is ready."

Nathan grinned in spite of himself. "This for the afternoon watch, weather permitting," he replied, trying to sound stern.

"Aye, Captain," said Thompson. As usual Nathan could not tell from his expression if this annoyingly competent man was happy or angry or feeling anything.

In a few hours, with the deck crowded, hammers would bang, capstan groan and blocks creak as a better topgallant was set up; and tarring mixed with the smell of pine and oak from the fresh-cut timber, would as always remind Nathan of his father's shipyard. The southeast-erly breeze would just enable them to claw close-hauled to the north-east—sinking Martinique's volcanic peak in their wake. If the wind veered to the north, they might have to make for Mona Passage, near Santo Domingo, where his first lover Maria Santiago was supposed to be. That would extend their run, but this early in the season the delay would probably be insignificant. If the wind did back to the south, it would help speed them outside the Bahamas.

Nathan recalled that Catherine had told him about the Philadelphia contingent, Beatrice Charles and the other rich creatures, the mysterious new major owner of what remained of Auster Shipping, Michael Fredericks. Catherine told him a great deal, but not nearly enough about what happened to who and why they would prefer it that way. Not a fond farewell. Nathan had signed everything over to his father as a kind of punishment—and most of that was now tied up in *Merlin's* cruise.

"Goodbye, Father," Nathan had saluted stiffly, "I hope you feel more disposed to speak when I return."

William Jeffries had scowled, then sneered and said nothing.

Catherine had briefly frowned and then shaken out her lovely dark hair. Nathan bowed deeply to her but with some sincerity, "Many thanks, Catherine . . . for all you have done."

She curtsied sweetly, smiling with those thin, curved lips. "Godspeed, Nathan. We shall miss you."

Tearing his eyes away from the whites of her eyes and teeth gleaming from her dark face, he had stared as he closed the door on the foundering drunk who had been the great hero Captain William Jeffries, U.S. Navy. "Thanks for nothing," Nathan bitterly thought, "except for advanced lessons in drinking."

Nathan knew that he had some mysterious benefactor who put up his share for the investment—$1,000—so that Nathan now presided over a remarkable cruise in command of *Merlin*. The crew, a handful, particularly one muscular sea lawyer, were hand-picked. Thompson was a true jack-of-all-trades, but in many ways he remained a stranger like many aboard. And *Merlin's* crew had performed brilliantly, every one—but no one could ever replace the crew aboard *Cormorant*. Especially her master, his beloved older friend and mentor Captain Turner, who had been a nobler replacement for Nathan's own father, now lost and unworthy of further infatuation. Nathan realized regretfully that no one could replace the all-knowing but still much beloved and admired Peter Hughes, now his blood enemy; "gone red," he had heard at Ram's Head, from the owner himself, Albert Highgate. But back to entrancing, young Miss Charles. Passion destroys life, Nathan realized now. Turner had been the greatest person in his life, except for his mother, Amy. All gone, and only an empty horizon.

"Sail ho!"

TWO

Fell's Point - *January 23, 1813*

Small front parlor of the Jeffries home at Thames and Hanover, near the heavily-trafficked briny basin.

CATHERINE CHARLES OPENED the front door and let the sunny afternoon enter the dimly lit house accompanied by the constant shriek of wind or wheel or rigging, and elusive odors in the breeze, some alluring, some most emphatically not—though the Patapsco mouth is not so bustling as it had been in 1812.

"The fools!" Captain William Jeffries was shouting to no one from his wheeled chair. "They still refuse to send every small armed craft possible to sea. The British will soon raid towns up and down the coast, and strangle all of our shipping—tightening the blockade with more brigs, frigates, ships of the line, from Maine to Florida."

"William, you are talking to yourself again," Catherine interrupted.

"Amy—Catherine! Must that man skulk about?"

From his chair edging the Tripoli oval rug, William Jeffries glanced around nervously at the implacable, impassive and massive black man standing near the hearth in the next room. William's expression reminded Catherine of an old woman. His mental failure since Nathan left had lately begun to alarm as well as sadden her. This man, Nathan's father, had once been a great man, now father of one of the best men she had ever known, despite the difficulties.

"'That man'? William, remember, Doctor Amos Anderson helped

save your life."

"When is Nathan getting back?" William asked. "Where is—"

"It is all right, William. Nathan will return soon, and we will square away."

"Amy—Catherine, you are . . . a dear . . . daughter; where is—is the ship ready to sail?"

"William, Enoch and the *Bucephalus* are gone, as you know, but I assure you Nathan is alive and well, and we are so proud of him, except—"

"Except . . . why did he leave us," said William, calmly, suddenly coherent. "Do we love him?"

"You promised not to—"

"Yes, yes, of course," said the captain, somehow, with his head sheepishly down, both mocking and apologetic. He was irritable and grateful over the prolonged presence of Catherine Charles, who most emphatically tried to enliven the house—but of course, most of the life had gone out of the Jeffries house when Amy died. Catherine had saved both men, this woman who had belonged to Richard Auster, himself now ruined finally, even as he paid the ultimate price for betraying his lover.

Men insisted that Catherine was hysterical, demented, dangerous. Once-legendary hero Naval Captain William Jeffries, now resentful, guilty, ashamed, drunk, disgraced, lost and lonely himself, was yet determined to save his son no matter how much it irritated Nathan. William Jeffries was also lucky, he realized, that in spite of their annoying qualities, Catherine had in some ways "adopted" Nathan and his father as her new family, although she spent mysterious time away from the house, and had the equally mysterious "Protector" skulking about; Doctor Anderson who helped save William's life. William knew more than anyone that he had become an enraged clown, a Don Quixote or a tortured fool like Oedipus, nearly divine but dying with some dignity in his blind, drunken, noble shame, comforted and disciplined at times by Catherine and her friend Doctor Amos Anderson.

Doctor Anderson was an expert Protector, part of a secret group, presumably financed from Massachusetts, consisting mostly of ex-slaves trained in security by abolitionists and the Friends. This large, massive, avuncular friend of Amy's, whose father, a friend of many black men who had crossed the line, had died a slave, knew more than almost anyone about the strengths and weaknesses of the human body. "We are like the Spartans—no, like Spartacus," says "Doctor Amos," a brown-skinned, jowly, slow-moving quadroon when not in action, with drooping eyes and cow-like face—not especially dangerous-looking except in size. "We would rather die than return to the white man's whip, Captain. Really not a very hard choice." Amos Anderson sounded like a scholar, an academician, a *white* doctor. Smoothly guided by his voice it seemed impossible to think of him as a Negro. He claimed to have been educated at Dartmouth College, Hanover, New Hampshire, as a special project, originally lead by the mad genius Professor Eugene W. Beatty, whose later protégés included Peter Hughes, whereabouts now unknown—but news stories abounded.

William Jeffries smiled in spite of himself. But more and more he feared for Nathan. And hated him for nearly eclipsing his old man in local fame as a sea warrior—the very career he had always dreamed for his son, a chip off the old block, but now the old block seemed to be—

"William," she yelled.

"What, Catherine?" he asked irritably, breaking his reverie.

"Please, please stop talking to yourself. We love you and we will take care of you."

How many times he had promised that to his crew—and then his own son?

"We do not always agree, Captain," she was saying. "But you and I are proud of Nathan, and furious that he left against our—your earnest urgent wishes. But you are both lions of a sea."

Again he smiled. This damned woman—practically read his mind, too damned smart.

Had the captain become a querulous old man? Only upon occasion, she decided. Mostly Catherine enjoyed matching wits with this man whose son she seldom tolerated when she was not craving him.

Proud, exasperating, Catherine nevertheless captivated William Jeffries, and the younger version, who both had to admit (to themselves alone) that she was the only woman they had ever known, with the exception of Amy, who had more intelligence, ability and courage than they—not what William told the men at Blind Jack's, or the new No-Name ale house, where there were far too many Irish. But he could argue from the regal comfort of the special wheeled chair that black magician Anderson had gotten him, with other beached sea fighters, about the efficacy of carronades over long guns, about 1801 when the navy lost the election, about 1807 and *guerre de course* and their hopes for a better leadership in William Jones, the new navy secretary, who could have been building the commerce raiding navy even before then.

"I have been invited up by Minerva Rodgers, wife of Commodore John Rodgers, to Havre de Grace, in time for May Day," said Catherine.

"Have you now?"

"Yes, William, and Amos is our Protector. Remember that when I am not here. No one knows his true origins; he never lived in Africa. But some of his friends made our defeat of Auster possible, my articles were—thanks to our Friends."

"I know, I know. Instrumental in our dealings with—who is the new threat, you said?"

"You know very well his name is Michael Fredericks."

William and Catherine even argued about the effect of Commodore Rodgers' squadron—two of which, *Congress* and *Chesapeake*, seemed especially unlucky.

The Friends of Amy had effectively shunned the wayward, reckless William Jeffries, to no one's surprise—otherwise he might have hoped for substantial financial assistance from Amy's branch of the Kemp families. The captain railed against their perfidy, but no one else blamed the Quakers at all for finally shedding William's "propensities for sinful problems." And even William Jeffries had heard the name Michael Fredericks, before and after the Austers themselves slipped their cable. Would his son prove the master? Would he?

Vitriolic newspapers, even (or perhaps especially) the *National*

Intelligencer, and the more ancient bitterness from the *London Times,* printed utterly fictitious quotations about the war, recognized as fraudulent by William because he had heard himself from the source. But he had to admit that Catherine's own comments on her "darker brothers" were actually understating their courage and resourcefulness.

"Captain Jeffries!" An ominous note from that lovely throat. William, hauled up tight, towed back to her world or towed to safety by her. Used to be—saved my life, twice! But I mind my own business. Except, dammit, the girl is right about Washington City, too, and Baltimore, Commodore John Rodgers, Captain Joshua Barney—but she helped Nathan leave, she said she agreed with me but she helped him.

"Captain, sir, I shall return presently. *Please* mind your manners with the good doctor."

But those mesmerizing deep brown eyes, that light brown face, tight lips, were not asking.

"Yes, my dear," was all he could manage, croaking like a dead man. He was entirely too sober. The new ale house that used to be Richard Pittsman's, the No-Name, would not open for another hour—and that girl had found and confiscated all of his bottles, even the "Short Fuse" jug behind the hearth.

Hard over, come about, he thought. Let's return to my course, my assessment. Captain James Lawrence, young commander of *Hornet* and had still to see combat in this war, but seemed to be trusted by his men. *Argus* might go to William Henry Allen; he's a fire-eater. But will he follow orders and attack only merchantmen and weaker vessels? Jeffries felt himself to be a marked man and despaired over the early demise of his beloved navy in this war. His city remained, like Boston, New York and other seaports, in a state of euphoria as plans were made to send frigates and smaller navy vessels to sea again. But there were no frigates, and few of even the smaller warships by now. Songs and poems were composed honoring the heroes of Old Ironsides, *Wasp* and *United States.* But soon he knew "all six" of the frigates would be captured or bottled up for the duration, from Maine to Florida, Louisiana, the entire east coast of North America, except perhaps not for the small fry,

unrated warships, schooners, brigs and corvettes—and not the Caribbean. Our Chesapeake and most ports were much too easily guarded
by a few British frigates and 74s. Not to mention brigs, sloops—but
their small fry were no match for our small fry! If only we had built
those purpose-built naval privateers, we could call them; 20 guns tops,
light carronades mostly, and the British merchant fleet would have no
chance. Even without cooperation from Bonaparte—or what is left of
him. Hull is a fine and aggressive sailor, William thought, but then he
gave his ship, Old Ironsides, to Hard Luck Bill Bainbridge. Bainbridge
was lucky the entire crew did not mutiny. Isaac Hull never once flogged
a member of his crew; not once and they loved him for it. Bainbridge
was a Jonas. And the blockade would soon be tighter than Hull's
breeches. And what about Nathan's next cruise, if he survived *Merlin*
with reputation and hide intact? William, struggling through his own
misery, envied his own son's recent adventures as a sea warrior—even
as he hated his son's catastrophic timing. Jehova! What would dearest
Amy think now? When would Catherine return?

And of course the privateers were capturing already ten times what
the navy had—in a good month! Perry, Porter, Blakely; all likely lads.
MacDonough too, some good men; same young firebrands who survived Prebles' adventures off Tripoli in '03, right after that quasi-squab-
ble with the French. The Caribbean is *our* back yard. So Old Ironsides
had gone on another cruise, with the sloop of war *Hornet* and Captain
Lawrence as her consort. They hoped to rendezvous with Porter's *Essex*.
It would be the Cape Verde Islands, then probably South America, and
here Captain Jeffries floundered a-sitting in a savage sea of windtorn
newsprints, broadsides and *Magothy's Monthly* serials, hunting down
every shred of information about the war from every source, including
the *Naval Chronicle*. Rodgers and *President* had sailed from Boston with
Congress in early October. And Decatur and *United States*, the "Old
Wagon," had sailed with *Argus*, the two ships operating as a separate
unit of the squadron. But soon it would be every captain for himself.
Since she was ready to sail earlier, Rodgers had ordered the sloop of
war *Wasp*, Master Commandant Jacob Jones, to rendezvous with his

squadron off the Delaware capes. *Chesapeake* was not yet ready for sea; *Constellation* down near Norfolk would never be.

Catherine and William often discussed Barbara, Peter, the Austers, and how Nathan tracked down the survivors of *Cormorant*. Captain Matthew Turner would not recover, but Tom Howard and Mister Jack Logan had survived and joined him aboard *Merlin*. After losing his father's ship *Bucephalus* to the *Scourge* back in '11, and his depredations at the hands of Auster and Coxe, then saved finally by Old Ironsides—and then to lose Amy—and still Nathan had gone on about this business.

William had warned and begged a bitter, deranged Nathan from going to back sea in any capacity. So had Catherine, bless her soul, so of course Nathan got a privateer of his own to command.

Both he and Catherine had been stunned by the change in Nathan, now a block of oak, angular; his flat face seemingly bland. But when angry his face and big muscular body terrified those unlucky enough to arouse that feeling. But in the light of the waning cantaloupe moon, Nathan's sun-whitened hair, blue eyes no longer warm or sensitive, now painted shutters against sun dark oak and brick of his face, revealing only a lonely house with no candles or lamps lit; inside there seemed to be deliberate and quiet activity. Nathan still did not excel at pretension—politics by another name, he said, blocking both sides.

It had been a still night, with an occasional, gentle evening breeze rising, as Nathan prepared to leave his home for the *Merlin*. A bright and quiet night; a carriage pulled up in front of the Lyman mansion up the hill—no, that was Caleb Codman's mansion. William rolled back into the shadows, inside the Jeffries' two-story Federal home bathed in orange moonlight. He remembered the early summers of fresh cut barley, trembling, fluttering young beech leaves, the feel of Amy's soft strength, her warm hands on his face, her cool, caressing voice; all gone, gone forever, as he heard Nathan clumping down from his bed chamber. A lit candle leaned down to him—the prodigal son. "Well, this is what you said you wanted, Father—more or less. Damn it all!" Nathan whispered.

"Get Gloria!" William had croaked. "Help take me upstairs, please!

Doctor Amos! My son wishes to add salt to the wounds—he has learned that much in his travels." Nathan shook his head in fury, threw open the door and slammed out of the house. Suddenly William knew that he must follow him to plead once more before it was too late. Calling to Doctor Anderson for his carriage, he rushed out.

Coming back to the present from his reverie, William felt that he had thrown everything away, wasted his life, a small pebble in the ocean; it sounded loud and fuzzy in the night. A dog barked once, followed by more canine challenges, like a Congressional debate in the House. Why in hell Jones turned Jefferson down in '07? Nathan would have been a midshipman then.

William looked around in the black shadow. Had Catherine removed his pistols too?

THREE

Frenchtown - *January 23, 1813*
Near the River Raisin, Michigan Territory, just before dawn

TOO OFTEN NOW THIS would recur, Peter's childhood ability—a curse—of seeing into the future. And he always shivered in the cold, the frozen white mantle. More than the direct and immediate consequences, according to the Professor, whose lovely mind and generosity had been the saving grace of Hanover, New Hampshire when no one else really wanted him there—well, except the electrifying Serelea. Samuel Occum, the Indian leader at Dartmouth, was betrayed; but we all betray someone, Peter thought, a Negro, even a dirty savage. Actually educated at Dartmouth College, Hanover, New Hampshire, as a special project by the mad genius Professor Eugene W. Beatty, whose later protégés included himself, Peter Hughes, whereabouts now unknown. What he had done to Nathan—his betrayal of his spiritual kin on the "white side." And now, he was reaping the rewards of his own wayward loyalties; torn loose from moorings, as Nathan would say, those he was most indebted to, now dead or enemies.

After the rout at Frenchtown, many of the hundreds of American prisoners were wounded. Two hundred drunken braves, he thought bitterly, watched over by a few terrified Canadian militia. Shawnee leader Tecumseh left with the Wyandot chief Roundhead; Roundhead returned alone, and met with chief Walk-in-the-Water. But how many of these young drunks were Shawnee, Potawatomi, Ottawa, Delaware,

Miami, Winnebago, Creek, Sauk? He knew only a few of the warriors. And now, Tecumseh insisted that Peter stay in Frenchtown after the battle, along with the ridiculously inadequate guards for the wounded prisoners. "General" Procter was not a British version of the despised William Hull, but still fell far short of General Brock, who had been killed at Queenstown Heights. Peter's definitive foreboding deepened as he studied the open contempt of some of the braves, even whole tribes, mostly Chippewas and Saganaw; he would not be able to control the situation.

Here, of course, in the savage wilderness there were more ingenious and exotic tortures. If he could save even one helpless human enemy, Peter, the brilliant, bitter half-breed, maybe "worse than an octaroon" as that enemy would say, would he remain angry with Tecumseh who was not the man he thought he knew? Did he know the insane hero Captain William Jeffries and his perhaps by now insane son? Poor Nathan. How he had betrayed him, his lifelong friend, who tends never to forgive. And here was Brigadier General Henry Procter, commanding the British Army around Detroit, including hundreds of tribal allies under Tecumseh. Tecumseh himself of course knew better than to get drunk and behave like the white man. Although he knew that many braves felt this necessary because they anticipated death every day, as he did. Best friends dying every day. Becoming friendly with death only a breath away. To the rankest white coward, or a great chief. Or himself. Well, Peter thought, I have always found myself at war with some others.

Then he thought of Catherine Charles, her Doctor Anderson, and his remarkable Protectors; the Austers themselves were no more, but what about Barbara Steward, her father and her brother? Not to mention his own seemingly dead-end search for his putative father, the naval lieutenant Hughes. Peter still mourned his beautiful, quiet mother, Elizabeth. One big happy cabal, he thought; yet he was still determined to find his mysterious father. He had heard that someone, maybe a Michael Fredericks, now controlled Austers' Cabal, but not of course under his name. Beatrice and her husband Jonathan Charles in Philadelphia knew everything, except for Nathan's success or failure as a privateer.

The Frenchtown battle itself had begun as a route and ended in butchery. The American commander, James Winchester and his men, awakened by Procter's three-pounders on sledges, were overwhelmed from the start. The enemy prisoners were hacked apart by the Indians as they surrendered, some running through the snow in their stockings. Barns and houses burned. Too many enraged braves were out of control, with musket, rifle, tomahawk and knife—and blood littered the snow. Peter hardened his heart against these unfortunate victims, but nothing could prepare him for the final disposal of those too injured to move, cut up and fed to the hogs or screaming in the flames—screams that would haunt him for the rest of his life. He finally his legs to move to the last building not on fire, where he knew some friendly Wyandots; knowing this was hopeless, that this massacre would fuel the American cause like no victory possibly could.

He stumbled over a freshly mangled leg, being dragged by a hungry pig, and almost vomited; then saw Blue Wing, not much of a leader but a very likable young man, who smiled and moved in a reassuring swagger toward Peter.

"Still aggressively sober, Peter Hughes?" he slurred happily. "Scout for the Governor General Prevost, Procter and his British minions and Provincial Army in Michigan Territory, not to mention advisor to Tecumseh himself—how are you?"

"My friend, we must some how put a stop to this . . . behavior unworthy of a warrior."

"Pthwough, you fool, you foolish man! Tecumseh left us, remember—do *you* know who is in charge? And you want to come between 200 drunks who think they're avenging their friends by feeding the whites to the pigs? Let'm have a little fun! Go bother someone else!" Then Blue Wing slapped Peter on the back and laughed again.

Peter had a sinking feeling as he lurched away from this man and rushed toward the last survivors of the last blaze, with all the assurance of a dead man. His horrible slow-motion trajectory moved him through a crowd slicing up those who had survived the fire, as he was ducking and leveling too many drunk savages, faces painted red and black, bloody with whisky-fed surgery, even some Pottawatomie. As he fought to save the last whites, Peter was pushed against a large sea chest, filled with papers and bloody body parts. He let his spirit loose and it was marvelous to behold, but what a waste.

But Peter soon left his soul behind, and by the next attack the pain finally convinced him to open his eyes, and admit that the terror was real. He was tightly bound hand and foot by angry warriors. Jolts of pain shot up to his consciousness every time he tried to move. He flew through the drunken binds, prescient, determined never to surrender. Through blood, warm and gurgling, strong arms held him down againas he thrashed until he finally broke their grip. He screamed and yelled those gasping breaths, but they laughed and argued about drowning or burning for this "white Shawnee." As they turned away to decide his fate, Peter felt the chill grow until the roar of musket and shotgun in his ears deafened him, and he thought he saw in the firelight, of all people, petite Serelea, dragging him into the darkness—or was he merely passing out?

"Peter!" he heard. Then he did stumble, and found himself first on the ground, leaning, then propped up near a smoldering wall; Serelea was actually by his side, holding his head and efficiently studying his injuries. It had never gotten completely dark; the half moonlight was inching up the alley, and Peter would slip half in and out of consciousness, his savior a diagonal shadow as she moved. A big brave approached and quickly backed off when Serelea produced a pistol and knife. Behind him, Peter could see three pale bodies, still intact, lying on the ground, and one recently stabbed Fox, dark skin and even darker blood against the snow.

"My God! Are you—"

"We must get you out of here now. Can you walk? We must see to your injuries."

Serelea helped Peter walk away from the commotion, and he looked back again where bodies and body parts lay motionless on the ice.

"Damn it," he said. "The dead cannot tell what happened here; this is all my fault."

"No, it is not. But it is fortunate I was here to save your life, Peter."

"Yes, well . . . Here, what is this?" He picked up a black object from the ground.

"That is my logbook. Give it to me."

They staggered to a small cabin, only scorched on one side, with few footprints around it.

"This will be safe for a while," she said, once they were inside, laying him on a makeshift bed of straw and cowhide on the wood floor. Her lovely brown face, strained in the dim light, studied Peter's bruises and injuries. After a few more minutes of examination, Serelea made her pronouncement, covering both of them with a gray wool blanket.

"That left eye will be closed for a week. It is black and blue already. But remarkably you have nothing broken—except maybe your head— and you should be recovered enough to walk this evening. You were foolish to take on dozens of men by hand at one time."

"But how did you get here, why are you—"

"Listen to me," she ordered. Serelea opened and closed her mouth, and started to open her leather-bound journal, then put it down after wiping off a spot of blood. "You are no longer just being hunted by those marshals from Ohio Territory. You are hunted as a renegade traitor and known ally of Tecumseh himself. You are wanted as a dangerous killer of more than just those two white trash. They are even looking at your association with the professor, and Robert Fulton, and—"

"Please!" said Peter, looking at her with his good right eye. "How do you know all this?"

"After the Professor's funeral, I tracked you down and, with my contacts in Baltimore, followed you. I heard everything. And if I can follow you, so can others."

"Yes. But why are *you* following me?" He felt like a fool, his thoughts still somewhat addled. Her dark beauty did not help.

She looked away. "I am not sure whether or not any of these men here were ordered to kill you," she said.

"Ordered to? Only Tecumseh wanted me to—"

"Certainly. I tell you, Peter, never trust any man, white or Indian."

"But . . . who else would have ambushed me, or had someone else —aaah!"

A wave of nausea overcame him as he tried to rise, and it was some minutes more before he could look his nurse in the eyes again.

"Peter, Catherine and I have—"

"*Catherine* . . . and you!"

"We agreed that I should tell you everything, even now, as you seek—"

"You know what I seek—that killer, my father. I will track him down."

"Listen to you! What have your vaunted abilities done for you?"

Peter shook his head. "They—I—seek the truth only. And you! What did the professor say when you told him about me—and Barbara? And . . . others? I am sorry, Serelea. But you are a stunningly brilliant woman, and better than some men. I must thank you for—"

"You foolish idiot!" She stared at Peter's red, impassive face, more ruddy in the faint light. "I love you!"

"You . . . love—you do not know who I am. I hate—have no other mission in life beyond killing my own father! And other white men!"

"And what about your friend Blue Wing? For now your mission is to . . . help me, Peter. And yourself. Now, listen. We wait till dusk. I have food and fire and weapons. The rising moon will offer sufficient light tonight, even with clouds," she said, her eyes blinking in amber, and gone was the arrogance he remembered so well.

"Serelea!" She looked down and he gently raised her chin.

Her tremulous voice began again. "This winter the British will certainly launch some kind of attack against Oswego, too, small as it is."

"Why?"

"It has excellent harbor and ramps for ships—and the roads are better."

He saw the tears in her brown eyes, darting in every direction, and finally boring into his. He sat up now, gripped her shoulders.

"Is there anything you don't know?" he asked.

"Yes—how can you resist me, Peter?"

He grabbed her violently and feverishly kissed her on those sweetly parted lips, delicately upturned at the corners, suddenly softly wet, eager, as she bent to his battered, muscular body.

FOUR

Dominica Channel - *January 23, 1813*

Course SW by W. Sun at noon but now partly cloudy. SE wind freshening.
Large sail now hull up to the east, could be Minerva, *crossing Dominica*
Channel—options rapidly diminishing—Thompson may be right but I must
use my own best judgment. Mostly he has been a brilliant "de facto" second-in-
command. Blast that man.
N. Jeffries, master of privateer schooner Merlin

AT HIS CABIN DESK, for a brief time, Nathan could feel that cursed
sense that he was truly doomed, and damned to hell, even, for his many
failings in life. But then his mother's indomitable spirit would rise and
shout to quit whining and lead his men as best he could. He hoped they
could accept their dubious fate—and especially that they would not be-
grudge their leader if he finally, inevitably, permanently, let them down.
And then he snapped out of it, walked up the few steps to the wheel
and got back down to business.

He knew what he must do. If *Merlin* did not lessen her draft, she
would not make it across the reef. Some of the crew knew already, so
he would make no further pronouncements. The crew would follow his
orders—mostly, anyway.

Save the men then the ship, in that order. There was no other.
Nathan could achieve both. He pounded his fist on the rail and looked
back to the east to hide his tears. What could he ask of the lovely *Mer-*
lin, this sea witch about to undergo torture in every timber?

"This is madness, Nathan!" said Mister Thompson, at his side, this short, powerful man who seemed to know everything. "You must yield to that ship. She will rip us apart—or the reef will!"

"You will address me as Captain Jeffries, Mister Thompson. And when you gain your own command, you can surrender it whenever you see fit." He looked aloft.

"All hands to furl topsails, and reef the main!" Nathan ordered. "And at two bells, furl all. Hufman, make ready to lower topmasts!"

"Captain, without more sail we hit the reef for sure. You must—"

"Silence, Mister Thompson!" Nathan turned and ordered the waisters to "get the lead out!"

There followed a flurry of orders barked and volleyed, as the men clustered around the boats.

"Sway out the longboats, captain's gig; the launch can handle the rest! Capsize and secure the long boat—all other boats away!"

"Man the boats?" asked Mister Thompson. "But—well, if you refuse to surrender—will you hide on the island? But if we cast off with the . . . but the cargo, Captain! The men; most will drown."

"Cut away!"

"No!" The shorter man quivered in fury. "This is absurd, Nath–Captain! We must come to. Do you want to lose everything? All of us? Now our boats—"

"We have less than two hours to ready the ship, but we will discuss this later in my cabin after—"

"After?" Mister Thompson laughed. "There will be no *after!*" He nearly screeched this last, "You must—"

"*You* must follow orders! Right now I need you to take most of the larboard watch and rig the main to hoist out most of the cargo that's ready to haul out and throw overboard!"

"Captain, I—"

"Mister Thompson, do you need an escort below?"

"No, sir! No escort necessary!" he snapped.

"Good. We are going to strip her nearly empty and with just enough ballast to prevent a capsize, but I believe she can ride over it.

The British can try to salvage our cargo and supplies. Now get to it!"

As *Merlin* drifted with wind and current toward certain disaster southwest of the Dominica Straights, the crew sweated in the brief calm to lower the topmasts, cast off the boats, heave the guns over the side. Some of the crew groaned in distress at the fortune feeding the deep.

"Silence! Keep at it, men! First the guns, Hufman, then the treasure. Then haul up the water casks and ballast and start pumping!"

The already weary crew shook their heads, tossing everything overboard, especially anything heavy—gold, spices, furniture, glass, porcelain, silver plate, guns, water, supplies—nearly everything that could be quickly run out and released to the wild, tossed sea. But as afternoon waned, and there was still no sign of another vessel, Nathan's hopes and spirits slowly started to climb with the moon. The late sun, now nearing Guadeloupe's peak and sinking below that ridge, became an orange bubble in a frothy russet sky. With a gibbous moon rising, the clouds to the west now red in that sunset of faded prophetic light sat on that rise looking down at the impatient moon, inching higher in disdain. Jib and staysails and shred of a driver were filled and pressed with wind as the brig's stem and stern rose, rolled and dipped through the steep seven-foot crests. Every man stumbled and staggered, alow and aloft, from the pronounced roll their poor ship now entertained.

"Harris, ease that lift! Hoist the topsail and brace together! Mister Thompson, keep a better eye on those three maintop men!"

"Aye, sir," said Mister Thompson.

Pungent-smelling oakum and tarring for the standing hemp, mainchains, deck beams whirled and wafted in the confused air, mixed with the scent of briny white pine, oak and fresh-cut blocks for the remaining spars. Nathan's father had taken him to the shipyards before he could walk. At least he had tasted love, and enough loss in Antigua; Nathan began to breathe the memory of entrancing Maria Santiago again, but she was gone. They could not make for Santo Domingo, and even if they could, he would never find her inside the Caribbean, Antigua, Martinique, St. Lucia, Tortola, Puerto Rico, Cuba, Barbados. He knew he was doomed to hunt for her only in his dreams. Memories rose up unbidden of Barbara's and Catherine's lustful affections, that forbidden intimacy the naïve call love.

Pointe-a-Pitre is less than two leagues from here, he thought, weakening in his resolve. We could reach it by noon tomorrow, maybe sooner, if we are not caught by our determined pursuer. We will have a good, fresh breeze abeam till we get abreast of north side of the island, then quarter around the south end of Basse Terre. But there was no reason for Nathan to stay north, inside, until the Gulf Stream, giving most other islands a wide berth as well. Wind's out of the southeast, he thought. If we can stay afloat we will have an even chance to run fair and free for Perdido, Savanna, or—

"Water casks ready to hoist and drop over, Captain," shouted Thompson, shattering Nathan's optimistic dream.

Nathan sighed. "Make it so."

In two hours of exacting labor, the topmasts and topgallants had been sent down and secured to the caps and crosstrees; the main and fore shrouds and futtock shrouds rewove to the tops, lifts, clewlines, buntlines, halyards, braces and parrels, lines from under an inch to over nine inches in diameter, and anchor cable, were mostly stored in the cable tier or the orlop deck and not expendable. Finally, the rigging was taut, yards run down; nearly every sail housed. Most of his cabin, except the lockbox, were secured below the pantry.

"Good work, Mister Thompson. You and the men have done well."

"Thank you, sir."

"Send the watch below for dinner and rest," he said to Thompson. "You get some rest, too. We'll stay ahead of the ebb."

"Aye, aye, sir."

Merlin, now grinding, groaning and screeching, her cracking timbers heeling so far that larboard gunwales were nearly awash. That hateful ship out there, not an American, though heavily sparred, many more guns. He would need more men below as she made the reef, no matter how terrifying the sounds, but in any case every man now commended himself to prayer and faith. *Merlin* would make it—or not. Still better than damn British flogging or prison, Nathan and nearly every man aboard told himself.

"I am very sorry, Old Girl," he said, returning aft, where Young Warren at the helm nervously glanced at him, then at the acting third mate, Hufman, to windward, then back at Nathan. Most of the men began to stare transfixed at the oddly calm waters, rippling through the coral. In a clear current soon to break her back on the coral or— only gently again *Merlin* began to heel, then more sharply in her deep, tortured stern. Poor *Merlin*, already damaged, but with her load much lightened, dragging her wretched keel, across the reef.

Oddly enough, after tamping down thoughts of his vessel seemingly doomed to destruction from cannon shot or coral teeth, Nathan remembered those earlier months when Thompson waxed enthusiastic about his study of the harlequin beauty of the toothy predatory world below that aquamarine surface, glittering, sometimes peaceful, even intoxicating—also bizarre and dangerous with creatures and plants of the reefs even just off the beach.

How many miles of this can she stand? The exact width of this reef was unknown, but it was vast, stretching miles southwest into the southern Caribbean Sea.

"Ease in her weather; let her stern fall off," he said to quartermaster Warren Graham and Oldesal, the master's mate, who nodded calmly. With only the jibsail and staysail, a patch of the main as brake, the bow swung slightly away as hands stationed for and aft, alow and aloft, ready for "suicide rocks," throwing lines and looks his way. There were still several hours of overcast light. It was comforting to see the blue and white swallowtail "Peabody Pennant" on the main, more than sufficient assurance that *Merlin* needed no pilot. Interference, quarantine and prompt payment of condemned cargo—with sufficient documents to complete—would still be paid handsomely, even with catastrophic loss in the next hour. Six bells in the afternoon watch, no later, their voyage could still remain very profitable; even if only one of the British merchant ships *Merlin* had captured, the merchant ship *Elizabeth*, with Mister Logan, Tom Howard and the boy, Jason, managed to reach an American port safely. All told, those prizes were worth more than $100,000—and Nathan had entrusted most of the valuable cargo to his friends.

Nathan turned to the maintop, roaring, "Any company besides our friend there?"

"Nothin' yet, sir!" The lookout shouted down. The other ship was full-rigged, lower sails furled, her reefed top hamper straining. She was almost certainly the British *Medusa* or *Minerva*, standing on and off, a simple onlooker at this point, less than a mile distant, her twenty guns silent.

He had to see and judge for himself, and he clambered up the fore ratlines quick as you please, and saw that she was going to hit and the best possible broad reach, and might possibly—now, he must return to the deck, must return, must survive if only for the sake of this crew in his hands. His mind calculated, his father's mind.

A high-pitched scream from the drone forward interrupted them. "Mark twain! Shoaling fast now, Cap'n! Sand and shell, broken coral!"

Good, he thought. A sudden cliff, a steep underwater wall rising to shallows, would have been fatal—it is gradual and we have a chance. A channel would have been a more convenient escape route, with his ship facing possibly catastrophic flooding, heeling, keel dragging, scraping, ending up holed and capsized by 50-foot coral heads.

Then he saw one directly ahead. *Merlin's* maintop whipped suddenly as she ground to a spinning stop, turning to starboard, threatening to send her stern underwater. There goes the bowsprit, he thought, as the mast whipped again and then finally shook him loose. And like Icarus, Nathan fell.

Except that he bounced off the leeward shrouds before he plunged into the waters of the reef and hit nothing hard. He had nearly hit the side of ship; now he desperately swam over to those rocking, twisting, nearly submerged mainchains and held on against the current and shrieking torture of *Merlin* herself.

He could see the bosun's mate, Evans, shouting down at him from the wheel. "Mister Thompson!" shrieked the normally taciturn Evans, pointing frantically as Nathan turned to look behind him, locking his arm to the mainstays to save himself from plunging into the surging waters, nearly under the leeward counter, but could see nothing but reef and ship. To weather, her vast and tortured side and keel must be nearly all exposed, full of jagged holes, yet hidden from view by any aboard. She will not come back this time, Nathan groaned inwardly. And he had seen safety, the blue depths, within a cable's length; a few hundred yards and the tide—

A ring of coiled topgallant line dropped over his head like a collar. "Captain! Tie this to your waist! Mister Thompson, he fell overboard—he was half a cable's-length behind you. Are you secure, Captain?"

Then he realized what he must do. "Hurry!" he told Evans. "Bend a dozen more fathoms on to my line! Double French bowline, make sure there's no bind." He stood on the larboard gunwales midship, awash in the bubbling current.

"Clear the way aft, lead me there once I have Thompson." He shouted to Evans, stripping to his trousers and bare feet, as some of the crew forward pointed to where they saw the lifeless body of Thompson drifted to the south.

It was now or never; *Merlin* still temporarily hung up, grinding, thumping, groaning and cracking, on the coral. He launched himself a few minutes later. If he lost the line to the *Merlin*, he would drown, shredded to death on the reef, food for sharks. The terror nearly froze him in the tropical water, but then he saw the lifeless body, seemingly peaceful, head down, in contrast to the monstrous healing, keel-dragging, desperate scraping of the ship. Nathan could see clearly the dark coral heads seemingly inches below, and wondered whether each silver flash presaged the crushing bite of a shark or other predator.

Nathan swam one hundred yards to the lifeless body, exhausted, and tried to turn it over; suddenly it came alive, pulling him down in panic. But Nathan jerked away, hit Thompson on the side of the head, grabbed the stunned man's hair and began to tow him back, with the help of the men at the other end of Nathan's line.

What happened next seemed miraculous. At first Nathan could

not believe his eyes when *Merlin* began to right herself, slowly veer so that her stern, now nearly balanced, turned away from Nathan to larboard, and her bow clearly nosed toward the southwest, free of the reef at last, in deeper water. Then she steadied again, like a trained horse. Nathan felt a final burst of energy as he swam toward the ship, low at the stern but even keel. It did not take long for young Captain Jeffries and Mister Thompson to get hauled along side—getting back aboard was the worst part, and possibly rib-breaking. But the ship was saved.

Later, on a well-secured cot in the day room, Mister Thompson, still pale blue but breathing regularly, reached out his hand to his visitor, Nathan. "I doubt my rib is cracked, Captain. How will I ever repay you for saving my life?"

"Help me save the *Merlin*," Nathan said. "Trust me that, with your help, we can get home."

"Captain, I can only say that—"

"Don't say anything more now. We need you—just don't fall overboard again! Repairs aboard the ship will be extensive, but I think we can make it to Guadeloupe; and, with any luck—"

"Haul out that cable! Bring the longboat alongside!" shouted Evans just above them.

"By the mark seventeen!"

"Silence!" Evans roared. "Cap'n's still with Mister Thompson!"

A peaceful, plashy, creaking silence as *Merlin* drifted north, with a comfortable seventeen fathoms underneath. They had survived the Devil's Teeth. For the time being, the biggest problem—

A knock on the open door. "Pardon, Captain," said Hufman. "Orlop's nearly awash, Sir! Five feet in the bilge aft."

"Can you—"

"Pumps are holding their own, same level. We'll keep 'er afloat as long as you need 'er, sir!"

"Thank you, I'll come," said Nathan. "You rest for now, Mister Thompson."

Back on the quarterdeck, he bellowed to the crew, "Men, we need to get farther away from this reef now. Starboard hands prepare to rig

topmasts and set sail. Hufman, make ready to sway out the longboat."
There were only the slightest southerly airs now. The late sun now
touched and would soon dip below Guadeloupe's Pinot Ridge. Nathan
squinted at the ruddy clouds, knowing that most of the exhausted crew
were looking at him still.

"Tonight," he cried, "we careen her at the beach south of Trois-
Rivieres. Plenty of fresh water there, and we can get to work on putting
Merlin a-right. If every man aboard pitches in, we will soon make for
Mona Passage, with the wind free. And we still have aboard our haul
from Barbados, lads, and Mister Thompson assures us that all our nar-
row sacrifices weren't in vain! We *will* reach Baltimore, alive and rich!
Mister Evans!"

"Sir!"

"Do you think you and young Warren could find the remains of
our spirits aboard? Double ration for every man aboard! Huzzah!"

"Huzzah!" the crew cheered, every man bone-weary, but relieved.
The master of *Merlin* had done it again.

FIVE

London - *January 23, 1813*
Admiralty Office, Whitehall, at dusk

IN SPITE OF THE weather, the vast long hall, the offices of Lords
Commissioners of the Admiralty, were alive with liveried attendant
escorts, mysterious men in unfamiliar uniforms, civilians, officers both
seated and on the move, servants and clerks of various grades—especially around the offices of First Lord the Right Honorable Robert
Dundas, 2nd Viscount of Melville, William Domett, Sir Joseph Sydney
Yorke, William Dundas, George Johnstone Hope, Sir George Warren-
der, John Osborn, and Henry Paulet.

A young British naval lieutenant, stocky, ruddy, filled with newly
commissioned self-importance, strode in the waiting hall, marched
directly to the fire, swept off his navy blue greatcoat and fore-and-aft
cocked hat and gave them to the waiting coat man to brush off snow
and hang. His shining blue-and-gold uniform was obviously new and
immaculate. He studied the various military and civilian men scattered
in various chairs, then picked out a handsome man of perhaps forty,
not tall but well-proportioned. Impeccably dressed in dark silk fashion
with a snow-white cravat, the gentleman sat on a long polished bench
away from others waiting to see Ministers or secretaries to Lords of the
Admiralty.

This man's sharply-etched face was calm and bland, yet alert, like
a resting hawk; his hooded eyes studying other men, mostly military,

in the vast chamber, checking the icy tall windows, the long mahogany and walnut tables and remote doors, the heraldric tapestries, the brilliant glass lamps and thick rugs on the oak floor. He wore no uniform, though his burnished complexion suggested sea duty. His beaver hat sat beside him and his black hair was fashionably short. Brazen, square-jawed, but just another man with his hand out, perhaps to beg and whine about his mistreatment by the navy, reading from a small book called *Childe Harold, Cantos I and II*, by somebody named George Gordon, Lord Byron. For some reason he was sitting alone, no one else even close to him. The lieutenant could almost pity this lonely loser.

But orders were orders. Approaching, he said quietly, "Sir, are you Mister Michael Fredericks?

Fredericks glanced up, then went back to reading.

"Sir!" the lieutenant said sharply, "Please tell me if your name is Michael Fredericks!"

Fredericks looked up at the lieutenant, and smiled. "Roll on, vain days! Full reckless may ye flow," he said, closing his eyes. "Since Time hath reft whate'er my soul enjoyed, And with the ills of Eld mine earlier years alloyed." With this, he returned to silent reading.

"My good man, I am Lieutenant Donald Simms Dupont."

"How wonderful for you," said Fredericks.

"My dear sir, Mister Whoever you are, as one *gentleman* to another—"

"This will not be like the duel between Castelreagh and Canning," said Fredericks wryly.

"I assure you," said the huffy lieutenant, "I have their Lordships' complete confidence."

"I'm delighted to hear it," said Fredericks.

"And you are . . . ?"

"A gentleman minding his own business."

The pompous young officer leaned over and stared at the man. "Sir, that is hardly an amiable response."

"Your astuteness is admirable." Fredericks yawned, and went back to reading.

"Sir, a gentleman should take care to avoid unnecessary ill manners."

Fredericks sighed, and looked up at him again. "Lieutenant, a fool would let his feelings carry him into disaster. Be off with you now." Fredericks actually waved him away, as one would an annoying pest.

The lieutenant rose and stiffened. "I must ask—"

"Mister Fredericks," intoned the liveried clerk just six feet away, "to see Secretary of State for Foreign Affairs, Lord Castlereagh, and the Right Honorable John Wilson Croker, First Secretary of the Admiralty!" Fredericks frowned briefly at the announcement, but quickly resumed his usual bland expression as he stood up and walked around the dumbfounded lieutenant, leading the way for the clerk.

"Then . . . you are, then—" he stammered.

"Apparently," said the now-less-mysterious Michael Fredericks, without looking back. This had already become much too public, but the new Prime Minister, Lord Liverpool, following the assassination of Spencer, had insisted that Foreign Minister Castlereagh meet Fredericks in London, to hash out this next move. Robert Stewart, the Marquis of Londonderry and Viscount Castlereagh, the minister most critical to North America, and Admiralty Secretary Croker's sympathies were critical to Fredericks' plans. The young liveried attendant clerk escort ushered Fredericks into the secretary's chamber, their pounding boots echoing somberly in the great hall, and the dignitaries both rose even before the gentleman was announced. Fredericks bowed and stood silently before them. Castlereagh still favored a white wig and wore a dark suit similar to Fredericks. Croker, middle-aged, wearing a light blue suit and old-fashioned, long pomaded hair, was shorter, once handsome, developing a slight paunch; he tried to smile.

"So," said Castlereagh, "this is the elusive Michael Fredericks."

"Yes—but first, did not we discuss this matter, John, my Lord, of publicly using this name?"

Croker, First Secretary, reddened. "Michael, I—I—Your Grace, my Lord, please allow me to—"

"Yes," said Castlereagh, gratingly, studying a fellow duelist of considerable notoriety. "Mister Fredericks is quite right. But may we dispense with the formalities now and hear your report, sir, if you would be so kind."

"Indeed, and what a great pleasure to see you again, my Lord," said Fredericks calmly. "Men in America customarily shake hands like this."

Foreign Minister Lord Castlereagh could only comply.

"We have met?" The two men then bowed again to each other, as all three moved to sit at the long polished oak table nearby, allowing Fredericks to delay his response.

"You perhaps do not remember the . . . less pleasant aspects of Copenhagen, in '07, my Lord."

It was Castlereagh's turn to redden. He did not speak.

"I deeply regret," said Croker, "that none of their Lords Commissioners—"

"I fully appreciate Lord Melville's priorities," Fredericks interrupted, eyes boring into Castlereagh's. "And of course Lord Liverpool's, please convey my respects and congratulations to him and Sir George for their appointments."

"I shall do so—uh, Admiral Domett had expressed the possibility of a meeting later this week."

"That will not be necessary," said Fredericks, curt and severe.

The three men seated around the table, the silent Castlereagh looking preoccupied, bored and annoyed by turns.

"You never responded to my last letter, my Lord," said Fredericks. "You know that the British—"

"Need I remind you that the British navy can never surrender its authority to search any vessel on the high seas and in some cases return a seaman to his—this fundamental law cannot be abridged; you know that. Especially now."

"You mean, impressment as a God-given Anglican right?" asked Fredericks with a twisted smile.

"Bah! You sound like a rebel Yank," Castlereagh cut himself off, his patience exhausted already.

"We shall get right to that after the first point, sir," said Croker in appeasement. "What news of the American feelings regarding the war, my friend?"

"In spite of Detroit, Queenstown Heights, and their other Canada disasters, I do not believe a separation of the northern states is possible at this time," said Fredericks. "I must give Barclay on Lake Erie my personal attention. The Americans do not understand that they will be defeated. They see those victories at sea as somehow decisive of the war. The lack of any military leadership does not faze them. A small regular army from England could burn any of their cities. These farmers are like simple children; those who can read pay little attention to the other party. And I would not expend a great deal of energy now on any further private 'treaty' efforts at this time.

"However, once their country is invaded, once Cochrane and Cockburne raid in force into the Chesapeake, once Warren blockades the entire Coast—except perhaps New England—their attitude will change. Remember, just as the Austers did, my colleagues will continue to cooperate fully with the Crown—rise up, even. No one really wants what my colleagues call the frog-eaters meddling in—actually, I misspeak myself. Many of the wealthier ship owners in Baltimore, Boston, New York, Philadelphia, of course, being traders and nothing more, that is another matter. They trade with Bonaparte now, even, as soon as they trade with any country, friend or foe, their secret agreements with England notwithstanding. That is why I will not give up on some of my many experiments. Like the Jeffries boy, now that William Jeffries is finally nothing more than a crippled drunk. My concern is with—"

"Can you *trust* your men—your colleagues—of the old Cabal?" asked Castlereagh abruptly. "You said that you would crush the opposition, and apparently that has not occurred. Indeed, the erstwhile Auster Cabal is the one much weakened by the war and the accusations from its enemies—most of whose identities remain unknown, Federalist or Republican. And just where are the influential ones you say you are intimate with?"

Croker frowned at his superior's rudeness, but said nothing. There was awkward silence.

Fredericks finally turned to Castlereagh. "What you may not real-ize, sir, is that the politics of America bear little similarity to those here. Most merchants, like the Austers, are concerned solely with profit."

"That is not unique to—"

"Whether they are Republicans or Federalists," interrupted Fred-ericks in turn, "the Americans, perhaps more strongly in New England, tend to oppose anyone in the national government. And these rebels no longer pay lip service to more lofty ideals. Many Loyalists will remain very useful to us, but they nevertheless admit that they cannot control their own political representatives, or the farmers. Americans have a unique aversion to outside control, nearly all of them, and if pushed too far are apt to run amok, take matters into the own hands. And then we lose more control."

"Then I take it your meaning is—"

"We can discuss specific names later," said Fredericks. "For now I want to merely remind you of that individual whose case is illustrative of my point. William Jeffries, the Revolutionary naval hero, has inspired someone whose accounts of Auster's activities damaged the Cabal considerably—yes, I know, he remains unidentified, although we have all conceivable sources under investigation. But the most remarkable persistence of the son, in spite of damage to *his* own business—fortu-nately since my . . . since Amy's death the son and the old man have but a few maritime friends in the trade. Any more, their income has trickled away. But ruining him financially, again, has been surprisingly difficult, not to mention the son.

"Forcing a crippled man to your will is distasteful, but one of the exigencies of this is the quite promising son, Nathan Jeffries, who did in fact survive to the role of privateer master; successful, for all I know—or will be. Young master Nathan Jeffries is a project of mine," concluded Fredericks with a chilling, satisfied smile. "I believe he will prove to be an asset to us."

"How so?" asked Lord Castlereagh. "Excuse me, please summarize that earlier report."

"The best way to get rid of the William Jeffries of the world is to breed them out. We still hope to bring all of Baltimore into the fold, and the full endorsement of the Jeffries and their cronies. You'll see young Nathan, one way or the other slipping his cables and heading into our fold."

"Excuse me, sir," said Croker. "Even though he hates everything British and Auster?"

"Auster is dead. Nathan's hatred of any country is dead," said Fredericks. "He is quite estranged from the family, again. He gambles a great deal—though not as much as the old man, William. They disagree and fight about everything. The son is now fairly compliant on matters of trade with England."

"Excellent!" said Croker. "The son revolts against the father!"

Even Castlereagh nodded.

"But there are some problems," admitted Fredericks. "The old system of trade lords is no longer . . . popular, shall we say; many merchants having to trade now in foreign vessels, even in local routes, never mind the Caribbean. Trade lords knew when to accommodate the right side—British, French, Spanish, Loyalists, Rebels, Republicans, Federalists—they would follow orders, gauging a man by his acumen in money matters or power. But the Baltimore mob, especially—a population difficult to predict—is mostly volatile against us, against appeasement. Brilliant shipbuilders, fastest I've ever seen. But then they seem to turn a blind eye to French deprivations. And that mysterious supporter of the Jeffries—we know that Negroes are involved, so we suspect someone south of Washington City, probably one of the wealthy slave-owners. And of course many of them finance the privateers and letters of marque. Privateering is especially lucrative out of Maryland, New York and Boston, but conditions change. I anticipate a continued healthy trend toward British licenses, especially in New England. Unless . . ."

"Unless what?" asked Castlereagh.

"There are disquieting rumors emanating from Washington City again, concerning the possibility of complete interdiction with purpose-built smaller craft to enforce it. There could be trouble later in 1813."

"With hundreds of American merchantmen clamoring for licenses? No! Surely that is unlikely," said Croker.

"They could conceivably conduct a no-quarter reprisal on all vessels, British or American, contravening belligerent's rights in a sea war against Great Britain. We both know that their offensive war has failed, but they are finally beginning to prepare for a defensive war, even though at present they have virtually no effective navy or army."

"But then—?"

"But practically speaking they could create such a *guerre de course* fleet in a matter of months, less than a year," said Fredericks smoothly. "Comprising both converted vessels and new ones. And they *could* create an effective corps of regular troops. We cannot hope to defeat Napoleon in that time. His majesty's government seems ill-equipped at present to reinforce navy or army assets on this side of the Atlantic."

"Ridiculous!" snorted Castlereagh. "Napoleon had his opportunity, but England and the Alliance—not to mention the Channel Fleet—frightened Boney, and the Americans' opportunity is lost now."

"I would not underestimate the potential American fighting ability or their connections in Europe—especially their friends in Russia, who want to play diplomats to the world," said Fredericks calmly. "Their army has been a laughingstock, a disgrace, in Canada at least. But at sea, their privateers and navy—"

"Their navy?" Castlereagh laughed humorlessly. "A few ill-deserved victories and they think, with their rafts and handful of ill-disguised ships of the line, a bit of striped bunting—"

"That is a foolish attitude," said Fredericks, taking Croker and Castlereagh aback. "American frigates and sloops are few, but superior in every way to the British vessels, whether or not of the same rate. I have seen them handled. And their corps of officers, though small, is a highly dedicated and skilled elite, motivated, for the most part, with a signal desire to prevail. Look at their behavior in the Tripoli engagements."

"A bunch of undisciplined rascals, no better than those Moham-medan pirates," Castlereagh scoffed. "Nelson's praise was excessive."

"These are the Corsairs whom you thought it more prudent to

bribe than fight," said Fredericks.

Castlereagh's face was reddening, again, his voice rising. "So that the weak navies, colonials like the United States—"

"Yes," said Fredericks, "'fir-built frigates' the *Times* called them. Not bad for Yankee rebels manned by ruffians, eh?"

"Everyone knows the *United States, President* and *Constitution* are really Line of Battle—"

"Yes," Fredericks snorted, "and when two equal warships engage, the winner proves that his country is the better one—and they must be frigates?"

Castlereagh fumed silently.

"Gentleman, please," said Croker. "I know you do not agree on some matters of maritime policy, but let us move on."

"Good God," muttered Castlereagh. "Did we not repeal the Orders in Council in June, and waited till the middle of October before beginning general reprisals? It is obvious that those blackguards are ambivalent about the war, and surely our concessions are enough. No British government at war can afford to suspend impressment. Of course, I am sympathetic to their seamens' rights, but—"

"They are not going to be satisfied with the accommodations of a Fox and Grenville."

"They would have been tarred and feathered for what we have already conceded," Croker observed.

"Nevertheless, I recommend that you continue to favor the New England ship owners with the most lenient attitudes and circumspect treatment at sea."

"You mean, those individuals—"

"I mean help retain those merchantmen already licensed, or willing to risk United States interdiction, and encourage others to do so, to become sympathetic and even active partners, if the New England coast remains open for trade. Much as we plan to facilitate exchange through St. Bartholomew."

"And the possibilities, if we leave her alone, of New England rejoining old England," Castlereagh ventured.

"Our navy is sadly afraid of a dirty peace with Jonathan," said Croker. "More than 500 British merchantmen have been captured, mostly by privateers, costing millions. The trades are already screaming. Their letters of marque are cutting out ships from Caribbean harbors—even in the Channel here."

"By God, licensed trade or no, we will blockade their coast until they howl. Blackguards! This would not have happened with Pitt, even. Jonathan thinks he is immune."

"Jonathan is no different from ourselves, gentlemen," said Fredericks, masking his dislike of the derogatory British epithet: "Brother Jonathan" was the British nickname for the greedy New England seamen. "Nathan Jeffries will be our child, a son of Albion, make no mistake, with all of the brilliance and greed—or he will cease to be."

"They are mere venal ruffians."

"They have the same preferments, the same board patronage and politics, the same orders, the same secret arrangements with customs agents and captains with 'prizes' shared with magistrates collecting fees from those trading with the enemy. False musters and trumped-up charges for one percent, and the same elite cadre. An inferior officer rarely challenges—"

"But it was Napoleon and his damn decrees," said Castlereagh. "And the Orders in Council are no more! We struggle to save not just England but the free world against the tyrant; they will beg for peace! You told us they spend thousands for licenses—Sidmouths, Prince Regents, they call them. Almost a million barrels of flour has sailed on American ships to the Peninsula this year. We can defeat Napoleon—after Moscow—in Spain and Portugal, but we must have crews; our navy is desperately undermanned, and it has for centuries been our time-honored custom—"

"This 'time-honored custom' as you put it," Fredericks interrupted, "is an outrage and affront to international law, to the United States; a custom which you must know they can never accept without dishonor. Let us face facts: however grievous the peril to England, you, sir, are in the wrong. Nathan will never tolerate his rights scuttled in this way—

until he is one of us."

"I cannot believe that you are in sympathy with these knaves—cowards."

"It is reckless, my Lord, to view them so; I am no more sympathetic to them than you are."

"But, surely, sir—"

Croker cleared his throat loudly. "And what news of the Administration, Mister Fredericks?"

"The Republicans are still firmly in charge. Madison defeated Clinton, and J. Q. Adams. Henry Clay and Albert Gallatin are off to Europe for a peace commission. Changes in his cabinet could affect our position—at sea, especially, and the Great Lakes. *Chesapeake* makes ready for sea, as do *Hornet, Congress* and the *United States*. What you won't read in their newspapers and broadsides is how many in the crew die of the scurvy—and how nearly two thirds of those crews are English, British tars promised better treatment, better pay and better grub. Soon enough *they* want to melt into the population ashore, to escape any sea duty. Most American politicians simply indulge in wishful thinking that there are abundant and loyal American crews for even the few American vessels available."

Fredericks studied his interlocutors and smiled. "The northwest could be extremely problematic for us, especially concerning the Indian question. Our forts in the territories on the Canadian frontier helped foster the prevailing attitude among most westerners that England is the one true friend. But many tribes are not enemy to the Americans; they know that no white man will look kindly toward anyone who favors their own expansion to the West."

"Broke is still in Halifax with *Shannon* and, as you know, we also have *Africa, Junon, Centurion* and more than a dozen others." Croker explained.

"By God, I wish we had 'Copenhagened' these rebel rascals in '07—that is what they feared more than losing one of their business profits!"

"The colonials are like cubs," said Fredericks. "They possess a terrible power, but they can be housebroken. Not by bullying, which will only make them wild, but by training: careful, judicious, patient. The last thing we need now, gentlemen, is to extend the conflict any longer than necessary, regardless of Bonaparte. Your biggest trading competitors are the colonies, so you jettison the Orders in Council but not impressment as necessaries while fighting Napoleon. These Yankees were working according to our plans without realizing it, until you let the puppets talk: then they leapt to the other side, if only to annoy us. The Federalist Party is doomed. You will find that you have paid too high a price for these American seamen."

Croker nodded. "We have paid a too high price already. If it weren't for Bonaparte, we could teach Jonathan some manners. Of course, we had hoped such measures would be unnecessary, but France threatens the world, except for Wellington. That is Boney's Achilles heel—"

"Just as America is mine," said Castlereagh.

"But both seem to snatch victory from defeat," added Croker. "And British fighting men 'bleed forever to save our empire from invidious men.'"

"Let us hope not," said Castlereagh.

"Meanwhile, gentlemen, I have another engagement I must attend," growled Fredericks. "You have my written reports here, and recommendations. I have been staying at Wentworth's. For now, if you will excuse me." He bowed, and left. The sky outside the window had darkened to night, the light having faded prematurely, auguring another storm.

Croker sighed and looked at Castlereagh. "Shall we conclude this discussion over brandy, my Lord?"

SIX

Ogdensburg, New York - *February 23, 1813*
Federalist Judge Ford's house on the southwest side of Oswegatchic River and the St. Lawrence River

SERELEA HAD JUST RETURNED from the main part of Ogdensburg, slamming the heavy door shut and sliding home the bolt before she shook off her bearskin overcoat and looked lovingly at Peter, swaddled in bed. "Macdonell's Glengarry boys are drilling on the ice again," she said, "Hundreds of 'em, just out of range of our north battery of two 24-pounders."

"Well? They like marching in the snow," said Peter in a wheezing, scratchy voice.

"Something's different this time," she said.

"Listen," Peter croaked, waving a newspaper. "From the *Republican Gazette*: 'Privateer schooner *Merlin* still has not returned, long overdue and feared lost along with *Saucy Jack*. But prize ship *Elizabeth* from Jeffries' earlier cruise did arrive commanded by Mister Jack Logan, with a crew rich with prize money and stories, expecting to see their Captain Jeffries . . . *Minerva* and *Medusa* along with *HMS Bellerophone* catch up with . . . still no news of . . .'" His weak voice trailed off, as if he were falling asleep. His right shoulder had started to bleed again through the cotton dressing.

"I understand you miss your friend," said Serelea, stroking his hair. "But right now we need to get you well, so you can–"

"Serelea, I want you to–"

"Silence. Our journey here from Frenchtown has opened your cut again. Lie back down and rest quietly," she commanded, and he obeyed, still recuperating under the brilliant and relentless care of this unbelievable "squaw," Serelea. They struggled toward some destination he knew not. In his recurring delirium he would see her beautiful brown body under the colorful beaded deerskin blouse and breathe her intoxicating love. Since fighting against the Americans was no longer palatable, Peter felt tormented by memories of the part he played in the disasters suffered by Nathan and his parents, Barbara Steward, Catherine Charles and the more-or-less innocent lives lost through despicable behavior of Indians—even some Shawnee, though never Tecumseh himself.

The not-so-innocent American town of Ogdensburg, founded by rich and powerful Federalist David Parish, refused any Army intrusion from either side, daily trading over the river with the enemy, and trading raid parties that were punitive or profitable, not military. Sporadically, the small British/Canadian regular infantry force marched back and forth through the snow and ice out of Prescott on the frozen St. Lawrence River.

"But they want their horses back," she said. "They want blood. I talked to the colonel myself—"

"You did what? How?" Peter asked, astonished again.

"I passed myself off as a young man."

"And they believed that?" Peter demanded weakly.

"Shut up," she said. She jabbed at lightning speed and grabbed his face, hers deformed into a nasty scowl, wolf-like, brutally, fiercely kissing him, her small lips expanding and tearing at his, her hands clasping iron-like around his body. Then she wrapped her legs, that small perfect body around his, and his pain seemed to dissipate. Her lovely round face, huge dark eyes, lips wide open. Peter stirred.

"Do you want me to stop?" she whispered sharply, biting in his ear.

Suddenly they heard the popping of British six-pounders and the roaring crash of 18-pounders from the Canadian side of the St.

Lawrence.

"Stay!" she ordered, and ran to open the door.

The vision confirmed her worst fears, and she closed the door again.

"All their batteries are firing," she said. "The entire column is attacking across the ice. I saw shots hit the Courthouse and Parish's store. Everybody is running, including Forsyth and his troops. The Canadians will be here soon."

"Serelea, I—"

"You just lie there and stay quiet!" she hissed. "We will soon be bereft of any Americans, and our company will be—"

Gunfire intensified briefly, and they could smell the white clouds of gunsmoke outside. Serelea felt Peter's pulse and temperature and knew his fever had reached its crisis.

She placed her hand over his mouth and, with a stern look, turned away and walked back to the door, nodding at what she saw before closing the door once again and rummaging through the large leather bag by the bed.

When the squad of troops reached her door and pounded on it, Serelea strode out with two loaded pistols pointed at the corporal. "What is it you want, sir?" she said.

"Listen to this one! Get the wench! What is it we want? Hah! You, for starters, my pretty squaw!"

One pistol exploded as he walked toward her, leering. He fell backwards, away from the blast, his chest a gaping red hole. After a stunned moment, another soldier screamed, "Get her, men! Get the bitch!" and charged the small, sweet-looking woman, whose face remained eerily calm. The next soldier's face dissolved in red mist as the second pistol ball crashed through his nose and jerked his head back as he toppled backward.

As a third soldier crept up behind her, Serelea dropped both guns and whirled around with a naked stiletto blade glinting in the sun, and in the blink of an eye that blade sank up to the hilt in the hapless man's eye socket. Serelea jumped back to avoid the initial bloodspurt and then retrieved the knife. No one was near her now, but more would soon come. She went back inside to reload and see to her man, then quickly returned to the door.

Now a British lieutenant strutted up to her, the remainders of the corporal's squad behind him.

"What is the meaning of this?" he asked her, beginning to draw his own bloody sword.

"This is Judge Ford's house," said Serelea. "Get out of here!"

The young officer blinked in the cold, his breath slowly dissipating in the mild air, filled already with gunsmoke.

"And you are . . . ?" he asked.

"Perhaps we better talk to your Colonel Macdonell, *Lieutenant*!" she barked.

This soldier, all British, was nonplussed, as she knew he would be, and began to retreat back toward the town.

"I . . . I will talk to . . . the colonel," he stuttered, and left her with no one nearby.

She dashed back inside and began packing. "Time for us to leave, my love," she said to Peter. "If the British don't burn us out, their Winnebagos will. At least you have had *some* rest."

"I d-doubt they will touch the Judge's house, but I . . . I can't help you now, Serelea," he croaked. "I think you had better—"

"Oh, the arrogance of the man," she cut in. "I am saving *you*, Peter Hughes—or Walpalaneathy as some know you. Now get dressed and, if you can, help me gather up our supplies. We must ask Orange Moon to save us one more time."

Her remarkable pinto pony had gotten them this far, unaided by white men or Indians, and was now ready to resume the march through snow and ice.

"Damn them!" she growled, "Your Americans could have captured Quebec or Montreal and ended this mess. Instead, Queenstown Heights, Detroit and Ogdensburg! If you can't trust the enemy, who can you trust? Everybody is the enemy here, Peter my love. We must go southwest, upstream to the Lake, and resume your recovery at Sackett's Harbor; we can meet up again with Forsyth! But I must also complete my letter to Catherine Charles, and post it somewhere."

"What are you two planning now?"

"I will tell you later. Make sure we have everything—ride this way, if you can. Orange Moon doesn't mind, she likes you. Once I tie you on, we are ready."

The town was almost deserted now, with the soldiers nearly completed in their thorough work at booty, burning and killing of the wounded. No one could be trusted. But fear seemed alien to this brilliant, relentless and petite Indian leading the pinto. Peter said nothing, wakefulness already slipping away, fearing he had met his match.

SEVEN

British Guyana - *February 23, 1813*
Aboard Merlin

"YOU LEFT THEM IN Grenada? Extraordinary!" a darkly tanned Lieutenant George Steward exclaimed.

"St. George's, yes. Thompson was the only one who was causing trouble, insisting that we return to Baltimore immediately after our repairs—after I'd saved his hide—when all the time he was planning to take over the ship. He'd been furious with me for dumping so much treasure in order to get *Merlin* across the reef, and obviously wanted to seek revenge," said Nathan. "And by then, he was in fear of a keel-hauling. The only others we were forced to put ashore were four British tars."

"But the rest of the crew—"

"Fortunately for me, there were a large number of Spanish and blacks aboard. Hufman and I treated them fairly . . . explained to them that we had 'discovered' that Thompson and the others wanted to take command, run the ship into the Ivory Coast, turn her into a slaver and sell the crew to a plantation—why are you laughing?"

"You are remarkable! Such a story, and the crew believed it! But the British in Grenada . . .?"

"As far as they were concerned, *we* were British. Of course, Thompson threatened me, and them, but we had prepared the way grandly—I believe they might still be convinced that Thompson works for the U.S. government! He had done poorly at hiding all of his papers."

George laughed again. It was incredible that, while sailing off Devil's Island near the French Guiana coast, *Merlin* had spoken, of all ships, the sloop of war *Hornet*, two of whose lieutenants, Shubrick and Steward, had recently transferred from the *Constitution*. But there had been no time for lengthy conversation over the water. Nathan had waved eagerly to George, and noted Commander Lawrence's disappointment when he realized that *Merlin* could not become his prize. Another sail had been sighted to the north, and both ships dashed off in pursuit.

Merlin and *Hornet* had lost sight of the chase and of each other, continuing north along the coast of Surinam, but then on 21 February, just beyond the mouth of the Demerara River, British Guyana, their luck returned. A large armed barque, which turned out to be *Mishouka*, from Liverpool via Fayal and Paramaribo, was caught between *Merlin*, in shore, and the *Hornet* several miles out. Before the latter appeared in a timely fashion, a number of broadsides from the two remaining vessels had injured crew and rigging. One *Merlin* crewman later died, and several on the *Mishouka*. There was little hull damage.

On the whole, although Nathan regretted the loss of life, the meeting and engagement were completely fortuitous; but Nathan was sure the prize would rightly be shared by both American vessels—in fact, prize crews from *Merlin* and *Hornet* were aboard *Mishouka* now, with strict orders to mind their manners. The prize and *Merlin* anchored in six fathoms, within sight of the fort and a league from Corobana Bank. Nathan knew Lawrence, also without a pilot, was as nervous of shoal water as he was. George, coming aboard *Merlin*, told Nathan that Lawrence would interview him shortly, receiving him on the sloop.

"But how did you find yourself with Thompson?" asked George.

Nathan told him about the events leading up to the cruise of *Merlin*. Thompson's appearance at Fell's Point with a solution to his problems over getting a ship had been too neat, all too easy; the timely offer by a mysterious benefactor, in Nathan's view, was too well orchestrated. Why was there not another commander? Why risk offering *Merlin* to Nathan, a man with relatively little command experience, and even accused of cowardice? His suspicions made him uncertain about taking the ship, but a decision seemed to crystallize that night Nathan lost thousands at the gaming table, money he could not afford to lose, gambling at Blackistone's. Besides, the list of ships that would not take him, the people to whom he owed money and the taunts led him to the desperate hope that in this last gamble he had gauged correctly.

George was incredulous. "You mean you deliberately risked further ruin, knowing the offer might just be another part of the plan for the destruction of Nathan Jeffries?"

"I suppose it was foolhardy. I struggled with Thompson from the beginning, and decided that I would gain the loyalty of the strange crew, with the help of my trusted friends aboard. Hufman overheard Thompson bragging how gullible I was in believing that he hated the Austers as much as I did. I considered several options, once I began to expose his plot: I could sink *Merlin*, give it to the Portuguese or the French as a prize, or merely threaten to do so.

"Finally I made it clear to Thompson that there would be no more tricks, that his choices were to tell me everything, or he would lose the ship and his life, in a most unpleasant fashion. I raised the ante, you might say; the stakes, he was convinced, were too high for him to bluff. He finally confessed to the plan, to make me a British privateersman, a clever plan devised by a man who is a British associate of the Austers. Even Thompson does not know his real name, but knew him as Fredericks. This British agent told him that the Admiralty brings greedy American privateersmen into the British fold through men like Thompson, to prey upon neutrals, or their own countrymen, any vessel *but* a British one. The New England coastline and ship owners are left alone in the hope that New England will rejoin Old England."

"I am glad you refuse to plunder your own country," said George, trying to hide the sarcastic tone. "But your poor father; William must be—"

"He hates me now, I have no doubt. Hearing the scuttlebut about my voyage and thinking the worst."

His father had said nothing about losing their money, but the painful memory of his escape, slipping away from Long Wharf, just as William's carriage arrived to stop them, would haunt Nathan forever. His father, held in place by two men, staring at his son in the gloom of dusk, a son whom he had warned, begged not to return to sea, especially not as a smuggler. But Nathan would stop at nothing to beat the Austers, for once and for all ... and they needed money again, did they not? He did not tell George that, to help destroy the Austers, he might *not* draw the line at attacking U.S. ships. He would plunder any vessel, if necessary, but preferably not American. He also did not talk about Barbara, his hatred for her, even as he still yearned to hold her in his arms; how much did George know? That seemed long ago, another time, before he lost his mother and lost his mind.

It was a dangerous game he played, but Nathan had won aboard *Merlin*, thanks to his earlier practice. He and his mates aboard had won over most of the crew Thompson thought hand-picked, so it had been easy to convince them to work for Nathan as somewhat more legitimate U.S. privateers with suitable certificates, pardons, protections. He would operate exactly the same as they would have with Thompson—except that they would concentrate on British merchant shipping. And they had been successful; shortly after removing Thompson and company, they had cut out several merchantmen from convoys, dodging their escorts—one was a rich Indiaman, which stood an excellent chance of reaching an American port. There had been a few narrow escapes for *Merlin*. Once a determined 74-gun ship, under wind conditions favorable to the larger ship, had chased them for two harrowing days before giving over. *Merlin* seldom required that long to make her captures; her victims expressed astonishment at her speed. Once a large armed schooner, *Tobago*, had had the temerity to fire at them; she quickly dropped her colors after several *Merlin* broadsides on her quarter cut her up badly. Ironically, *Tobago* turned out to hail from Savannah, Georgia, though carrying forged papers and British goods. Nathan let them go.

Their last prize, making eight in all, was the London brig *Ellen*, they captured south of Trinidad at latitude 8.40 north and roughly 61 degrees west longitude, almost to the mouth of the Orinoco. Some might be recaptured by the British; but if only three or four of these vessels returned safely, Nathan would be a wealthy man—especially if he benefited from the *Mishouka*. Of course, there were also the hazards of Thompson and his cronies, legal complications in Boston, and more; but he decided he would talk to one of the shipowners, William Gray, and ask him to intervene with his partner, Peabody. With their support, Nathan hoped that he might succeed.

During their run down the islands, a mooring at Tobago had proved fortuitous, too; they had made their offing, but then almost lost the rudder, cycling in a trough in a strong wind off the coast. Any earlier, even a few cablelengths, and *Merlin* might have been laid on her beam ends. As it was, the weather had turned fair, the fates favorable; there had been a southerly breeze rising that would just serve to ease them into a deserted cove. Ten days work for the carpenter and rewoven tiller ropes made the ship as seaworthy and maneuverable as ever. There had been no need to run into port, which had been problematic even before 1812. In an issue of the *Naval Chronicle*, Nathan read of the Mexican war for independence, still dragging on, and Hidalgo's death, and of the uneasy relationship between Spain and the U.S., which had been that way since long before 1807, when the Spanish in exile joined the British against Napoleon. This unease existed even during the days of the Continental Navy, according to his father. The war between the U.S. and Great Britain apparently remained a sideshow to the latter, but it had become a more urgent sideshow.

"But why did you venture so far south in your search for riches?"

"It is simple, George. I wanted to sail across the Line, and see the Amazon. It might seem strange—but see, we still found each other, and made another capture."

George shook his head and smiled. "No prisoners aboard? No cargo?"

"We have done a little trading since Grenada. We've some molasses, Madeira, salt and coal—oh, and of course, specie and valuables. But I sent most of the prisoners north with their own vessels. Some we paroled in St. Martin and Martinique."

"Hmm. Risky." Nathan could tell George disapproved of much of this. He shrugged.

Nathan's mate Hufman stuck his head in.

"The wind is backing northerly, sir. Other than the prize and *Hornet*, there are no other ships in sight. Will we weigh anchor, make for the open sea?"

"No . . . no. Maintain a good watch aloft, though, Mister Hufman, and let me know if we get any east in the wind. We might have to move then, if necessary, but not before."

"Aye, aye, sir." That young face, not merely flat, but almost concave, dish-shaped, revealed little; so competent, so homely. When Hufman did grin, it revealed protruding, haphazard, frightening teeth; he wore his hair unfashionably long, in a pigtail, like an old tar. Nathan loved the man, and had learned to trust him completely—with secrets, with managing the ship, with his life.

"And tell Carter to stop that caterwalling above me. If he must butcher the song, have him do it in the foc's'l."

"Aye, Captain," Hufman sighed.

As the sun slanted up and down, they could hear the creaking and groaning of the old hull, and then singing on deck, the music of a horn-pipe lost up among the spars; bare feet slapped and drummed on pine, and the rigging hummed along:

. . . I thought I hear the Old Man say,

Leave her Johnny, Leave her; you may go ashore and

Draw your pay. And it's time for us to leave her . . .

The singing suddenly stopped.

"But tell me, George, more about this great victory of yours, off Bahia. Begin with your cruise south to the Line."

George told Nathan how ill fortune or worse had continued to plague the unpopular "Hard Luck Bill" Bainbridge, infecting the *Constitution*, the sloop of war *Hornet*, and probably the *Essex*, as well. Even with Bainbridge in command of the squadron, every American knew that hot, bloody action was in store, especially with Lawrence in command of *Hornet*. But their cruise south had been marked by more frustration and misfortune than Nathan had ever dreamed. Weeks had gone by as Bainbridge and Porter played an ultimately pointless game of false messages and invisible ink, with letters deposited with and picked up from the governor of Fernando de Noronha. They had not sighted *Essex* at Cape Frio, Rio de Janeiro, Bahia or any of the other points of rendezvous, and by the time they lay off Sao Salvador, Brazil, on December 13, both commanders were obviously nettled and itching for action as much as the crew. The Portuguese governor was officially neutral but in fact was a British ally, and the British 74-gun *Montagu* was another threat reported in the vicinity.

Their hopes had soared when they learned that the British brig *Bonne Citoyenne*, roughly equal to the *Hornet* in size and firepower, was at anchor in the harbor, loaded with over 200,000 pounds, over one million dollars in specie. As Bainbridge searched the coast for other prey, pledging not to interfere with *Hornet* and *Bonne Citoyenne*, Lawrence tried to coax the British into leaving port for a fight in international waters.

But it was all to no avail. Finally *Constitution* had left *Hornet* to watch the enemy brig, a one-ship blockade, and sailed to the southeast. Some thirty miles off the Brazil coast, *Constitution* met up with a British frigate, *Java*, and destroyed her.

When Nathan heard this story from George, he burned with envy; then he felt a chill, whether of anticipation, excitement, fear or prescience, he knew not. The *Java*, roughly equal to *Guerriere* in firepower, had also been a French prize, but was newer, faster, and more maneuverable. After two hours in the clear, light afternoon she was similarly left a riddled hulk "with nary a spar standing." She was also blown up. The American damage and losses were somewhat heavier than in the earlier battle: nine killed and twenty-five wounded, including Bainbridge himself, wounded twice, once when the wheel was shot away. But on *Java*, sixty were dead and one hundred wounded, including Captain Lambert, whose sword Bainbridge returned before Lambert died. When the heavy frigate had returned to Sao Salvador on January 2, she carried 400 prisoners and incredible news.

Bainbridge was the hero of the hour now. "Henry Chadds, the senior British lieutenant," said George, "admitted the *Constitution* was handled in a most masterly fashion. He said it made him regret that she was not British." Nathan had met Bainbridge some years earlier, and had tried to avoid a tendency to stare at the pompous man's enormous sideburns and incipient jowls.

"But Captain Hull is still the man for me," George said. "He would have accomplished the same ends more cheaply, though I'll not gainsay Bill's courage and capabilities. I simply do not like the man, that is all. He treats officers and dignitaries with all that courtly aplomb, but the crew he says are dogs. 'Tis a flayed back for the least offense, the last man down. And now they return to Boston, supposedly to refit and repair, but really so that Bill can bask in glory."

And that is what happened, after the prisoners were taken care of. George had stood with Lawrence on the quarterdeck of *Hornet* and watched Old Ironsides sail north to more glory back home. *Hornet* had continued her patrol off Bahia. Lawrence, a big, powerful man, was very popular among officers and crew, but allowed now a little of his anger and hunger for battle to show through. "We shall take that damned brig," he said, "if it takes another year!"

But *Bonne Citoyenne* refused to come out, and after *Hornet* had captured a merchant schooner with a cargo of specie they learned that the 74-gun HMS *Montagu* had arrived. George knew how much Lawrence hated being chased away—the entire crew did. But under the circumstances they were forced to prudence to evade the ship of the line and run north at night.

The rest of January had gone by, and in early February, off Pernambucco, near Recife, they captured the English brig *Resolution* of 10 guns. But for most of February, there was no action of any great significance, and Lawrence apparently felt near despair. Now here they were, approaching the Demerara River in British Guyana, not 400 miles north of the equator. George did not get along particularly well with Lieutenant Stuart, indisposed on the sick list, but Lawrence was not unpleasant to him, and Shubrick, the first lieutenant, and Connor and Newton, acting lieutenants, also trusted him. But George had felt the frustration eating at all of them; what had happened to Porter? Where was the *Essex*? Where was the enemy? They had a number of lightly armed privateers and merchant prizes to their credit, now this *Mishouka*, and thousands in specie; but they hungered for a worthy opponent, "the way a newborn hungers for milk."

"You do seem to be born to the life, George; but then people like you. I make enemies."

"You do sometimes have an abrasive way about you, Nathan," George grinned, patting his shoulder affectionately. "Sometimes you may gain more by showing a little more tact."

"Possibly," Nathan grinned back. "But in this business I feel it is necessary. I regret, old friend, we cannot always be discrete and subtle. Diplomats are not paid by weight of merchandise."

"Still, there's more to life than pounds and barrels, Nathan." Suddenly George began to sing:

Onward she sails, my love from the sea,

into the dangerous waters of my soul;

that passion, the curse of young and old!

On a bold course for my lover and me.

Then he stopped, embarrassed by his exuberance. "That is only the first verse," he mumbled.

Nathan stared at him in amazement. "It is fine, truly! An excellent ode, and well-executed. Who wrote that?"

George coughed and cleared his throat. "I must confess I dabble in poetry, myself, to while away the hours sometimes."

"I am most impressed," Nathan said. His voice was solemn with the encroachment of inebriation.

"Nathan, I—"

"You are a truly gifted soul, George. A generous soul and a great friend."

They were luxuriating in fresh dairy produce, fruit, vegetables and meat, thankful to be relatively free of the fetid odors and walking hardtack. Nathan thought again of Peter's gift to him, Lind's *Treatise on the Scurvy.* On this southern voyage, *Merlin* had lost two men, one to a fall and one to the fever. Another two were ailing, but there were no other injuries or sicknesses at the moment, a remarkably happy state of affairs. Two dozen of the crew were sailing north in the prize ships, but that still left more than enough to work the ship. They had lemons and oranges, guava, fresh butter, honey, eggs; the list rolled along of the pleasures of the food available here.

Then he remembered another pleasure, one of the flesh, a fortnight ago, when he had *not* slept alone. At the Monarch Tavern, in Port-of-Spain, she had danced with various men, but her dark, sultry eyes had continually returned to him, flashing, brilliant, Spanish or Indian eyes, filled with passion. Her lithe, almost muscular form captivated and aroused him as they began to move together, to the unfamiliar, exotic music of stringed instruments and drums. Laughing, in broken English, she showed him the Mediterranean "Gregale," a dance named after the violent, dangerous northwest winds that blow destruction through the islands, around the equinox. It was unnecessary to fight for her; other men watched as they left together, no doubt envious but not jealous enough to challenge him or cause trouble.

She was eager and inventive. Their lovemaking exhausted him and brought him to the most mindless oblivion he had ever experienced. But in the morning she was gone; she had disappeared like the "Gregale" itself. And he looked for her, but did not find her.

Nathan and George overheard a loud voice nearby on the *Mishouka,* left the cabin and went up on deck to watch the man holding forth. He was an older tar, with sun-browned, tattooed arms, heavy crowsfeet and thick, salt-and-pepper queued hair.

"A brave and wondrous sight she wore too, lads, gliding over that still gray pond out there in the wee hours of the morning, with silver shining patches where the light shone through the clouds, every stitch o' canvas set, nary a breath of wind, her teeth showin' on both sides, the biggest, boldest frigate you ever saw. The *Constitution,* she was, I knewed her. Even the limeys respect her, though they hate to admit it."

To Nathan's disgust, he was not summoned by Lawrence that

evening, and bid a temporary farewell to George for the night, as he returned to *Hornet*. An hour later the three ships were still together; *Hornet* still hove to, and Nathan had gone below again, sitting at the table in his cabin. He looked with distaste at the chart over which he and the new sailing master, Tyler, had been arguing. Nathan had selected and promoted Tyler because he was intelligent, capable and stubborn enough to argue, even with his own captain, when he felt strongly enough about a decision. This made him the best man for the job, but also insured that they would constantly wrangle. Alone again, he sighed, and settled down to continue his journal:

Merlin is completely refitted and her bottom clean and provisions and stores complete. We had intended to complete our trading in Surinam and possibly West Indies ports on the return as per suggestions. I have included the losses from prior to capture of Mishouka *bound for Maranhao, and the list of names of replacements from Trinidad and the account I recorded of those earlier events. Re. our crew, it is in excellent health and spirits and I cannot endorse enough their work and enthusiasm and especially the skill and loyalty of mate Hufman and acting sailing master Tyler.*

Even allowing for expenses here our profits to date are sure to exceed $50,000, and re. Mishouka, *its condemnation and value are still uncertain but I will do whatever I can; re. cargo earlier on shore, most hogheads of tobacco have been sold or traded, only a few oz. of indigo remain, and we have extra arms and gunpowder, naval stores and ordinance aboard, plus some copper, corn, potatoes, onions, and wheat flour, mostly for the crew. In addition we have ten casks of Madeira, a roughly equal amount of olive oil, a barrel of raisins, two tons of sugar, over a hundred bolts of fine linen and silk, Talavera porcelain work and some that made its way here from China, Venetian glass ware, some leather goods and precious stones, jewelry, and specie amounting to four thousands, silver crowns and Spanish gold, mostly. All of the rum is gone, except that for our own use.*

Nathan decided to delay sending the report until he had discussed the *Mishouka* prize with Lawrence; then he would how much he could record in the ship's log, or in letters. Yes, he would continue his report when he returned from the *Hornet*. He suspected it might be wise to avoid mentioning *Hornet*'s part in the capture.

THE NEXT MORNING, February 24, the sky was bleak and pearly. It was nearly eight bells, the end of the watch, when Nathan and George finally dined with Captain Lawrence, his face already somewhat florid from the wine he sipped discretely. Nathan, even wearier than George, fought to restrain a desire to laugh at Lawrence's attempts to be a courtly, sophisticated host. He could not help but like the man, anyway; his handsome, long, slightly curved nose, open face, with wide, fleshy cheeks, gentle chin, and almost prissy mouth giving him a boyish, or even slightly girlish aspect, in spite of the fashionably immense sideburns.

"The captain of *Mishouka* told us that he was bound from Madeira for Maranhao," said Lawrence, eventually getting down to business. "They have aboard . . . let's see . . . coffee, jerked beef, flour, fustic, butter, and $23,000 in specie."

"Yes," said Nathan. At least, he thought, Lawrence is an educated man. Even in this small cabin, he noted—and envied—Lawrence's collection of Shakespeare, Pope, Swift, Hume and Gibbon, as well as Greek and Latin classics. He saw these old and vaguely familiar names, as well as new or unfamiliar ones. Jonathan Edwards, Kant, Edward Taylor, Rousseau, Byron, Goethe, Scott, Shelley, Coleridge, Wordsworth, *The Connecticut Wits*, de Crevecoeur's *Letters From an American Farmer*, at least two additions of Bowditch's *Practical Navigator*. He also noted a chronometer, sextant, letter book, order book, signal book, and various professional texts. A marble bust of Marcus Aurelius near the window seemed to wink and turn in the light from the swinging, gimballed lamp.

George began to speak. "Captain Jeffries, sir, would like to discuss a request—"

"A truly impressive library, sir," Nathan broke in.

"Thank you," said Lawrence. "They say the Enlightenment, the age of reason, has been swept away by apostles of the natural, free and romantic; dare to know has become dare to imagine."

George seemed annoyed, and cleared his throat. "I would like to explain to you, sir—if you will let me—Captain Jeffries . . . why he has a just claim to specie or cargo of *Mishouka* in exchange for expenses and loss caused by her."

"What loss? Oh, I see."

"It is true we came to the rescue, as it were, but who knows what would have transpired if we had not and no doubt, you have letters of marque issued by the Commonwealth of Massachusetts?" George turned to his friend.

"Of course! We were authorized as a privateer and letter of marque when we received new guns, against just such an event."

"Privateer?" Lawrence said. "Rather more than letter of marque."

"Our involvement does complicate the matter, sir," George added quickly. "Certainly, an involvement Captain Jeffries fully appreciates."

"Yes," said Nathan. "Without you, our fate was dubious at best, but I believe legally we are entitled to a share of the prize, as co-combatant. Is that correct, George?"

"I think we are on safe ground there, sir." George replied.

"Let us be clear here, Mister Steward. I shall decide what is proper here. We need no sea lawyers."

"It takes men of sense, sir," said Nathan loudly, "not sea lawyers, nor demigods, to decide what is fair and just."

"Do not use that tone with me, sir. You and your men are lucky to be free, and alive!"

"That is true, Captain, and I apologize for raising my voice but the fact remains, I have a duty to care for my crew, and look to the investment my employers have made in this voyage." Nathan chose not to mention that at present it was not clear who were the legal employers or owners of *Merlin.*

Lawrence leaned back and raised his hand in submission. "I have no more time to argue this point, Jeffries. I will see to it that you receive compensation, subject to condemnation of the *Mishouka.* What would you consider reasonable?"

The steward returned, and Nathan waited until he had sipped some coffee before answering.

"Seven thousand dollars, or two thousand pounds, whichever is convenient."

"Seven thousand, that is absurd, Jeffries! Impossible."

"Sir, that is—"

"If I receive the approval of the our nearest authorities, and the assurance of our minister, I would probably be able to release one thousand dollars."

"Captain, I cannot possibly accept less than four thousand. When you consider—"

"Three thousand, then, sir."

"Done, sir." Nathan did not look happy, but inwardly he rejoiced.

Lawrence grinned in spite of himself. "You turn me into a bargainer; you are a persistent fellow, aren't you?"

"The majority of benefit falls to you and this national vessel, Commander Lawrence—and I, after all, have helped and also have taken care of my crew."

"How convenient, that you can 'help' your country, and get rich off prizes, too."

"Sir!"

"Captain," said George, "may I remind you that our orders are to treat *bona fide* American vessels, merchant or privateer, with greater tact than our enemy did in peacetime, to exercise leniency in cases of doubt, and only detain ships clearly violating—"

"Unless I order it, Lieutenant. Any other comments?"

Lawrence was impatient.

"I will be honored to see you back in America, Captain," said Nathan.

EIGHT

Fell's Point, Baltimore - *April 12, 1813*
Hanover and Thames

THE OUTSIDE LATCH CLICKED loudly, the door slammed
open, and there he was, Captain Nathan Jeffries, swaying unashamedly,
his faded coat showing signs of recent Madeira, loudly proclaiming his
presence. His face more stern, commanding.

It was Nathan, the same blue eyes, sandy hair, flat, almost handsome features, now cured brown in the sun and salt; and yet the expression distant, as if it were not the same man.

It was just after three in the afternoon. Catherine had put William
to bed. The good Doctor Amos lurked somewhere. Their "protected" girl
Gloria was out, getting supplies up the Hill. Meanwhile her new guest
sat patiently on the small sofa.

But Catherine knew this was not the same Nathan who began this
cruise in October 1812; himself, by then battered, barely recognizable as
the frightened boy she had barely known. And now, eyes glazed, a mad
look that one does not resist.

The expression on her aristocratic features, now oddly pale, was
neither haughty nor contemptuous. She was shocked, almost frightened; perhaps her shock was even greater than his own. Nathan stared
angrily, impatiently, at those delicately curved lips, small and thin,
tapering at the ends; luscious, swollen and ripe in the middle, trembling
in the corners. He watched them struggled for control. Catherine pulled

him further inside and threw her arms around his neck. She kissed him violently on the lips.

After the two had recovered, he turned to the sofa. "And who is this lovely 'breed'?"

Serelea abruptly stood in her beautiful deerskin.

Catherine looked as if Nathan had slapped her. "Nathan! Please! This is Serelea, a friend of . . . Peter's," said Catherine. "My dear, this is Captain—"

"Ah! Indian princess wench to lead my traitor and betrayer half-breed to further ruination."

"Nathan!"

"I am now a-going to Canada," he sang, "And there I will get money; and there I'll kiss the pretty squaws; they are as sweet as honey."

He deftly dodged Serelea's lightning jab and picked up her squirming, exquisite body, winking at a frozen Catherine.

To his victim he said quietly, "Behave or I break your neck."

She nodded, so he tossed her on her feet.

"Why don't you go to my teepee and we will talk later?" he said, gently, as she staggered back.

Serelea looked at Catherine, whose eyes pleaded for understanding.

Nathan studied the trembling girl, who turned away and left.

"She is staying in with your father for tonight. Nathan, how could you—"

"Who in Jehova's oven do you think you are," he roared, "telling me what to say or do in my home?"

This was not a greeting she had ever anticipated. "I am just grateful you are back safe," she whispered.

Nathan looked at her strangely, his face even flatter, less revealing, as if she were indeed talking to a stranger.

"What are you reading?" he asked.

She began to read aloud from the *Baltimore Sentinel*: "The good Mrs. Evans of Cape May says a British Agent waved a .65 caliber flint-lock navy pistol in her face, and agents have been reported in Rehobeth and Bethany, and we learn more from Mrs. Rodgers, much-admired wife of Commodore Rodgers, about her husband's heroic search for the Jamaican fleet homebound, on the last page in an Incredibly Detailed report; and the British captured by our privateers and our frigates *United States* and *Constitution*—twice; and the tragic although triumphant loss of our sloop *Wasp,* and part of his report as well as Commodore Decatur's and Captain Hull's on the last page. According to the *London Times,* we gleefully quote, and gloat, 'Even after our righteous triumphs at Detroit and Queenstown, this is quite a disaster.'"

"I am sorry, dear Catherine, for my drunken rage. Please ask your guest to forgive me, and allow me to make formal amends in the morning."

"Nathan, I think it is better if—"

"With my esteemed father sleeping it off, I am the head of this house, and may I assure you in the name of my sainted mother I must make all the decisions here now—except for Doctor Protector." And indeed his voice began to mesmerize her, and she obeyed.

But when she returned to the parlor, he was not there.

Then suddenly, electrifyingly, he was: warm hands on her shoulders, caressing, soothing, and the waft of Madeira as he offered her the best stories of their cruise—including adventures on land she hated to hear.

"And I guess you heard," he said. "My Mister Jack Logan and his crew made it safely with a small fortune aboard. But it's about revenge for most of us," Nathan sighed, "and not only profit. The blockades tighten, the odds—but I estimated correctly how we could take the damaged and lightened *Merlin* for refit and take on fresh water in Le Saintes, in the Guadeloupe channel, take on more supplies, in this case in San Juan. We allowed ourselves another celebration on the town, then skirted the Bahamas; and I saved crew and vessel; think of it! After tearing the ship over the reef to escape the *Minerva*—we think it was that frigate—we careened the good *Merlin,* hauling out and repairing the ship in a beach near Terre-de-Haut, as my mate pronounces it, in the Saintes, off the main island of Basse-Terre." Nathan quickly ran through the incredible adventures with the *Hornet.* Catherine's black eyes widened.

"When we did return, we stayed in the Caribbean through the Mona Passage, then hugged the Turks and Caicos, Eleuthera, then we made Florida at the St. Mary's River, Fernandina, then ran up to Savannah, all inside the Gulf Stream. We traded some there, for supplies and more repairs; I wrote to my father and to the *Merlin* owners, then avoided the British again into Chesapeake Bay. Even with all that, we sailed from Guadeloupe just three weeks ago. And we still return with a highly respectable treasure—maybe $100,000! And nearly all of my crew survived to share my good fortune. My share will be at least $10,000, probably more."

NATHAN WOULD OFTEN WONDER at his naiveté during the next few days, blustering and confident and letting all his concerns drift downstream. A week later, settled into his shore side routine, Nathan was now behaving the larger-than-life hero, but Catherine sensed that something was wrong. He was more violent, drinking constantly, seemingly trapped in fear, mentally on the run again, chasing up from the Caribbean—homeward bound. His hopes were fulfilled, he thought, now swaggering and staggering more than ever.

"You drink yourself into bed with—whores," she cut sharply at him. "And you had said you wanted only—"

"'Em jus'makin' up fer lost time, mah darlin'!" shouted a swaying, drunken Nathan. "My dear father couldn't make it to Blackistone's today so I—a sip off the old block, eh?"

"Nathan, please—what has happened—so suddenly?" she cried.

"My dear, we—"

"No! Doctor—it is all right."

Nathan ignored the massive Protector behind him.

"Leave him alone," she said sadly to the good Doctor Anderson.

"Yes," Nathan admitted. "Years ago, I thought I loved Barbara. The bigger fool I . . . if only that were my worst sin! And trying to keep from disappointing that . . . woman. And you. Again, I am so sorry. And you, my angel— here all the—"

"Stop lying, Nathan! Make sense. Tell me the truth."

And yet she knew he had her, and she could not resist. Regardless of the fate of the Nathan she had known, this one was even more powerful and compelling; she loved him with all the glaring stupidity of a naïve farm girl, admiring Great Men from afar and learning too late what they really are up close. Nathan was even more dangerous.

There in the dwindling candlelight of the foyer, he was kissing and fondling her from behind. His hands were so clever; caressing first her back, then lower, and she knew it was so wrong, but she was his, she knew she was his. Those fingers and hands played with her neck, legs, mind; those madly addictive hands, that voice, reassuring, insistent, seductive. She was on fire, she wanted him; she hated him for making her this way, never wanting him to stop, those maddening hands all over her. Walking her up to her bedchamber at other end of second floor hall, they stood there outside the guest chamber. Then he guided her inside, and began to kiss her voraciously. Catherine's protests died stillborn as their kissing became more heated. He lifted her effortlessly and carried her to the bed. His lips were on her neck as he released buttons and began to disrobe her; she half fought, half helped him, and began to fumble with his own scarf, then whispered, then hushed, trembling in his warm wind.

Later, as they lay in her bed in the dark she asked him again, "Do you not want to see your father?"

"Not particularly. But I suppose when he suffers his morning draught, I can discuss some new arrangements here."

"What new arrangements?"

"The United States are doomed," he said. "You know as well as my father and I that Secretary Armstrong is an idiot; and there have been no preparations made, except in Baltimore, for British attacks up and down Chesapeake Bay and its rivers. If we had begun in 1807, instead of fearing a 'Copenhagen,' we could have had a fleet of purpose-built merchantmen-killers. The generation of my father's counsel, annoying as it was, has been silenced—except for Secretary Jones, but his entrance is too late. I will take care of my own, thank you, and sentimental patriot claptrap be damned!"

"Nathan, what are you saying? We are *Americans*. We must—"

"I must sell the house and find a small plantation far from the coast, away from this damned foolish war; it is every many for himself, you know."

"And every woman?" she felt like sobbing.

"We will pay the debt we owe you, Catherine, as I said—"

"The debt! You think I stayed here and helped you for—money?"

"I do not know what secrets you shared with my mother. I do not know why you brought that bewitching squaw—"

"Nathan, you must listen! Her Shawnee name is Taima and it means—"

"I don't care what it means, Catherine. I only care about people whom I can trust—or at least *tolerate*. For instance, normally, you know, on a cruise supercargo and mate are different. This time, with Mister Jack Logan away on the prize ship, Mister Phillip Thompson's share—did I tell you his name? I threw him off—"

"Phillip Thompson?" she cried, rolling on top of him.

NINE

Fell's Point - *May 9, 1813*

DOCTOR AMOS ANDERSON, the Protector of the residents and
Friends of 4 Hanover Street, off Thames Street, had always agreed with
his friend James Douglas, one of the ex-slave Quakers, when he denied
that the new world of nationhood was a hopeless ship of fools, and denied the fury to return some personal and political *favors* for the British.
It was an irrevocable vendetta, because to choose between the two was
like choosing between the devil and the deep blue sea. Only individuals
could be trusted to some degree. Peter Hughes had been their youngest
Protector, now somewhere near the great lakes, according to Taima. She
would not reveal his exact location, and Anderson did not blame her
enough to persuade her otherwise.

Catherine had insisted they add Nathan to their burden, and Doctor Anderson felt less hostile to the young fool after the *Merlin* affair—
Nathan hated everyone now, not just Americans, but at least he was
no coward. Like all Protectors Doctor Anderson unofficially honored
brave men, even his enemies. These days, some of the bravest Americans
happened to be friends of Amy's, the Quakers who did not fear the
government or anyone else. It was difficult to tell friend from foe, but
Anderson did have to admire Nathan's epic odyssey to save his men and
his ship; few mariners could have done it, according to none other than
Captain Joshua Barney. Nathan if nothing else was a natural-born sea
warrior, a raider, a fighter—and also a fool "sip off the old block," as the

Doctor's original master used to laugh about drunks.

In April, when a distraught Catherine had told him that Phillip Thompson in fact worked for Michael Fredericks, who reportedly ran most of the shipping companies in Chesapeake Bay, Nathan's triumph on his return rapidly shrank. The *Merlin's* owners were nearly as elusive as Fredericks and Thompson, but Nathan finally tracked down one of these gentlemen. He ended up running down the street away from Nathan, until the latter was pulled down and shackled by irate Baltimore constables. Nathan, briefly behind the thick rusty bars of the jail, finally thought he understood his father's lunacy. The *Merlin* documents proved, according to the court, that Nathan was entitled to no more than his "personal stores and valuables," which somehow the court upheld as precisely those valuables Nathan had thrown overboard to save the ship. Most of those in court were stunned. The rest of the crew would enjoy at least what they had signed on for. Nathan saw the smirk on the old judge's face.

"There is nothing more we can do right now, Nathan," Catherine had said. "Don't worry, and please do nothing . . . impetuous. We are working on that judge—his Honor, Ronald DeAbreu, a real swine. We are working on his mistress, too, that vixen-wench Tara Hart."

"That's fi—that is very comforting, I am sure," said a bitter Nathan. He ordered his men, especially Jack Logan, Tom Howard and young Jason Earleigh, old Enoch's boy, to do nothing and say nothing about his situation—no searches, no efforts at persuasion, so he at least could have the satisfaction of knowing that his men were taken good care of. Nathan felt the chill of that malevolent power, which was beyond his reach, and he knew his men were unhappy. Similarly, he had no control over Doctor Anderson at home, so he did not discuss anything with him. Other than his dubious presence, with Catherine away visiting the wife of Commodore Rodgers, if-you-please, in Havre de Grace with that uppity squaw, Serelea—or is it Taima?—he was alone except for Gloria and his miserable father. William had showed him the way towards full-term drunk, in his new favorite taverns, Saucy Sallie's, and White Horse, or Blackistone's, his home away from home. Here he drank his friends under the docket nearly every night, and finally ordered Gloria, who had begun to sound like Catherine in her relentless raking fire, to say nothing at all in his presence.

And his last battle with Catherine several weeks ago was particularly bloody, before she and Taima left for Havre de Grace. She would never accept his drunken gambling, "waiting for another ship" or "fighting for the *Merlin*" excuses. She could not silently watch him destroy everything.

"What is there left to destroy?" he had laughed.

"Stop acting like a child!"

"Stop trying to be . . . Amy!" he had snarled.

Or should he ask droopy, sad-eyed Doctor Amos Anderson to do something about it? With Catherine gone it seemed that he, rather than the Jeffries, ran this small house. In any case, Nathan felt that he had done everything he could, and should just surrender to the Sirens, and let the Thompsons and Frederickses of the world have their way. He would concentrate on savoring his breakfast and beer, and by noon be curled up to a heavily laden Madeira, or a brace of gin and rum that the British favored, or faro, so much to the better. Otherwise, there were always other ears and money to gamble at the White Horse or Blackistone's, and card-players galore. After a life-and-death voyage commanding *Merlin,* Nathan's shrunken share of the 145-day cruise only covers the costs to repair the schooner, pay his crew and other worthy causes, not just in the pockets of those bastards.

His father, secretly proud of his son's exploits, had always wanted him to join the navy, and even now railed on and on about Hull and Bainbridge on *Constitution,* Jones on *Wasp,* Decatur on *United States,* Lawrence on *Hornet* destroying the *Peacock*—who sank so fast she took some of ours with her. Even Catherine of the curling wave-like lips, mesmerizing, depthless eyes, even she was a voice crying in the wilderness, as Nathan dangerously heaved off into the night.

BUT THIS DAY STARTED with his father suffering a particularly bad fall, yelling at Gloria from the bottom of the stairs; he waved

Nathan away, his shouts crashing into Nathan's alcohol-ravaged-head like 32-pounders. No sooner had Doctor Anderson taken over that debacle and carried the old man upstairs when Nathan received the visit he had forgotten, had dreaded, from his one-time purser, the wizened little Endicott; the fat, slimy Highgate, now in partnership with another bastard; partner-in-slime, Captain Reynolds—the three noisiest swine who "represented the owners" including Phillip Thompson.

"Please have a seat, gentlemen," Nathan said. "My father is ill so I do not have a great deal of time."

"Yes, I, uh, I am sorry, Captain," said Endicott, "but we must proceed with uh, business. Mister Thompson wished me to convey—"

"Mister Thompson is no sea lawyer but a cracker jack attorney who knew how to cheat me."

"Captain Jeffries! We can—"

"Cheat me out of my rightful share of the—"

Nathan paused; Captain Reynolds and Highgate were smiling.

"Personally, Nathan," said Endicott, "I mean, Captain Jeffries, I praise your performance on the *Merlin* and feel it manifestly unjust that you receive nothing but a quit claim for $500."

"Captain Jeffries," said Reynolds, "we must remind you that as captain of *Merlin* your presence was requested and required for final restitution with Doughty, MacIntyre and their agents."

"Yes, *Captain*, and what about *my*—"

"Captain," said Highgate, "let us face facts. We are prepared to forgive your . . . debts to company and the house, including your—"

"Enough, sir!"

During their cruise, Nathan and his crew had captured one ship, two brigs, one schooner and one small sloop of war. "Do you really intend to go to sea again soon, Captain Jeffries?" asked Endicott.

"A plague of hubris is indeed rampant on the innocent land, sir," added Reynolds, "that a responsible patriot would risk his . . . family's good health for—"

"That will do, damn it!" shouted Nathan, his once-proud face, plain yet sensitive, even shyly heroic, too open and candid for effective subterfuge.

He signed the papers—signed his life away—and threw them back at Endicott. With the possible exception of this Captain Reynolds, Nathan could have easily laid this crowd to rest; but "his nose has been broken, so beware," as fighters say, as Peter Hughes had taught him—before his betrayal. Nathan threw them out, and Captain Reynolds laughed as he tossed five hundred dollars in coin on the floor. Nathan warned them to leave his father alone—at which point Endicott, also laughing, said, "Then he's to sea again, maybe Liverpool?"

Perhaps only the professional slick Highgate could see that if Nathan had had a pistol, he would have shot all three scoundrels, starting with the sub-Iago Endicott—but he was not the Moor in Avalon, only Baltimore, and he knew it was futile to resist. After the three men left, he trudged upstairs to his father's room, thinking how odd, of all times, to think of Peter's sharp, high cheekbones, striking, chiseled, intense, too swarthy to pass. Nathan had always been drawn to Peter's shrewd, burning dark eyes; a dangerous enemy, a trusted friend, he thought, and then the betrayal—now that bewitching Taima. The old man lay in bed quietly, still accompanied by the good doctor and Gloria, and Nathan looked down at the famous pale William Jeffries.

"Two letters arrived for yew, suh," said Gloria, handing them to Nathan. "I thought you would rather for me to wait till the gennelmen—"

"Yes, all right, Gloria, thank you," said Nathan, absently stuffing them in his coat pocket. "How is he, Doctor?"

"There is nothing you can do for him right now, Captain Jeffries." And that was that.

And then Nathan was on his way out to re-drink himself into oblivion at Blackistone's.

Sure enough, at two bells he had found his friends Jack Logan and Tom Howard at the tavern, and they made their report.

"Jason is with my cousin at Catonsville—he knows we'll send for 'im 'n we needs him," said Tom Howard.

Nathan nodded.

"Commander Lawrence's destruction of the *Peacock* is just about the only good news," said Logan. "*Constellation* fought off the British boats off Craney Island but the British are going to bottle up this bay. More and more towns are getting attacked up and down the bay, Delaware too—not to mention more disaster on our northern border, the Great Lakes. Looks like they're sending your friend Perry over there. And Lawrence's made captain on *Chesapeake* as reward for *Hornet's* 'Peacocking' that brig."

"No!"

"Look here for yourself, Cap'n," said Mister Logan, slurring his words and staggering as the earlier rye whiskey from Saucy Sally's finally caught up to him. The *Baltimore Federal Republican* and *Niles' Weekly Intelligencer* fell helplessly to the dusty wooden floor but were quickly rescued by Nathan, who was also working avidly on rum.

As he read about the great new hero, Nathan remembered meeting him for the first time back in '07 at the Stewards' before the Embargo, at that same damned ball, along with Perry. Their recent joint adventure in capturing a prize ship off British Guyana confirmed Nathan's respect for Lawrence. It made sense that Lawrence had climbed to captain of a frigate, no doubt a hero to his crew as well as to the admiring public.

"He wants us to join him, Captain. He can make you acting lieutenant; not the first, but he needs another lieutenant, and of course he needs us. We can make *Chesapeake* the first frigate victory of 1813! Also—maybe—prize money."

"What?"

"Should we sign up on *Chesapeake* in Boston, Captain? Some others in the *Merlin* crew are beached here, too—but some ships are still escaping northern ports."

"Let me first read these letters," said Nathan, still more or less sober.

The first one was from Catherine, and he instantly forgot about everything else:

May 3

Dearest Nathan,

I can only write briefly! It is early morning and Havre de Grace is under attack by Cockburn's British fleet—we recognized the frigates *Minerva* and *Maidstone*. The Commodore's wife, Minerva Rodgers, knows someone who can leave immediately before the invaders land, and avoid the iron shot and grape whirling all around, and explosions and people running from their homes. The Gibsons' is already a-blaze. The crashing and screams are terrible. We fear none of the town will be spared. Mr. O'Neill is the only one left in the Potato Battery, and those barges are filled with troops. Please do not try to come here, since by that time we will either be spared or not. I will return to Baltimore as soon as I can. Hopefully Taima will be able to return to Peter at that time.

I hope you and your father are well and that we will soon reunite.

Do know that I love you, Nathan, no matter what you might think of my behavior. I know with the growing British presence up and down the Chesapeake this spring you will do the right thing. Must get this to Mrs. Rodger's postal carrier.

Forever yours,

Catherine.

Nathan looked up at his friends, and did not bother to conceal his tears.

"What is it, Captain?"

"Havre de Grace has been attacked," said Nathan.

"What?" The two men stared at him.

"Here," said Nathan, quickly sobering up, handing Logan the letter.

Nathan meanwhile opened the other letter, curiously unmarked outside, in any way:

Captain J—

We applaude your exploits at sea but what a shame it is that man can get gored (hornd, as one might say) in his own home-towne. Though personally I never have guessed that your lovely Miss Catherine Charles, as she fancies herself, would be seen with the young R. Auster and now Mr. Fredericks! That you must take hard seeing as how you been robbed and legally falsified only now to be out-diallianced as they say with none other than the man you set to kill.

a Friend.

"Now I do understand," Nathan growled, crushing the letter.

"Captain, what did you say? What else is wrong?"

Tom Howard pulled back when he saw the look in Nathan's eyes.

"We will sort out and settle up our seachests tonight and sail or take the post-chaise to Boston tomorrow," Nathan ordered calmly, his mouth a slash in stone. "Round up everyone who wants to fight for his country. I may have to borrow a few dollars to help with the fare. We should be there in four days. Gentlemen, we're joining the *Chesapeake*."

TEN

Boston, Massachusetts - *June 1, 1813*
US frigate Chesapeake *sails to engage HMS frigate* Shannon

NOON—*CHESAPEAKE* HAD UNMOORED at 8 AM and was finally underway from President's Roads. "Deck there!" roared the lookout, "I make one sail beyond the light!"

"Captain?" Lieutenant Steward approached and saluted. "Sir, we have just received word from the pilot boat that there is still but one British frigate is in sight off the port."

The officers looked at each other, and grinned. Clear and light winds from the southwest.

"Yes. Thank you. Well, Number One, it is time to prepare for another British prize!"

"Shall we go through the formality of an attack, sir?"

"'Tis a pity, for all that pain and damage; but, yes, I fear it must be so. They must be convinced to surrender."

The British frigate was clearly leading her opponent away from Boston lighthouse to the southeast, while *Chesapeake* was still surrounded by well-wishers in civilian boats. The crew had complained about pay and prize money, but felt better about all the young female visitors in the crowds ashore, on the hills and in all manner of small vessels there to see them off and watch them capture another British frigate—whose topsails shone plainly on the eastern horizon. Thanks to Captain James Lawrence, one of the favored few, his mostly raw crew were heroes already, even before the battle. Everyone in Boston knew that the captain of the *Shannon* had sent away the other British frigate *Tenedos*, leaving no doubt that he offered Lawrence a frigate duel; and no one could be more eager.

Lawrence was nodding absently, no doubt as exhausted as everybody else aboard, gazing out beyond the light toward the enemy. Eleven days earlier, in conformity with his orders to put to sea at the earliest opportunity, he had taken the *Chesapeake* from Long Wharf down to the Roads. The Secretary of the Navy had left the matter in no doubt that, in the next few days, he should find an opportunity to slip his moorings and evade the two British frigates blockading Boston harbor. But when the pilot boats had reported only one frigate in the offing, Lawrence was ready to pounce—not on a mere merchant ship, but on a warship nearly identical to *Chesapeake*, at least on paper. Lawrence read from the Navy Department letter:

"Our esteemed Mister Jones writes that 'It is impossible to conceive a naval service of a higher order in national point of view, than the capture and destruction of the enemy's store ships with military and naval stores destined for the supply of his armies in Canada and fleets on this station and the capture of transports with troops, intended to reinforce Canada, or to invade our own shores.' He wants us to evade the warships and sail directly to St. Lawrence. You realize that a frigate action will necessarily violate the letter and spirit of our orders."

"Aye, sir."

"Muster the men aft, please, if you can pull that boatswain's mate and gunner's mate from their money—like grumbling women."

Lawrence strode forward on the spar deck and stood proudly in the waist, where most of the men could hear him. "Lads, today we add that enemy frigate yonder to the laurels of our great nation. She will be ours, just as *Guerriere, Java, Macedonian, Frolic* and *Peacock*, and so many others fell to our courage, skill and guns! Let us win more glory for our country and ourselves—not to mention prize-money for our pockets! There she is, challenging us to a fair plain fight off Marblehead. We will fire our guns in salute of these foolish challengers; Captain Broke of the

Shannon has sent his consort away, and waits for us."

Wearing his second-best uniform, his devilishly handsome face alight with anticipation, graceful, a little under six feet in height, a fine figure with dark side whiskers combed up, Lawrence spoke from the heart.

"Make ready to send down royals and t'gallants! Before nightfall, we shall be entertaining new British guests. 'Peacock' her, my boys!"

The cry was taken up by every man aboard. "Peacock her! Peacock her! Huzzah! For the captain and the *Chesapeake*, huzzah! Huzzah! Huzzah! Peacock her!"

By the time the cheers subsided, Acting Lieutenant Nathan Jeffries could see that Lawrence's eyes were filled with tears.

"Beat to quarters, Mister Steward," said Lawrence. "Clear the ship for action. Mister Budd, Mister Jeffries, make ready your broadsides."

"Aye, aye, Captain."

The lieutenants ran down along the guns, making sure they were ready. The crew aloft and on deck were eager and needed no persuasion. Tampions, cartridges, buckets of sand, round shot, extra flints—all was in order as the ship settled into deadly silence. The short, stubby carronades were primed, loaded and run out. The enemy ahead of them, flying the British ensign, bristled with all guns run out.

"Clear the ship for action, Mister Steward," said Captain Lawrence. "Round shot and grape in the guns. Decatur didn't use canister or bar shot, and neither will we. Secure those flags on all three masts."

Amid the noise and bustle, Nathan, near the mainmast, took a moment to admire the red, blue and white ensigns against the white clouds of canvas and the clear blue sky. At the forepeak, he could make out "Free Trade and Sailors' Rights." Under all plain sail and light airs from the south, the frigate's press of sail slowly narrowed the gap between them and the enemy.

4 PM—NATHAN COULD not remain silent. He returned to the quarterdeck and approached James Lawrence.

"Captain," said Nathan, tipping his lieutenant's fore-and-aft, "I know Number One—I mean, Lieutenant Steward—doesn't agree with me, but this crew is not ready; we have not had enough practice with the guns."

"You disappoint me, Nathan," growled Lawrence. "You already provided me with your assessment of Broome and Russell, Ballard, Hardcastle, even Lieutenant Budd, who has considerable training, as you know."

"Sir, Number Two and I agree that most of the midshipmen will perform satisfactorily, but Broome is a . . ."

"A drunk, Mister Jeffries. Let us face facts."

"Yes, and he is not alone, sir. The purser is no coward, but—"

"Chew is a good man. These men will fight for me and their country."

"Yes, sir, of course. But with so many jumped up lieutenants, warrant officers, and midshipmen—"

Lawrence waved his hand dismissively. "You know, the *Hornet* still has plenty of foreigners and raw crew; ask Commander Biddle."

"Yes, sir, but he is not facing a well-trained frigate."

"You sound more and more like our green third, Acting Lieutenant Cox," said Lawrence with his "do not continue this" taut smile.

Nathan did continue, anyway. "Sir, the *United States, President* and *Constitution* were highly trained crews and heavy frigates. Your great success in sinking—"

"We want to capture, Jeffries, not sink. We must make sure not to sink this frigate! We will take *Shannon*, is that clear? I met Broke, her captain, you know—"

"Sir, we will not find this as easy as some earlier duels—not to mention the secretary ordered all commanders to—"

"Lieutenant Jeffries, that is quite enough. It grieves me to hear a Jeffries talk like this. Please, Nathan, I apologize for any pejorative suggestion. Please return to your station, Lieutenant."

Nathan had bristled during this line of talk. Now he simply saluted. "Aye, sir."

When he saw Logan and Tom Howard again, he shook his head. "It's no use—this fame and glory has gone to his head. And here Secretary Jones has ordered all warships to make war on the merchant men and not other warships—but there is no glory in it."

Logan nodded. "Most o' the crew feels—we need to kick a few rear ends as well, gettin' these boys to behave, these newborn tar babies. That bugler Brown is more likely to hide than sound his—"

"Yes, I know. I worry about Cox, too."

"Cap'n, if you'll pardon, you and Miss Charles—" Tom Howard began.

"That's in the wake and well forgot," said Nathan, with a deliberate attempt at sounding anything other than hopeless. "Her dalliance with Fredericks made fools of many of us; certainly the Jeffries."

"But when you return home, Cap'n—"

"I have no home, Mister Logan."

The men shrugged. Nathan also didn't like the fact that Jason Earleigh was now a powder monkey—although admittedly all the small youngsters aboard shared that honor. He yelled one of the gun crews into silence again. In effect, Nathan commanded the entire larboard main gun deck, because the youngest lieutenant aboard, acting Lieutenant Cox, was obviously ill-equipped to handle the men or the guns. Nathan knew the British had the same enormous 18-pounders, and only their "big three" frigates boasted 24-pounders on the main deck, not to mention the 32-pound "smashers," carronades, on the quarter deck and foredeck. He knew Lawrence was making a mistake, but Lawrence commanded this ship. Nathan could only hope that the general optimism would prove justified, now that the captain had practically accused him of cowardice.

5 PM—THE AMERICAN frigate crept up on a parallel course, as close as half pistol shot range, the enemy top hamper looming high overhead, through the open gunports; there she was, ready to fight under topsails alone. But instead of bearing up for a rake, Nathan saw to his dismay that Lawrence was bearing down to parallel *Shannon's* course, a simple slugfest with no delay, in late afternoon. Nathan raised his arm for the first volley. The broadsides of 500 pounds—nearly 30

carriage guns firing on each side—would be devastating. Their bow-sprit suddenly passed the enemy's stern, too quickly. He could see they were less than three leagues from Nahant Bay—would he ever return to shore again? He looked at Logan, nearby captain of the number four gun, who nodded. Tom Howard was now serving one of the carronades above on the foredeck.

5:45 PM—THE MOMENT had come. "Fire as your guns bear!" Nathan's arm swept down; the first broadsides rippled down the line, killing and wounding dozens of men. The deafening thunder and gritty smoke erupted down the line, but too quickly. They had too much way on. And then the awful explosion of crashing metal, tearing splinters and flesh. Nathan could feel the *Chesapeake* backing her stern against the foreshrouds of the enemy. One of the arm chests above blew up, and Nathan could hear men above running from their guns—flinching, and who could blame them? Lawrence played Broke's game for him.

"Run in! Sponge out! Reload!"

Another exchange of broadsides crashed out, this time less on the American side; more and more guns dismounted as the ship turned her helpless stern to *Shannon's* forerigging and held. Nathan could see shot smashing her planks and frame as *Chesapeake* was holed regularly, the deafening blast of cannon and small arms continuous as they were riddled on the larboard quarter with a raking fire.

Most of the great guns became ominously silent as a small arms fighting became more intense. Nathan ran from the aft companionway to the quarterdeck, as a cheer rose from the British boarding party.

Nathan tried to reach the quarterdeck, only to see Captain Lawrence being carried below, yelling, "Don't give up the ship! Fight her till she sinks!" Lieutenant Cox was carrying him below.

"What are you doing here?" he yelled at Cox.

"My God! Can't you see? There is no one left to command!" he yelled back. "It is hopeless!"

Nathan heard the triumphant shouts of *Shannon's* boarding party, and knew he could never regain the quarterdeck. He ran forward, and finally reached the foredeck.

Nathan heard a scream, and looked over as the American flag was pulled down, and the British ensign raised, the sky in full late bloom of hope, smashed wood, cut rigging and torn sails fluttering feebly in the light wind. Ghastly horror, blood and gore, ruined men and their creations, faces bloody black with powder and tar, white and red streaks slashed across the filthy deck, the terrible carnage by injured men laying all over. And then the *Chesapeake* chaplain swung a saber down on the head of a man in a round hat, only to be cut down himself in turn. Nathan blindly charged into the scene, cutlass and pistol drawn. "Never surrender!" he shouted to no one in particular. Those British before him fled, but he saw a British marine near the mainmast aim at him with a musket. He saw the flash, the smoke, but never heard the shot as he felt the electrifying pain of the lead ball entering his right side and passed into blessed oblivion.

WHEN HE REGAINED consciousness, the pockmarked, ugly young face of what must have been a loblolly boy was staring down at him.

"Boy, is you lucky, Yank," he said, with a Cockney drift.

Nathan tried to sit up, and sharp pains shot up and down his right side. Wounded men lay all around him.

"Lay back, my lad. You'll start bleeding again—'e got all of the lead and cloth out of yer side. He did a good job, Yank, especially yew the enemy and all."

"Where—cockpit!"

"Aye! We got the whole berth deck full up now, with you upstarts!" He stopped smiling and looked less ugly, if no more genial.

"You fought well, most of ye—give yew that—butchers bill were—"

"Never mind that, I must—"

"You must do what I tell you, laddy-buck! I'm Hal—"

"Reece, get over here!" The orderly, rudely summoned, left Nathan.

Nathan lay in an ooze of pain and nausea, and then he heard a familiar voice.

"Captain! Hey, here you are!" It was Mister Logan, swilling from a jug, which he offered to Nathan.

"Where are Tom Howard and . . . Jason?" Nathan's asked, his voice sounding shredded.

"Captain—"

"Where are they, Logan?"

"Tom Howard, he were cut in two by a round shot, Captain, getting—"

"Where's the boy?"

"He's here, sir, the Doc's. We've—Nathan, what are y'doin? Over here, Cap'n."

Reluctantly Logan helped Nathan up, groaning in pain, over to the table right aft, behind a bloodied, yellow canvas mainsail.

There, on the bloody table, with half his face missing, poor Jason lay drowning in his own blood while the exhausted surgeon barely glanced up from his useless ministrations.

The young man, now robbed of a future, seemed to recognize Nathan. Jason gurgled and then rasped, "We done ya proud, ain't we, Cap'n?"

Nathan watched the eyes now staring at him. He turned away and fell to his knees to vomit, and then found himself sobbing, once again an abject prisoner of the damned British, without anything to show for his bitter misery. He had managed to get Jason killed, and even Logan had wandered off. It was all Nathan could do to lie down near to poor Jason, his side opened and bleeding again, the exquisite pain such a relief to his own vile thoughts, before they took him away in the darkness. Nathan, not yet 23, bitter over Catherine's betrayal, found himself wishing death could overmaster the pain along his right side, knowing that his wounds would not heal.

"Berate him," said Nathan, delirious. "And then thank him. Praise us. At least take us to Bermuda, not Halifax! Logan, you're acting lieutenant now, the best seaman I know—Peter, damn you! Father . . . don't give up the ship," he groaned, and gasped again in pain.

ELEVEN

Philadelphia - *July 4, 1813*

CATHERINE FELT AS IF her entire world was falling apart—again. When she returned to Fell's Point, Baltimore, there was no information from Nathan himself, none at all. Doctor Amos Anderson told her that Nathan had gone to Boston to fight aboard the frigate *Chesapeake*, which was captured in sight of Boston onlookers by British frigate *Shannon*. Nathan was either dead or a prisoner. William Jeffries was out of his mind most of the time now, and no one in town would or could help her—most military and civilian notables were on the verge of panic with the increasing number of raids along the tidal waters of Chesapeake Bay, and a growing numbers of the enemy were using Tangier Island as a base. She decided she must ask the Charles in Philadelphia for help, with the excuse that she wanted to help parole the captured Lieutenant Budd, whom she knew slightly, and other officers from the *Chesapeake*—not Nathan, whom she knew her "parents" would never want to help. Captain Lawrence and First Lieutenant Steward had died before *Chesapeake* reached Halifax, and they were now martyrs for the cause. But Budd and others had survived. The Charles probably knew nothing about Nathan's actions since he left the *Merlin*, and that was all to the good. How much did they know about her relationship with Michael Fredericks?

Catherine had decided she would implore Beatrice and Jonathan to help her, and perhaps find out other information involving Nathan, and Fredericks, whom she had not seen for months.

So here she was, drinking tea once again with her putative parents, Philadelphia royalty, in the all-too-familiar game room of the mansion on Beacham Street. She discussed the dismal war news with Beatrice and Jonathan, surrounded by the enormous portraits of the dynasty, all lace and gold and brocade finery, the heavy curtains of the enormous west windows closed against the early afternoon sun. Beatrice's blue silk gown failed to obviate her increasing corpulence, her pale, round face floating on vast jowls as she tried to convince Catherine to surrender her loyalty to the dissolving United States. Jonathan, more skeletal than ever in a dark suit with snowy white cravat, spoke little, his insipid smile hiding—what? Catherine would be hard pressed to decide which annoyed her more; Beatrice's fluid and confident absurdities or Jonathan's unsettling silences.

Yet today Beatrice seemed a little less condescending, less arrogant and more talkative than ever. She sat on the Hepplewhite sofa, Catherine in a Chippendale armchair.

"Surely you can see how hopeless it is, my dear," she was saying, Jonathan nodding. "The United States cannot even defend their own borders, let alone—"

"The leadership has been lacking, Beatrice," said Catherine. "I agree with you there, but—"

"Frenchtown, Havre de Grace, Georgetown, Fredericktown burned. All of Chesapeake Bay blockaded. Admiral Cockburn will capture Baltimore as soon as he and General Ross have a few more troops at their disposal. Detroit in our—in British and Canadian hands, more American failures at Queenston Heights, Odgensburg, Fort George, Sackett's harbor; once Bonaparte is finally defeated."

"Not all of the battles have been American defeats, Beatrice."

"No, indeed, my dear, and not all of the American coast has been blockaded—yet."

She smiled and looked at her husband.

Catherine followed her gaze. "Jonathan, do you—"

"Excuse me, Madam," said a light brown-skinned servant from the door. "They are here."

"Thank you, Susan. Please show them in."

"I do not recognize that woman," said Catherine.

"Susan Morgan is a new . . . acquisition. When Hope died, I took her on as a favor. A bit slow, I am afraid, even compared to—"

"Well, look who is here!" said the new visitor.

Catherine stared in disbelief at Michael Fredericks, and on his arm, Barbara Steward.

"Welcome, sir," said Jonathan, who stood as the two men bowed to each other. Barbara stared at Catherine, her green eyes burning into those of her one-time friend.

Barbara's full, generous lips and perfect complexion had not abandoned her, and in spite of her shock Catherine had to admire Barbara's resilience. She had lost none of her voluptuous grace, glowing in her golden hair and sky-blue Empire gown.

"How delightful to see you again, my dear," said Fredericks with a slight smile. He kissed Catherine's hand as his mistress sat across from her.

"Catherine, you look lovely," said Barbara, with the tone of a highwayman accosting a four-in-hand. There was an awkward pause.

"I know everyone knows everyone," Jonathan began nervously.

"I was so sorry to hear about your friends aboard the *Chesapeake*," said Fredericks to Catherine, taking over the room. Beatrice remained curiously silent—she and her husband were clearly nervous.

Catherine's dark eyes opened wide. "Why is that, Michael?"

"Bravo!" cried Fredericks. "You are bidding in the game now." He was no longer smiling.

"What do you mean?" demanded Barbara.

"Let's not mince words," said Catherine, ignoring her. "You and Barbara, the Auster Cabal, these Philadelphia royalists—you are all traitors and belong in prison or in Europe, like Barbara's friend Betsy Bonaparte."

"How dare you . . . you ingrate!" cried Beatrice, now red in the face.

"Not another word," said Fredericks. "Catherine, when the United

States dissolve and return hat in hand to the British Empire, you may wish to reconsider those spiteful accusations."

"We will not succumb to England," Catherine said defiantly. "And even if we do, I for one will never be subject to the Crown."

"I am disappointed in you, Catherine," said Fredericks, now smiling again.

"Perhaps we should change—"

"I wonder if Catherine and I could have this room to ourselves," said Fredericks, standing up.

"You want to be alone with *her*, Michael?" asked Barbara bitterly. "I saved that foolish boy Nathan for this woman; mostly for you, and I know how much you hate Nathan, and now—"

The withering stare from Fredericks silenced her, and Catherine knew and understood the source of the information leaking over to her enemies.

Fredericks bowed to the women and Jonathan as they left the room and closed the double engraved mahogany doors. Fredericks smiled again, and Catherine hid her fear.

"Do not surrender the ship, eh, my dear?"

"I do not know what you mean, Michael."

"You would have been a fine poker player, Catherine. You have courage, even though you are nearly as naïve as the Jefferies themselves were."

"I am so glad you are disappointed in me—perhaps it is that way with all of your 'conquests.'"

Fredericks nodded. "And you saved the Rodgers home in Havre de Grace—and that braggart Irishman, another noble and useless gesture. And yet you, the well-known mistress of my eye—"

"Shut your lying mouth, Michael. Don't play with me—unless you want to tell me who wrote that."

"Oh yes, who wrote, or whispered, or said through gritting teeth that Mister O'Connell was saved by his own daughter, who was able to convince that odious Cockburn—"

"You want to—do you want to make sure I pay for what I did?"

"The Admiralty has shown remarkable constraint, you know, Catherine, against this annoying infant collation of a nation that declares war and cannot even defend its own borders. Now what are we going to do with *you*?"

The beautiful woman felt a chill, but looked at her putative lover in those large gray eyes, and ignored the question.

The pleasantly round-faced Fredericks continued. "The hypocrisy of these farmers does bother me. Freedom and equality? Perhaps for the wealthy white landowners! Anything for the coin. The southern states already contain more slaves than the West Indies! Without French help, the United States could still be properly managed. Once again British must take over, offer enlightened governing of the Indian populations, and resolve the slavery problem sooner or later, depending on whether Parliament can ever appease the plantations."

"Yes, enlightened management," said Catherine sarcastically. "I wonder how the Austers slave trade was crushed."

"Here we go again, my foolish beauty. Auster was reckless and I am glad he is gone. He was stupid enough to flaunt his power and lust, and ignore the volatility and stupidity of the Stewards. But Barbara has her . . . qualities. It matters not, dear Catherine. The American greed and failures will only facilitate Chesapeake's falling totally under British control. New England has understood and tolerated the need to provide a few prime seamen for the Royal Navy, and those merchants will peacefully return to England's fold—and there you have it."

"That will not happen, sir, and there will be no civil war."

"The only competent member of Madison's staff is Navy Secretary Jones. He knows how to conduct operations, but he has no fleet to work with. The others, and Madison himself, are ignorant cowards, no better than their poor illiterate country folk, with no sense of aristocracy, nobility, sacrifice."

"Epitomized by great men such as yourself," said Catherine.

Fredericks laughed. "Sometimes I hate you more than Nathan Jeffries himself! Now that I have destroyed old William, I am going to miss you, Miss Charles. I surely will. What a shame you associated yourself with bugs we needed to squash, like that drunken cripple and young Nathan."

"You do not know that he is dead," Catherine interrupted again, stifling a sob.

"Dead or as good as dead, my darling; they die fairly quickly in those rotten prison hulks, regardless of their health when they arrive there."

"The American sailor has been underestimated before, Michael—remember calling American ships 'a few bits of Paltry Striped Bunting, manned by bastards and outlaws'? Some men can be trusted, and not all of them are venal, corrupt cowards like yourself!"

But Fredericks was unflappable. "Tish—what a war woman! You mean, ship owners such as Peabody and Gray? But most of them are ready to throw the United States to the wolves. Remember Captain McAndrews,? 'Old Mac?' That Scot who would not back down and he would not come forward. The captain told us that whenever he needed help from the owners, he would just as soon come to us. And he got as good he gave. Nothing speaks louder than life—and money. The Boston *Columbian Centinel* listed half a hundred powerful Americans against the war—same in Providence, New York, and even in Baltimore. We rely on upright citizens such as Abraham Steward, blessed with not one trace of courage or creativity—but awfully clever with figures and profitable uses of bonds, notes and specie. It was his greed that helped us through the obnoxious spies that printed all those lies in the newspapers."

"I despise the Stewards for many reasons, Michael, but mainly for their betrayal of—"

"You are the one who is disloyal; to your own kind, you lovely fool."

Did Fredericks know all about *her* involvement in the intelligence gathering? Why else have her name and reputation smeared in public?

"Those *spies* to whom you refer only printed the truth, Michael—they were able to help Nathan, William, other traders, such as Gray and Peabody, to side against you and the Austers primarily because you betrayed everyone, had no scruples against foul play even among your own kind. Most ship owners opposed the slave trade, and those spies provided proof of such activities, financed by a British partner, whether Rhode Island, Delaware or Connecticut."

"The British disavowed this, but it did hurt the Cabal, I will give you that, as did various charges of piracy and smuggling. None of which ever occurred to your friends, I am sure."

"Of course many captains resorted to illegal trade during the Embargo, if only to survive," said Catherine. "But even the slimiest is a saint compared to you."

Her manners flew away in the strong wind of her anger, fear and resentment, but he merely shrugged and stared at her imperiously, while still admiring her trim, dark blue gown and red ribbons at waist, bare arms and neck. Her dark hair glistened in the light and her smooth light brown shoulders complemented her brow, only furrowed slightly at his rude silence; her slightly arched, sharp nose, which widened at the tip in a button, flared at the nostrils now. Her dark brown eyes opened a little more.

"You lovely simpleton! Even with that useless Earl of Liverpool as Prime Minister, we have accomplished a great deal. You and the Jeffries and the other sniveling cowards have done all you can against us—which is damn little, really, considering the assistance from my lovely Catherine."

Fredericks reached over and flicked her hair dismissively. She cringed, and then glared at him. The hate flickered in her eyes.

"I have long been aware of *your* betrayal, Catherine. Did you really think I did not know, my dear? The pitiful 'patriotic' efforts of you and others like you have caused some inconvenience and delay, but this glorification of 'sacrifice to the states' is laughable. Few men— or women—are foolish enough to still believe in the survival of this country, and what does it matter? Profit speaks louder than patriotism. *My* services will always be wanted more, needed more, though I grant it is uncomfortable for Lloyd's at present. After the war, we will make arrangements to continue from where we left off; you have been only a slight nuisance, you and your supporters. Matters will be easier when New England rejoins Old Mother England. But in any case it is time to deal with you and your Protectors."

Catherine laughed derisively. "Please explain exactly what you shall do, Michael. I am only sorry that Nathan will never forgive me for allowing you to think you could seduce me!"

"How touching!" said Fredericks. "You *allowed* me to flirt. You reveled in it! Almost as touching as Barbara's relationship to the half-breed—yes, and Nathan, and—to think, Peter's natural mother, a Shawnee squaw princess! Elizabeth Hughes—"

"Where is Peter! Do you even *know*?" she shouted, her back twitching, knowing that Fredericks yearned to destroy her.

"A half-breed mistress—even lower than the Jeffries! The father—well, you know, he may have been a young British naval officer and spy during the idiotic rebellion. But Elizabeth Hughes did not become a problem, Catherine, until another bastard was actually conceived! Think of it. And the pompous fool threatened me with *my* indiscretions."

"*You* are a bastard, Michael."

"Catherine, don't—keep silent, my love! Such eloquence! As I was saying, how convenient. In any case, where is Peter? I neither know nor care. But we know where you are going—surprising, in a way, that you fell for this obvious trap, after slipping through all the others! Take one last long look around, Catherine. Not a scene that you wanted to sacrifice, perhaps!"

And she actually did gaze around the room with the keen eye of that ultimate strangeness, the unique fear, terror of death. She admired the Federal and Empire styles, the beautiful mahogany, maple, and oak grain patterns in the Hepplewhite, Sheraton, and Queen Anne furniture, the six long thin legs and lion's paws of the sideboard, with its slightly curved front and severe but immaculate central brass handles, the discrete Sevres porcelain, the arched Palladian architecture of the front portico, the shining balusters and newel posts, the warm and beckoning landing, the carved and painted panels to match the wainscoting, square sections of skylight, the plain but handsome dark walnut trim.

"It is amazing, I must say," Fredericks was saying, "that you have played the game as well as you have. Such surprising cleverness for a young, ignorant woman—of course, with considerable assets, strong friends; in many ways Nathan has come far. Too bad you are such a fool, we could have—damn you, and damn your . . . Jeffries toadies!"

Catherine smiled calmly. "Amy is dead, 'Sir' Fredericks. But her secrets remain in a . . . safe place. And Nathan has already outstripped you, wherever—whenever he . . . they—so are you going to try to stop me?" she asked, wiping a tear. "If not . . . I have much to do."

TWELVE

Presque Isle, Lake Erie - *June 29, 1813*

BY THIS TIME MANY in the northeast knew his reputation, and according to the scuttlebutt dockside, ". . . when Cap'n Nathan was asked, he would just shrug and say, something like, 'today's hero, tomorrow's goat'—and that ain't some phoney sugarfoot, neither—I seen him offen a feller just for annoyin' his supper—swear on my mother's grave, if'n she had'n one, I mean." News from the east did not reach Buffalo until the end of the month. Nathan's luck, it seemed, had not run out, even though he was the bearer of terrible news.

Young Jeffries himself had to marvel at his own "luck," getting himself paroled as lieutenant with Bush's help in Halifax, himself and his last friend on the blue earth, Mister Jack Logan, the best seaman Nathan knew. So how can we fight the British at sea? His answer from the secretary: on the shores of Lake Erie. It seemed ironic that their mission now would be to crush another fleet, albeit a mighty small one, with a fresh-cut, green pine fleet not yet in existence.

To Nathan it was clear: it was the Secretary of the Navy and veteran captain William Jones, virtually alone, vs. Jefferson, Madison, Armstrong and the other autocrats, who now whined for a strong naval force, the idiots, after years of deliberately dismantling it. No need for large military or naval forces at the Capital, assured Armstrong, over and over, like a demented mantra. Now these benighted, besotted knights of the Democrat-Republican Dynasty were given full and foul play. ". . . and what about this rumor of these mysterious and beautiful women, often seen together, Catherine Charles and a bewitching squaw, Taima, associated with the damned rascal Nathan Jeffries? We hope the last of a inglorious reign, and herewith challenged to a gentleman's discussion of suitable grounds and means to execute a fine and honorable duel agreed to by parties and their designated seconds. Physicians Mark herein embossed."

Logan was foraging, mainly searching for the actual identity of this annoying Michael Fredericks. Meanwhile, Nathan's hardbitten escort of frontier settlers and Kentucky riflemen had left him there in the rude log and pitch canvas "village" at Erie without a word, and there was no one in uniform nearby. The chopping, banging and rasping of hammers, adzes and saws on the boats and ships, both in stocks and afloat, echoed through the clearing. The bright sun streamed through the thick forests of fir, cedar and hardwoods above the nearby lake as Nathan knocked on the green-planked door of a rough-hewn log cabin that served as the house and command headquarters of Master Commandant Oliver Hazard Perry. Or soon-to-be Captain, or even Commodore Perry, as Nathan was told he already preferred, in deference to his proud command of a small squadron of vessels currently being pried, hewn, sawn, chopped and cut out of the raw, immense pine and oak forests. It was early morning, hazy but clearing, and the air was already buzzing with black flies, hard and dusty, yet humid and beating down with the promise of an oppressive summer day. Nathan swayed with fatigue from his long journey posthaste north and the residual effects of his fever. Everyone had warned him that it was likely to recur in this climate; lake fever had killed many men.

"Come in," said a clear, mellifluous voice.

Nathan was surprised that no one had escorted him to this building; a carpenter, already at work on one of the brigs in the harbor, had merely pointed up to the cabin. Several people had stared at him as he slowly made his way there from the shore, but no one had accosted the somewhat dilapidated lieutenant. But even at dawn, Perry was not alone. A big Negro was helping the handsome, dark-haired young commodore into his uniform coat.

"Ah!" he said, glancing at Jeffries' filthy new uniform. "You bring news from the secretary?"

"Yes, sir," said Nathan.

"Thank you, Hannibal. Some coffee, Lieutenant?"

"Jeffries, sir. Yes, please. Uh, excuse me, Com–commodore, this is urgent news from the secretary."

"I remember you. We met at the Stewards' in Boston. And then you had your . . . difficulties with the Austers. I heard something about your extraordinary adventures last year. Would you bring two coffees, Hannibal?"

"Yes, suh."

"I have been anxiously awaiting more men for these ships," said Perry. "As much as your presence is welcome, I had hoped for fewer excuses and more—oh, thank you, Hannibal."

Nathan nodded as he was handed a cup of coffee, and with an apologetic glance at Perry, drank thirstily. The personal aide or manservant had disappeared again with Nathan's bag, and a deftness amazing in one so bulky.

"Sir, I am afraid the news is—"

"Orders?" said Perry, holding out his hand for the packet Nathan carried.

"Yes, sir," said Nathan, handing them over.

But Perry merely placed them on his desk. "I will read them after we make a brief inspection of our small town and the Presque Isle defenses, Lieutenant Jeffries, if you do not object. I know you need to rest. But first, I would like to hear from you as we walk."

"Certainly, Commodore. But I must tell you—"

Perry coughed, seemed unwell; his features were pale, romantic like Decatur and Lawrence, with his sharp nose, high cheekbones and sleepy, almost feminine, olive-colored eyes. The fleshy, almost petulant lips, cherubic cheeks, enormous forehead and long eyelashes belied a palpable air of intensity and determination. The heavy eyebrows matched the obligatory sideburns, which were full and bushy, almost reaching his lips and chin. Still, a gentle, compassionate face withal, thought Nathan; but at the same time an intellectual energy, a touchiness barely kept under control, seemed to exude from him. Not a man to trifle with.

"Finish your coffee first, sir."

The man's consideration, and the unspoken compliment in seeking Nathan's report before even reading the letters from the secretary, told much. Nathan had never served with Perry, but his charismatic presence was known by most officers. Detractors called him a martinet, and "Rodgers' pet," but his abilities were held in high esteem in Washington. His father, like Nathan's, had been a *bona fide* Revolutionary naval hero. In February, at his own request, he'd been ordered to Erie from Newport, where he'd commanded twelve gunboats, the "hog troughs" which had been proved so manifestly useless.

"You just arrived from Sackett's Harbor, Mister Jeffries?"

"Yes, sir; by longboat, traveling mostly by night. We saw a schooner against the loom of the land less than two hours ago, but we were not challenged." The British controlled western Lake Erie as Perry worked desperately to complete the work on his two new 20-gun brigs, and get enough men somehow to man them. Ships from the British fleet under Barclay would sail out of Fort Malden on the north shore, harassing smaller vessels and "bearding" Perry by hoisting British colors, taunting him to come out. But in spite of the risks, travel by water was much faster—if you weren't captured.

"Excellent," said Perry. "No doubt this package also contains messages from our Great Lakes commander, Chauncey, and from Elliott." His nose twitched in seeming distaste. "But tell me, sir, what news? What news?"

Nathan took a deep breath. "I am sorry to have to report, Commodore, that *Chesapeake* was captured outside Boston by *Shannon*, and almost hundred of her crew, including Captain Lawrence and George Steward were lost."

Perry's cordial mood changed suddenly. His brows knitted together. He turned away from Nathan and walked over behind his desk. His frown relapsed into a merely bland suffering as he slowly sat down.

"Jim is dead?"

"Yes, sir. Killed in action. I have been trying to tell you, but . . . he died trying to rally the men, Commodore. He died a hero, with the undying love and gratitude of his country."

Nathan hesitated.

"Yes?" Perry was only 28 years old, struggling alone against fearsome responsibilities. Nathan felt for him, and knew that discipline was not needed now.

"I also have lost my friend," Nathan said. "Lieutenant Steward; had you met him since the ball in '11?"

"No . . . no, I am sorry," said Perry quietly. "Yes, actually, we did splice the main brace together, at Decatur's birthday in Washington City last year. I did not know him well; seemed a decent, determined fellow." Now his head rested in his hands. "But I know how you feel. James Lawrence was . . . irreplaceable."

"Sir, it is all covered in the reports and newspapers, but . . . before he died, Captain Lawrence said over and over again, 'Don't give up the ship. Fight her till she sinks!'"

Those sleepy eyes suddenly came alive again, burning briefly, as he looked up at Nathan.

"Don't give up the ship!"

"Yes, sir. His defeat was also a glorious call to—"

Perry shot up, and Nathan stiffened to attention. "You were aboard, from Boston, when *Chesapeake* sailed?" Perry asked him.

Nathan looked into those defiant eyes. "Yes, sir. I should have died with—"

"Ridiculous—you are needed here."

"And I will fight here, sir—Commodore—but one would prefer to die with friends."

Perry thought he detected a kindred spirit. "Not all of our enemies are British," he said.

"Yes, sir. No, sir—Commodore, I was not the injured one, but now I would drag myself. Excuse me, sir."

Perry almost smiled. "Your mate's condition must have been very serious"

"The fact is, we had not yet even joined the navy, sir—I was a privateersman!" He could hardly keep the bitter pride and shame out of his voice.

"I understand, *Lieutenant*." And then his compassion shone through again, in an odd way. "I know we can offer you a worthy opportunity here at Lake Erie."

"Thank you, sir."

"We can dispense with the formalities in private, Mister Jeffries—Nathan."

"With pleasure, Captain." Nathan hesitated. "No doubt you have heard of the various charges preferred against me—accusations of criminal acts and cowardice."

Perry held up his hand and shook his head impatiently. "What I have or have not heard up to this time means nothing," he said flatly. "You are one of my lieutenants, and your actions will henceforth be judged accordingly."

"I am much obliged—"

"I shall still read these missives later," said Perry. "Let us talk while I make my rounds."

The two men, studied carefully by militiamen, workers, seamen and other residents, began to walk around the small hamlet of Erie. Feeling glum and pessimistic at first, Nathan was pleased with this man's seemingly indefatigable confidence.

At first, Perry wanted more information from the south, and Nathan found himself giving a detailed report on his perspective on the war. They discussed the spring campaign—or lack of it—and friends or colleagues such as Hull, Bainbridge, Decatur, Jones, Porter, and Lawrence. Nathan described the sordid sicknesses, the secrecy in Boston, the petty attacks that weakened the benefits of the few successes in 1813.

He shrugged, "They must make attempts, Commodore, as you know, even if no one is sure . . . and the news is that the country will soon be at a standstill. It is bad on all fronts now, with most of the harbors bottled up. Most states seem unaware of the sacrifices of the few; Isaac Hull's own state of Connecticut refuses to honor him. I wanted to be at sea again; they would like to give others a chance, and yet after their two years are up most crews rush to the privateers, where they hope to gain more prize money. In any case, there are no ships, sir. Old Ironsides is still undergoing repairs, and may be blockaded in Boston for the duration."

"I know," said Perry. "I served as lieutenant aboard her in the Mediterranean, from late '04 to '06. Those were exciting times. And now, Allen's given command of *Argus*, and the *Hornet* went to James Biddle. There are always new commanders, but precious little experience. What of the *Constellation*?"

"She is blockaded in the Chesapeake Bay, sir, fighting off British incursions. They have made several retaliatory raids, because of depradations against Canada, I heard."

Perry shook his head. "There is no honor in attacking civilians."

"No, sir."

The commodore pointed towards the two brigs. "Jeffries, I . . . good God, I have just remembered your father is Captain William Jeffries!"

"That is so, sir."

Gradually, Perry pulled the details from Nathan of his father's recovery after delirium from the loss of his mother, the strain with his father day and night, the arguments; he revealed much more than he would have thought appropriate.

"You are not married?"

"No, sir, but . . . I . . . well, there is no one, no one."

"That is a pity; or perhaps I have just been fortunate. Betsy is the love of my life." Elizabeth Champlin Mason was a beautiful Rhode Island belle Perry had married just before the war.

Perry looked again towards the ships anchored just off shore. "Mister Jeffries," he said, "Nathan, we have accomplished a great deal this year, but we are chronically short of men and supplies; and the unseen enemies here are boredom and disease. The strongest men of all can find themselves laid up in the army, the militia, and among my navy lads. The swampy ground of Presque Isle there has helped reduce my active force by more than 30 percent, thanks to the ague, chills and malaria. And the coast of Lake Ontario and Lake Erie, even the town here, is rife with cowards, intrigue, greed and corruption. Lice are apparently a sign of virility. But here at least my men work hard."

He pointed to the west. "It's about 250 miles to Put-in-Bay of South Bass Island near the south shore and about another sixty miles to Amherstburg and Fort Malden on the north, that's Canada. It's about another seventy-five miles further west of the Bass Islands to Fort Meigs; that's where General Harrison is now. Pittsburgh is about 250 miles to the south, and Buffalo and the east end of the lake are 120 miles to the east. About fifty miles further north, as you know, lie Forts George and Niagara, and beyond that, Lake Ontario, Commodore Chauncey's headquarters, in Sackett's Harbor, and eventually, the Saint Lawrence River; just three turns around the longboat, and a pull at the scuttlebutt." He sounded bitter.

Nathan began to grow discouraged; but he had nevertheless pledged himself to support Perry.

"Everyone knows the navy has been desperate for men and supplies, especially up here, sir," he said. "I have had experience as captain and supercargo, and as second-in-command, I may be able to act as your clerk."

"Excuse me, Mister Jeffries, but I fear you are mistaken; there are two men who outrank you, in addition to myself. But of course your assistance in all matters of preparation, as ordered by me, will be greatly appreciated."

"My understanding was that I would be senior lieutenant."

Perry's temper began to flare. "Mister Jeffries, do not make conditions more difficult for yourself as well as—"

Two men approached and he fell silent.

"Pardon me, Commodore," said a lean, grizzled man with a slight stoop. He wore a faded captain's coat. "We were wondering if you had heard from that damned scout. The supplies from Pittsburgh are two days overdue."

"I know, I know," said Perry irritably. But then he smoothed his scowl. "Captain Dobbins, Mister Brown, please allow me to introduce Lieutenant Jeffries. The lieutenant will be joining us for our next actions against the enemy; probably he will serve as my second lieutenant. Dan Dobbins is our sailing master and Noah Brown and his brother Ira are the best shipwrights in the United States. When it comes to designing and building vessels, they are geniuses. Their next mission is to build a fleet for MacDonough for Lake Champlain."

"Thank you, Commodore, for the undeserved accolade. A pleasure, sir," said Brown.

Nathan nodded, and shook hands with both men. Dobbins looked at him suspiciously, but then softened.

"I trust you are listening carefully to the commander, my lad?" asked Dobbins. They all laughed.

"I am certainly here to learn as well as work and fight," said Nathan.

"But Mister Jeffries brought news I must share with you," said Perry, suddenly sad again. "The *Chesapeake* was captured in a single ship-to-ship action. Lawrence is dead."

"What?" said Dobbins. "Dead? The frigate defeated? How could it happen?"

"The reports are inside. And no doubt Jeffries can fill you in, later," said Perry. "My friend Lawrence was hit several times, and did not last through the battle. But his dying words were, 'Don't give up the ship. Fight her 'til she sinks.'"

"Ah!" said Dobbins. Then all three men were silent.

"Mister Brown," said Perry, after a moment, "please find Lieutenant Yarnall and ask him to find suitable accommodations for Jeffries. We shall have the men wear black armbands in honor of Captain Lawrence's sacrifice. And Captain Dobbins, I have a special request to make of you."

"Sir?"

"I would like an ensign made to fly on my flagship, navy blue with white letters large enough so that these words can be read from at least a cable's length distance: 'Don't Give Up The Ship.'"

Nathan gulped. It was an inspired idea, simple and brilliant.

"Very good, sir," said Brown, then grinned through his solemnity. "Much better than *'vox clamantis in deserto.'*"

Perry smiled in spite of his sadness at the moment, and turned to Nathan.

"A private joke—we thought an appropriate motto under these circumstances would be 'a voice crying in the wilderness.' And Dobbins, we have already named one brig *Niagara*; I have just decided there is only one name suitable for the other: *Lawrence*. Now, gentlemen, if you will excuse me."

Within the next half hour, Nathan had met stolid, big-nosed Lieutenant Yarnall, his immediate superior; had eaten some cold venison and apple cider; and had settled into his quarters—a log cabin shared with a Midshipman Bannek. Though exhausted and not on duty, he could not rest with the activity in town and in his mind. He walked beyond the perimeter of the town, to the south, on a path that led to the main wagon trail that in turn joined up with French Creek and the Allegheny River.

The sun streamed down through the branches on this clear day, but through the thick woods, he could no longer see the blockhouses, hospital and storehouses on either side of the winding, shoaling channel, the sandy, sickle-shaped hook of seven-mile Presque Ile, the peninsula and small Misery Bay where most of the fleet was snuggly moored. They were secure here, apparently, from enemy attack; but the sandbar that guarded the entrance to the bay was often less than a fathom deep, sometimes a shallow as three feet. How would they get the brigs into deep water?

There was still a great deal about the situation that Nathan was not familiar with, but Perry had mentioned General William Henry Harrison, "Ol' Tippecanoe." At least the man was willing to fight. But Nathan thought without pride of the seemingly inevitable extermination of the Indians, regardless of the outcome of the war.

A voice at his back startled him. "What is your business here, mister?"

That voice . . . as Nathan whirled around, he heard laughter. There, six feet behind him on the trail, wearing the floppy, broad-brimmed hat and the tanned and tallow-darkened, fringed buckskin of a trapper or scout, stood Peter Hughes.

Thirteen

Presque Isle, Lake Erie

HE HAD NEVER BEEN so angry and happy to see any one, damn it. Peter dropped his Kentucky rifle and held out his arms with another laugh. Nathan grabbed his friend's shoulders, shaking him violently. "What the hell are you doing here—on our side? I thought we had lost you forever, damn your eyes! It has been more than a year. How long have you been here? Why did you—"

Peter's smile faded. "I have been here since Perry arrived; I left Tecumseh and the British at Ogdensburg, not long after the Raisin; but that was the winter. Early spring. Much has happened since then. Have you heard from—"

"Oh yes, Catherine has been well," his tone sarcastic. "But come, we shall compare our lives at leisure."

"So, my friend, you do . . . forgive me for—"

"No," said Nathan, but he began to laugh. "Of course not, Peter, but we have both no doubt learned much since then about women."

"Ah, yes," said Peter, trying not to laugh. "And there is a poor excuse for a tavern here."

Though both men were exhausted, neither would admit that he needed rest, more than anything else. They returned to the "town," a clearing of about three miles and seventy-six homes, cabins and assorted tents and lean-tos perched high on a plateau above the lake. The war had killed the salt trade and the local population of 400 was declining. And just beyond the town, they were surrounded by the seemingly infinite expanse of dense, impenetrable forest that might conceal armies of Indians and British.

"One of my duties is to prevent such surprises," Peter said. "We have a larger patrol tonight. Would you care to—"

"Of course," said Nathan, again.

The tavern, where Peter seated Nathan and handed him a mug of cider, was filled with casks and barrels of spirits, raisins, hardware, bread, boots, crockery, tinware, cutlery, nutmeg and basil re-shipped from Lynn, calicoes from Lowell, salted cod that came up the St. Lawrence River and sacks containing other assorted supplies, which covered almost every inch of the crude pine plank flooring.

"See these iron corner nails? They're from Pittsburgh. By the time they arrive, it would have been cheaper to build another new forge here." He gestured vaguely around the room. "We just returned from Pittsburgh. That is part of my regular duty now, seeing to the safety of our supply route."

In the lamplight, Nathan pointed to what looked like crusty blood on the lower part of Peter's ear. "What happened?" he asked.

Peter sighed. "Friends become enemies, and the war damage is permanent; we were attacked by a small, roving band of Ottawas, not ten miles from here. I think I recognized some of them. My 'brothers!' We drove them off, but I was nicked. Fortunately, our other wounds were equally slight."

"Peter, I am grateful that you are here, south of the border. But why . . . how is it that you—"

"I know; you are curious regarding my loyalties and affections. Well, like the prophet Isaiah or perhaps more like the prodigal son, I wondered through the Ohio Territory, mostly, telling myself to give up on reprisal, on finding and avenging my mother. I would live some times with my Shawnee relatives—though we do not get along well— sometimes tracking for the British. I thought I had cut off the curse of my white heritage. I might even have lived with the fact that I was unable even to prevent the butchery by the Raisin River: Winchester's wounded prisoners, mostly Kentuckians, massacred. So look at me!" cried Peter. "I condemned you for indirectly helping white men arm themselves against my Indian brothers and then I—"

There were tears in his eyes. "I helped supply the weapons to the British and Indians. I helped them find Winchester. If I had known, oh, God, Nathan, this is my own purgatory."

Nathan reached over again to grab his arm. "Peter, you are right about purgatory; you are doomed to suffer for all of your crimes, believe me! You are the most evil man I have ever known."

"Thank you, Lieutenant—or Captain, is it?—Jeffries!" Peter grinned, then frowned. "I am not smart enough to be the most evil man you ever saw, even in your small circles."

The wide arc of Nathan's fist was too obvious to Peter, but when he ducked, Nathan's powerful forearms were squeezing his head like a vise. Then Nathan backed away and bowed.

"You have improved, my old friend," Peter said breathlessly. "Very impressive."

But then he looked away. "I wonder if I am doomed, but if I *am* doomed, at least in this life, there is a savior, an angel, you know . . . do you remember the girl Taima that you met in Baltimore?"

"Yes, I do. But wasn't she from around here?"

"I somehow ended up around here. I don't remember much of it, but I finally came here and decided to help Perry. They probably should not be told about many of my earlier actions. I am the enemy. Where do I belong? No matter who wins the war, the Indians will lose. My people lose their land and their lives; doomed, as I am, like Cain, to kill my brother, wandering a blood trail of betrayal—but after the massacre, I could not wash my hands of the shame. You were right when you said everybody sells guns, Nathan; as many of them go to tribes fighting *for* Tecumseh as against him!

"The Potawatomis; many tribes have massacred women and children on their hands. Indians have learned too well how to commit crimes that betray their own people for . . . Tenskwatawa, The One that Opens the Door; he is nothing, a false prophet. Tecumseh is a great man, Nathan, but he has changed. He is so bitter and single-minded, and he still thinks British are the key to hope for any tribe. He is wrong; he is the bravest, most intelligent man I know, but he is so wrong, he—I could no longer follow him, even though I love him. It is no longer hopeful—white Americans will win even if they 'lose' this war. The Indians will lose, and Tecumseh fights the fight of the hopeless even now believing he can somehow . . . save something of his people, their land. I found it convenient to change sides, that's all. I really hate no one—except for the man who destroyed my mother."

"I know," said Nathan. "Peter, there is something I must tell you."

"Lake Erie is the key to victory, for both sides," Peter said. "And I believed that Shooting Star, Tecumseh, was the key to the success my people would have with the redcoats; but now they're under General Henry Procter. Tecumseh's finest hour was the surrender of Detroit, with his British ally and friend General Brock. But his successor, Procter, is no Brock. The last time I saw Tecumseh, he was wearing a blue uniform coat, complete with gold epaulettes, a red woolen cap with one eagle feather in it, and a medallion around his neck, given to him by Brock."

"Peter—"

"Tecumseh has rallied many of the nations; many tribes and chiefs are still united against the Americans. Withered Hand, Stiahta, the Wyandot leader, Black Hawk of the Sacs, Four Legs, the great Winnebago chief—all here, joined with the Shawnee. I have seen, or heard of warriors of the Ottawa, Creek, Kickapoo, Potawatomi, Fox, Sioux, Huron, Ojibwas, Miami . . ."

"Have many Indians sided with Harrison?" Nathan asked.

"Oh, there have been a few, especially half-breeds, like myself; my Wyandot friend Between the Logs, for instance. A man named Anthony Shane, a half-blood Wyandot, who has been reporting on the councils on the north shore; and there's Mayar Walk in the Water, and Tarhe, who do not wish to remain with the British. But there are not as many fighters who wear medallions of the 'Great Father George' in England. The killings have been less since the British have offered five dollars for every American prisoner turned in alive."

Nathan nodded. "Before I left Halifax, I read an excerpt from *Nile's Register* comparing Admiral Warren and his Chesapeake Bay invaders to 'Water Winnebagoes.' There have been reports of rape, pillage and murder among the civilians in Virginia. Hampton and several villages were burned. But Peter, you do not know that—"

"Have there been no successes to the south?" Peter asked.

"None that I have heard of. The British are threatening the entire coast; our very capital may be in jeopardy, as well as Boston. The early triumphs at sea are still celebrated, but the only escapes and captures involve smaller sloops mostly, or privateers."

"How are your father and Catherine? Have you heard nothing?"

"Yes." Nathan had not been able to broach the subject of their friend. There were a few moments of silence.

"I suppose my father is the same; Catherine might be in Philadelphia," Nathan finally continued. "And apparently no one knows the whereabouts of your Barbara Steward and her friends; they have disappeared again. They might be sailing back to England, for all I know. There are so many lies, I weary of this . . ." His voice trailed off, then Nathan looked at his friend again.

"Peter, Catherine has . . . betrayed us; betrayed me, in any case, with this Michael Fredericks himself."

"No!"

"Yes."

"I can't believe it. Catherine, siding with the enemy?"

"I know Catherine is your . . . friend, but she is now his . . . mistress. Just as Barbara was Richard's, and—yours!"

Peter looked at him, eyes narrowed for a moment, then turned away.

"Would you care to rest now," asked Peter, "or should I tell you the news here?"

"Peter, did you understand my—"

Peter banged his hand so hard on the table that their pewter mugs of beer toppled off and rolled loudly on the floor, sending their contents cascading across the bare planks. A few men turned at the crash, then looked away. Peter quickly retrieved the mugs and placed them gently on the table again.

"I am sorry," he said. "I guess, the friend of my enemy is not my—I did not think of it that way back then, but I always knew Barbara, Abraham, Richard, Michael, Elizabeth Patterson Bonaparte, even. They are blood enemies—but I also treated you like an enemy, and that was terrible."

"Well, yes. The wife of my enemy is my friend, enemy? I am very glad that you feel guilt."

"Shall I tell you more about the Lakes?"

"I asked you a question, Peter! What about Catherine?"

"She loves you, Nathan."

He shook his head, scowled, and there was an angry silence.

"Please, Nathan, I know, you were right. Let's not discuss it now. I have no right to say anything about it, but at least I can tell you the news here."

Nathan felt chilled, but then shrugged, and yawned.

FOURTEEN

Presque Isle Camp - *July 1, 1813*

AFTER SLEEPING WHAT "SEEMED like 29 hours or so"—the exact amount of unconscious time as difficult to pin down as the battles on the Great Lakes, cooling down then heating up on every scale, land and water—this quiet morning Peter and Nathan were still alone in Nathan's tent.

"How did you sleep on that cot?"

Nathan smiled. "Sleep? Is that what it's for? And as to that lack of sleep, you never told me what happened to your Taima."

"Are you ready to take the trail east along the shore?"

"And what about Taima?" Nathan repeated.

"I don't think—"

"Where is she, damn it, man! Your guardian angel? Where is the brilliant Taima?"

"I don't know," Peter finally admitted. "Taima has disappeared and I miss her."

"All right, that's better. Maybe now that you have been on the receiving end," Nathan said cruelly, "you may be convinced to trust no one. Who can be trusted? Now that Catherine has betrayed me with that creature Michael Fredericks—and worse, betrayed the cause."

"What cause, Nathan? The cause of a more enlightened American independence. Without the unfettered ability to wipe out all indigenous tribes and nations that stand in the way of white progressional land-grabbing? More profits for slave-owning cotton growers from Texas to Maryland, even down eastern Florida now, with no resistance but a few do-gooders and northerners and Indian-lovers and those damned abolitionists."

"Shut your mouth, Peter."

Through the mesh of his own miserable guilt Nathan had finally understood how Amy, increasingly isolated from most of her community over the war, Indian and slavery issues, had long predicted the white tide pouring west in ugly conflicts, more people like Nathan's enemies, and Peter's "amok tribes." People in Washington City floundered and flipped; greedy, ruthless, disciplined, aggressive, clever, able to bend with the political wind like the light trigger on a duelist's pistol. Not all were cowards or fools on either side, but few could stand up to the rich company men.

"It's not just the loss you fear of this glorious Taima, it's the guilt you feel about being a murderer—and don't tell me to shut my mouth, Peter."

"There was once another man, a half-white man named Peter Hughes. Now I am honored to serve as a half-breed Indian scout," said Peter. "I have been spy, assassin, soldier, raider, *murderer.* You know of some of my sins. And there is little left for me to violate. Serelea—uh, Taima—seems to . . . seemed to—I don't know how much you know about the lake situation up here."

"It's because you have killed any number of whites *and* blacks *and* Indians, isn't that so, Peter?"

"During the spring, when Perry's boats and ships were on the stocks, the British controlled the Lake, but now—it has become impossible to feed, clothe and equip the regular army, let alone their Indian allies."

"Answer me! Tell me the truth!"

"Perry has performed a miracle in building that makeshift ship-yard and a small fleet to destroy Barclay's fleet and regain control of the Lake—possibly even win the war. Fortunately, we managed to sneak five small craft from Black Rock to Erie in May and June, hugging the shore en route. This southern shore is what you and I—"

"Damn it, Peter, *answer me!*"

"Naval control of the lake is the key—it could decide the entire war. All right, all right! You stubborn foolish white man, '*God Be Praised*.' Taima told me to follow her instructions explicitly. She told me to wait here for her, so I have *waited*. And yes, I have killed my whole life, my white friends, my red friends—my red and white friends—my black friends, my fellow Republican-Democrat-Federalists-Quaker-Friends. All is darkness. Does that answer all of your questions, damn you? *Here!*"

Peter shoved the back of his razor-edged tomahawk into Nathan's chest, the business end toward himself.

Nathan could only yell and slap down the tomahawk with his left then knock Peter down with a blinding right. Before Peter could recover, Nathan had his head in that deadly vice again, squeezing the life out of him.

Then Nathan released him.

"You're getting slow, *old man*," said Nathan, half in jest.

"*You* have changed, my friend," Peter gasped, struggling for breath. "Now that you have bested and punished me for my weakness and betrayal, can we go on?"

"Yes," said Nathan quietly. "*Do* go on."

"Perry desperately tries to get our two powerful warships ready for battle with the British fleet," said Peter, his voice still harsh. "If he can do that before the British fleet destroys us, we'll win. The British supply problems are critical. They cannot feed their Indian allies, and must come out and fight on our terms—unless they can some how get supplies over land. Lake Erie smuggling operations, whether for patriotism or profit, might just solve the British supply problem. There are rumors from Fort Niagara, Fort George, Black Rock and Buffalo at the far eastern end of the lake, all the way to Fort Meigs and Detroit in the west. Here."

Nathan took the drink Peter offered.

"Even on this side of the lake it costs $1.00 to fell and trim a tree. Ax men are paid 50 cents a day, sawyers $1.25, wagoners $3.25. Perry was been advanced $2,000 from Secretary Jones. Corn whiskey costs six bits a gallon. Rations are better than Canadians get, but still poor. Fortunately, pigeon, geese, sturgeon, perch and whitetail have been plentiful, with plenty of hunters. There is the tavern and a blacksmith. They got in the big guns, shot, powder, muskets, pistols, cutlasses, boarding pikes, lead, treenails, copper, iron, Georgia iron, live oak, oakum, all from Black Rock, Albany, Buffalo or Pittsburgh. A barrel of flour costs $100. And it costs $1,000 to ship the big guns, the 24-pounders.

"Wages should be enough for anyone to buy 500 acres and grow rich. Instead, we get the ingenious naval designs of Henry Charles Eckford—not "fir built frigates" but two brigs, 110-foot and 500 ton, the 20-gun *Lawrence* and 20-gun *Niagara*, now finally fully rigged with 32-pound carronades mounted. They also built four gunboats, the 50 ton *Porcupine* and *Tigress*, the 60 ton *Scorpion* and the *Ariel*, a pilot advice boat. All this built under the threat of a British attack, the fear that the ships would be burned before they were launched—never mind under sail, the fickle late summer winds notwithstanding—with Harrison's 500 militia for defense."

Part of the price paid for this remarkable speed, Peter had learned from Perry, was the thin skin of these vessels, made with black and white oak and poplar, chestnut, ash, pine, black walnut and red cedar stanchions, wide-spaced knees and ribs. It was barely two inches thin, allowing any sized round shot to pierce clean through both sides. Not exactly "Ironsides." Would the men stay at their great guns? Overnight, forests were made into ships—green wood, good for one good fight. Nathan's job would be to help defend, supply and ready the brigs, similar to the *Enterprise, Argus* or *Hornet* across the sandbar, which offered both protection and a barrier to larger vessels attempting to navigate the winding channel from the lake and peninsula.

The keels of the two powerful vessels had been laid on the beach; then they had been floated and fitted out in Cascade Creek. Their guns would have to be removed again to help lighten them enough to float over the bar. And now Perry's opponent, the one-armed British Captain Barclay, who had lost his arm with Admiral Horatio Nelson at

Trafalgar, was patrolling the lake and watchful for any opportunity to blow helpless vessels out of the water. On Lake Ontario, Commodore Chauncey, with over 400 men on his flagship alone, the full-sized frigate *General Pike,* could or would not send Perry sufficient numbers.

"But even more aggravating than getting supplies," said Peter, "and much more critical is the lack of men."

Perry had bombarded Chauncey with urgent appeals pleading for more crew to man his ships. Instead of the 700 men he had asked for as a bare minimum, he had received 120 officers and crew—some of them, thank God, veteran gunners from *Constitution.* And now Lieutenant Nathan Jeffries, whom Perry might even make commander of *Niagara.* But he needed 180 men for each brig alone, or at least some trained seamen. American Generals Winder and Chandler had been recalled in disgrace, but in June the United States had routed the British at Fort George and Fort Erie, near the Falls. Unfortunately these victories were not followed up on land, in spite of the efforts of General Winfield Scott.

But thanks to Scott, Perry and his second, Lieutenant Jesse Elliott, the Americans captured the *Caledonia, Somers, Ohio, Trippe* and *Amelia,* and converted them into warships, altogether but seven guns; and young Captain Barclay was on the prowl.

But now, with Perry's fleet almost ready (only a few long guns but carrying 65 good short range guns), all he needed was crew to man it. Commodore Chauncey and his British counterpart, Captain Sir James Yeo, were engaged in a building war. Combat on Erie did not seem a priority, according to Perry, and until he could obtain at least a few more trained sailors—or even landsmen—Perry, a fighter, paced and barked like a caged animal struggling for release.

"I was in the bombardment of the forts," said Peter with a grin, "but I returned here by another route. But Perry's voyage home with the five ships was miraculous, horrendous. He was chased by the 19-gun *Queen Charlotte,* 13-gun *Lady Prevost* and 10-gun *Hunter,* sometimes *towing* upstream, always with his lake fever. But fog helped. Perry's Luck held again. They barely reached Misery Bay, just west of here, before Barclay appeared in the offing."

"And no storms," said Nathan.

"Yes," said Peter. "There is always that possibility. York was sacked in April, by Chauncey's Lake Ontario fleet of twelve vessels and 1700 soldiers under General Dearborn, Colonel Scott and Perry."

"I read about that," said Nathan.

"The famous General Zebulon Pike was killed in that explosion at York. Then at the end of May, the British attacked Sackett's Harbor, but not much came of it. Chauncey in Sackett's Harbor and Yeo in Kingston indulge themselves in safe, retaliatory raids and depradations. Our friends to the north don't like the way we wage war in Canada. But the unseen enemies here are boredom, fever and intrigue—or let us just call it business. The agents, the clerks—did you hear about the traitors Stacy and Hogeboom? Spies are supposed to hang. In any case, corruption runs rampant here. I wonder how that the Canadians haven't pushed us farther south. The military is rife with Jonahs and cowards, collaborators and conspiracies, smugglers who send funds and orders to the government. Now that York is destroyed, the British say we owe them a capital, but Defense Secretary Armstrong has convinced those fools to do nothing to defend Washington City."

"I keep reminding you, Peter. You cannot trust anybody, not even your own mates. We read about the string of defeats on the frontier up here in Canada—while all along the same border Canadians and Americans get rich trading away. The blockade dries up trade along the American coast, especially in Chesapeake Bay, except that thousands of merchantmen are being captured by privateers. After 1807, our government could have built a large fleet of merchant-killers—purpose-built privateers, except *not* private, not ships of the line, not frigates—only ships of fifteen to twenty guns. That is one thing my father was right about. Speaking of naval matters, did you see the sketches by Decatur and Fulton? Torpedoes, they call them—exploded against ships, kegs connected to spars and lines, and delivered by a small vessel, possibly even a submersible. The British call them inhuman."

"Yes!" cried Peter. "The Professor and I had sent them some . . . inventions I had been developing with Fulton and I had also—there was work on a steam-powered warship."

"In New York," said Nathan. "A brilliant idea! But far from completed."

Peter sighed. "Meanwhile Congress hammers and harangues on the impressment issue, just as they did, just as impotently; please, don't press our seamen, they ask and offer concessions. By 1814, perhaps they won't even mention it.

"Here friends become enemies, priests order pests out of a field, lice are a sign of virility. We scrounge and beg for soldiers from Harrison, and he begs for us to sail out and fight. At least Fort Meigs is safe—for now. But here we wait in Erie, discouraged, pledged to a martinet. Oh, don't misunderstand me; Perry is a brave man, whether you love him, hate him or fear him. But nevertheless he is high-strung, too touchy, and his problems with Chauncey, Elliott, and the others could undo us. There is considerable tension, not to mention sickness . . . but Perry is determined, I'll give him that, and loyalty is his strong suit; and responsibility and sacrifice—and glory. The man is obsessed with his personal honor. He thirsts for redemption, even though he was fully vindicated for the loss of the *Retribution*."

"So he has you scouting for Yankees now."

"I have forsworn my promises to Indian and white, I admit to you, and it is torment." Peter lowered his head.

Good, Nathan thought snidely. Instead he asked, "The British supply situation is even more desperate?"

"It is now, said Peter. "But what happens when Napoleon is defeated? Great Britain could then send over thousands of additional troops, munitions, food, supplies—and the United States already faces economic disaster. It would certainly then face utter defeat and ruin, perhaps loss of territory—or even sovereignty. There is something else. Elliott and Chauncey seem to lead an unholy league to frustrate Perry, who must see clear victory. Elliott has long considered Erie his lake, since long before Perry arrived. He captured *Caledonia* and *Detroit* under the Fort Erie guns, though the latter ran aground and burned.

He plots and argues and undermines and insults, while Chauncey urges Perry to relieve Harrison—even though he knows he cannot, without men. 'We need success on both Lakes,' he tells Perry. Meanwhile, the enemy's flags and sails are in sight every day, mocking and challenging us."

"So we sit here," said Nathan, "all efforts sabotaged, while Barclay's ships beard us daily. He can't get in, and we can't get out."

THE REST OF JULY exhausted Nathan, mostly the arduous routine of supply and Great Gun drill with "smashers" (32-pounders), 24-pounders, and smaller guns—mostly carronades. He was also training ill and ignorant men to work a ship, to perform some of the tasks that would be needed aboard; to lay alongside, or at least within pistol shot, and destroy at close range. There was too much to do, with insufficient resources and men, but a few young officers—Bannek and Lieutenant Champlin, who would command the schooner *Scorpion*, and Malacthon Woolsey, and his bower anchors, Lieutenant Holdup—were making good progress. Nathan did not see much of the beleaguered Commodore Perry himself, or even of Peter Hughes, but he heard through Peter and through Perry's trusted purser, Hambleton, that Secretary Jones, as well as Chauncey, ordered Perry to assist General Harrison; and yet the reinforcements that he continued to beg for were few and far between—sixty here, seventy there, mostly landsmen. "A great many that came by Mister Champlin are a motley set: blacks, soldiers, and boys. I cannot think you saw them after they were selected—I am, however, pleased with anything in the shape of a man. Very respectfully, I have the honor to be Sir Your Obd. Servt." Perry also wrote to the Honorable Navy Secretary William Jones.

By the last day of July, after constantly watching half a dozen enemy sail to the north and continuously blockade Erie with impunity, word was that Perry would sail, fight his way out of the bag—even though he had only 300 men, half of what he needed, and many of those virtually useless because of sickness or lack of skill. The slow greenness of his ships' timber was matched by the raw greenness of most of the men. But the eyes of his superiors, and the public, were upon him. How he could delay? And boats might appear any night to attack his precious ships.

Then, a miracle happened—more of Perry's Luck. That Saturday morning, a little after sunrise, Nathan heard shouting.

"They're gone, sir! No enemy in sight!" They later learned Barclay had accepted a dinner invitation at Port Dover, below Long Point on the north shore directly across from Erie, thinking that he could afford to leave the trapped Perry alone for a few days.

Nathan and Bannek rushed out of their quarters and scanned the horizon. Sure enough, it was clear. Within the hour, Perry had assembled his officers and issued orders for anchoring all of the vessels just inside the bar. Peter was grinning at him.

"Are you ready for a little work?" he asked Nathan.

"But how are we going to—?"

"You shall soon see!"

Boats rowed back and forth all day and into the night; the ships were all anchored just inside the bar before dawn on Sunday, August 1. The channel's depth was sounded: less than six feet, and the brigs drew nine.

After nightmarish hours of work with kedge anchors and brute force, all of the shallower draft vessels were hauled over the bar into deep water—except for one gunboat, to protect the brigs. A battery of three 12-pounder long guns was also set up.

Meanwhile, Perry had ordered Nathan, already exhausted, to report to the four odd-looking scows that he had noticed earlier but never inquired about. They were box-like, 20 ton barges, 50 feet long, ten feet wide and eight feet deep, and curved inwardly on one side. When he arrived, he saw that Peter was there, and Lieutenant Yarnall with Brown's foreman, Sidney Wright.

"Mister Jeffries," said Perry, looking strained but confident. "I suppose your friend here told you about these camels."

"Sir?"

Perry almost laughed. "Well, it was his idea originally, and though you may come to curse it, these will enable us to lift the brigs into deep water across the bar."

"I've read the Dutch use them when their polders are stranded," said Peter.

"Excuse me, sir."

"Mister Wright assures me that these will work. You will act as liaison between Mister Yarnall, the crew, and myself, in putting them to effect."

"Aye, aye, sir," said Nathan; that was all he could say, though he was still mystified.

But not for long. During the next three grueling days, with hardly any sleep, Nathan learned the hard way about camels.

The watertight barges, shaped to fit against the hull of the *Lawrence*, were towed in place, then sunk, then secured with stout cable and spars passed through the brig's gunports. Then the camels were pumped dry; acting as pontoons, they raised the ship until she floated very high in the water. With every healthy body available for muscle, and after several snags and false starts, *Lawrence* finally slid into deep water at 10 AM on August 4; the men cheered.

"Remount her guns!" Perry ordered. Her sister ship, the *Niagara*, would be next.

Just then Barclay's fleet was sighted, standing in with a fair wind. One brig was helpless, the other still being re-armed.

Like the sands of the hourglass, it seemed that Perry's Luck had finally run out.

Nathan's and Peter's as well.

FIFTEEN

Lake Erie - *August 4, 1813*

"WE'LL HAVE TO BLUFF," said Perry. He ordered the *Scorpion* and *Ariel* to attack Barclay, firing their long range guns.

"Brilliant," said Nathan. "The wind's in the west now; they can see our sails filling and it could very well appear that we are ready in force."

The bluff worked. The British made off for Malden, and the next day Perry could write to the secretary that *Lawrence, Niagara, Caledonia, Ariel, Scorpion, Somers, Tigress* and *Porcupine* were ready to engage the enemy. Still seriously undermanned but with help from a company of seventy-two riflemen, they sailed on a shakedown cruise several hours before dawn on August 6, spurred on by a letter from Harrison pleading for help at the western end of the lake, with Nathan as acting commander of the *Niagara*. Peter remained behind in the virtually empty town. Waving goodbye to him, Nathan feared it was the last time he would see his friend, even as he wondered if he would ever be able to sleep for more than two hours at a stretch again.

But the enemy was nowhere to be found, and the wind failed, so they returned to Erie twenty-four hours later. Another letter from Harrison assured Perry that the army was no longer in any immediate danger, but the commodore intended to venture west and north again as soon as any additional men were found and extra stores for Harrison were aboard.

In early August, Perry received a letter from Chauncey in which the latter said, "I have yet to learn that the colour of the skin, or cut and trimmings of the coat, can affect a mans qualifications or usefulness—I have nearly 50 Blacks on board of this Ship and many of them are amongst my best men . . . complain that the 'distance was so great between Sackett's Harbor and Erie that you could not get instructions from me in time to execute with any advantages to the service,' thereby intimating the necessity of a separate command—would it not have been as well to have made the complaint to me instead of the secretary?"

Perry pounded his fist on the table, trembling to swallow his rage and pride. Chauncey praised Perry's "zealous gallantry," but rebuked him for complaining about the black sailors, and for complaining directly to the secretary and intriguing for a separate command. Chauncey had sent him the dregs, a trickle, and kept almost all sailors to himself; expected Perry to fight with a few officers, a sailing master, a handful of sailors, mostly non-seamen, militia and volunteers, with very little experience. It took months to get any response from Chauncey (which was why he had written the secretary). And now this insulting rebuke. It was hopeless, Perry decided, the agony of his situation almost overwhelming him, his sense of duty and anticipation of battle warring against his sense of outrage, humiliation and futility.

On August 10, Perry wrote to Secretary Jones again, saying that "I am under the disagreeable necessity of requesting a removal from this station. I cannot serve longer under an officer who has been so totally regardless of my feelings. Under all these circumstances, I beg most respectfully and most earnestly that I may be immediately removed from this station. I am willing to forego that reward which I have considered for two months past almost within my grasp—if, sir, I have rendered my country any service in the equipment of this squadron, I beg it may be considered as an inducement to grant my request. I shall proceed with the squadron and whatever is in my power shall be done to promote the interest and honor of the service." Perry's duty outweighed his pride, but it was almost unbearable to write this letter. But he would fight, if possible, until transferred, even with a fourth of his meager forces down with fever.

"Four hundred men for a squadron of nine vessels!" he shouted, and pounded his fist again, tore at his hair. Images of madness and rage, of a disastrous failure and court martial, flittered through his head like torturing demons. After all this labor and sacrifice, to lose his great chance.

Slowly Perry forced his mind to consider the situation. They would sail again off Sandusky; the British were on the defensive now, having missed their chance, and more afraid of him that he was of them. After the brigs were built, the *Queen Charlotte, Lady Prevost* and some galleys had exchanged a few shots with them. Their vigorous fire had chased off the British, who had returned to Fort Malden and Amherstburg. Perry was desperate for crews, but the British were desperate for food. They had 20,000 mouths to feed: 1,500 Indian fighting braves, civilians, families, perhaps 4,000 British troops, residents. Meanwhile, the surgeon's assistant yammered on about bilious remittent fever and influenza, suggested that mosquitoes had something to do with it, or drinking the fecal-contaminated water, or even something in the air.

Perry's mind, like a crazed compass, returned to the pressing matter at hand—insanely, he thought of revoking the paroles of the British in Erie, conscripting prisoners from anywhere he could find them, civilians, militia patrols. He would impress, just as the British had! They had achieved a remarkable thing, and created a powerful squadron. Now he must get men. He must get at Barclay, somehow.

"You were right, Lieutenant Jeffries," said Perry. "Thank God I did not take the coach or wagon south. What an opportunity for service to the United States, for we few. I shall have him!" he whispered. "Or he shall have me."

The balance of power on the lake had shifted once again, and Nathan, sailing with Perry and Peter Hughes—not to mention self-styled Master Commandant Elliott—knew that this showdown could be a hopeless contest, a trap, and not the desperate gamble it appeared to be. Peter had somehow managed to sail from the east with three schooners. Perry, now as corpulent as Isaac Hull, seemed oddly ineffectual now as they sailed toward their doom. They had a skeleton crew, barely half the number needed to adequately man the ship and guns. A dark-skinned man capered and sang on the foredeck, nonsense words that somehow spoke directly to Nathan.

"Mister Robert, he says, clew up, haul down, three turns around the longboat, and a pull at the scuttlebutt, haw, haw, humbugged, Jack! Helm up, head down you there at the main royal masthead truck–he bore up and run off, salute him, sir, Tom Cox's traverse, sogerin' we is, Jonathan's a blackguard, yes he is! We's sadly afraid of a dirty peace, yes we is! Keep your head down, powder dry . . ."

Why doesn't Perry silence that man? Nathan wondered. How odd! He is a Negro with blue eyes and red hair like a coxcomb curling over the top of his head; sideburns, ruddy cheeks, Roman nose. Now he is singing, "Old Robin Gray," "Bonny Jane," "Alloa House," "Love in a Village," "Hey, Johnny Cope;" the tars were dancing to the "Eightsome Reel," laughing at us; and there was my mother, at the ball!

THAT NIGHT, NATHAN DREAMED of his mother, Amy. "Why did you leave me, Nathan?" she asked calmly.

"Why did you have to die? Why did you leave us?" he sobbed, oblivious to his surroundings. "I think about you every day. You are still with me, not just from time to time, with me—"

"You know, the Protectors have been helpful, helping us to—"

"Oh God, no, Mother, it can't be! Did Catherine betray you, too?"

He heard Peter explaining to the officers on the quarterdeck that "he lost his mother, then he lost his mind, and this is a father and mother delirium; but he insisted on secrecy, so with the ague, flu, tropical disease, chills."

"Where is my father?" Nathan shouted. "He can save us."

"*She* will save us," said Peter pointing to the side of the ship. And Catherine climbed aboard, unattended, unaided by an arm or chair, and promised to rescue them.

"It is thanks to fever on the Lakes," she said to Nathan. "We have a surprise for them."

"This is another trick," Nathan said, "just as Barbara betrayed me."

"Nonsense," said Peter. "Remember my dream? Those tricks will turn around and bite the trickster! Tell me, don't you realize that Barbara betrayed Richard? And look at Catherine! Does she not look beautiful, even though you are no longer a man who has been without women."

"Mother, how can you be here?" asked Nathan. "You died, I never saw you again, and yet you—"

"Well, what of that?" Amy asked. "Here is another captain, a new man, your father, somebody near me, a servant, perhaps."

"But there is no one, no one—just stay with me, Mother!"

"But there was someone," she said, "searching the waterfront for Catherine."

"Don't give up, Mother!" Nathan sobbed. "I am alone!" He was sobbing, shouting. They were dragging him down again, shaking.

"Sir! Are you all right, Lieutenant?" A lantern blinded his eyes; someone was shaking his shoulder, and the threads of his nightmare shredded like mist in the dark.

"Who is there?" he groaned.

"Montgomery, sir—the corporal of the watch called me. You were . . . crying out."

"I am—it was nothing, Mister Montgomery, a dream. Please convey my apologies to the watch. It will not happen again."

"Very good, sir."

He remembered now. It was August 18, 1813, the anniversary of his mother's death. Someone at supper had mentioned the victory of the *Constitution* over the *Guerriere,* and Nathan had chimed in, choking down the other memory, swallowing his tears in beer and camaraderie. None of his other losses, not even his dear friends, caused the same guilt and panic. Now it had caught up with him; it seemed these days that once a fortnight or so the pain erupted and the emptiness overwhelmed him. It had been more difficult in the first few months, even while he kept busy. He could imagine a time, say, ten or twenty years in the future (if he lived that long) when the agony would be bearable and he would not sincerely wish to die. During nights like these, death appeared as a great release—even death at the hands of his enemies; there was some relief and comfort in that.

It was another, more physical kind of agony when Midshipman Montgomery woke him still later that night to inform him that Perry requested his presence immediately. He yearned for sleep but groggily splashed his face with water from the bowl and dressed as best he could. At Perry's headquarters, the same house in which he had met the man less than a month ago, he found Peter, as well as Sailing Master Taylor, a lieutenant he did not recognize and Jesse Elliott, whom he had disliked from the first moment they met.

"Ah, Mister Jeffries. You remember Captain Elliott, of course. And this is Acting Lieutenant Augustus Conkling. They have just arrived by boat from Cattaraugus Creek, with almost a hundred prime seamen!"

"Excellent, sir."

"We have also received some important news from our spies," Perry continued, nodding at Peter, "as well as from these gentlemen. But I will ask our scout to tell you."

"Barclay's new ship *Detroit* is ready to sail," Peter told Nathan. "She is stoutly built with nineteen guns of mixed types, mostly long range. I understand they must be fired off with pistols. That is why Barclay retreated to Malden. But there is more; apparently, there is a—"

"Barclay and Procter are having greater difficulty," Elliott interrupted, "supplying their beef and flour needs of their own forces—as well as the thousands of Indian fighters and families under their care. Most of their supplies are sent on the St. Lawrence and the Thames River, if they arrive at all. They are growing desperate, and now we threaten their line of communication even more. This we know. We also know that they have several American contacts providing shipments across the American borders to the south and east."

Elliott paused, his sleepy, arrogant eyes studying his audience. His uniform was immaculate, his pudgy cheeks and receding hairline only adding to his irritating manner.

"Through a friend perhaps more reliable than some of our spies," he continued, ignoring Peter, "I learned at Cattaraugus Creek—which you must be aware is a smuggler's haven—that a large number of cattle, wagons and carts loaded with supplies for the British are due to arrive there within the next few days. It is not clear who is involved, but the operation calls for a night rendezvous with British ships that will then carry the supplies to the Canadian coast. This I learned after sending a letter to the commodore regarding our success at obtaining reinforcements. In the absence of any orders, I deemed it prudent to proceed here, rather than attempt to interdict the smugglers."

"Thank you, Captain Elliott," said Perry. "As you know, Lieutenant Jeffries has performed well in accordance with my orders, and demonstrated his courage and abilities in independent command."

Looking at no one, Elliott actually scoffed dismissively.

Nathan could not believe the man's rudeness.

"Did you have a comment, sir?" asked Perry.

"No, sir. Pardon me," said Elliott. Nathan glared at him.

"I shall not sail again for several days, Mister Jeffries," Perry continued, "and, as much as I regret any risk of sailing without you, I feel you are the best man to lead a small party to Cattaraugus Creek."

"Sir?" Nathan was shocked.

"Captain Elliott as senior captain will of course take command of *Niagara*. But we hope fervently that you are successful and can return in time to sail in search of Barclay. I cannot overstress the importance of your mission, Mister Jeffries. We force Barclay to come to us if we strangle his sources of supply. His needs for men and food are at least as critical as our own, and now we can with one stroke secure the frontier! We now have just enough men to do it. When you are back, I will need you aboard *Lawrence* as my second, along with the men I am sending with you; but I need to cut off Barclay's and Procter's supplies more. They are growing desperate, and victory is within our grasp. There will soon be honor and satisfaction enough for all of us!"

"Commodore, I hardly think that I should remain ashore at a time—"

"Jeffries, are my orders not clear? You will take Peter Hughes and ten men and proceed immediately by schooner and boat to Cattaraugus

Creek. Hughes and his people will advise you as to precautions. We shall see you back here in two or three days. We must sail again before the end of August. The Bass Islands will be the primary rendezvous."

"Aye, aye, sir!"

Nathan saluted angrily and spun around, leaving the cabin without a glance at the other men.

Peter stopped him outside. "Nathan, please. We may have warm enough work ahead without your exploding."

"I had no idea that Elliott had even returned, let alone—"

"Orders are orders, my friend. And those the most involved are often the last to know."

"Perry offered to resign—I believe I will do so myself!"

"Be silent, Nathan! Come in here."

Peter dragged him into the tavern, where they sat at their usual table. "You must not quit now, my friend," he continued, "or even talk that way!"

"You are telling me what I must do or not do? And what about that bastard Elliott? He took the best men for *Niagara,* you know! That was *my* command, damn it. Perhaps I shall meet with him privately and settle—"

"And another thing, you cannot challenge a superior officer. You have no business dueling, Nathan! And Perry has expressly forbid it."

"Forbid an affair of honor! In any case, he and I are both nominally lieutenants."

"Nathan, your—"

"Pardon, sirs, this came for the gentleman here." The innkeeper, whose greenish, drawn face and haggard appearance suggested yellow jack, bowed and handed Nathan a letter.

"Two beers, my good man," said Peter. "What is it, Nathan? You seem awfully cheerful, damn it!"

"Well, at least we will be together."

"What do you mean?"

Nathan handed him the note, which said simply, "Cattaraugus."

Peter nodded. "Do you not recognize the handwriting?"

Nathan shook his head.

"Who do you think would write this?"

"I'm not sure. But let us be careful."

"What do you know? What if it's an ambush? Who is it—tell me!"

"Peter, I do not know, honestly, and we must follow orders—that is all I can say! This confirms—"

"What are you here for, Nathan? It is your duty—"

"Don't talk to me about duty! I came here to fight the British—did you?"

As if frozen in the pleasant breeze, Peter hissed, "I'm going to Cattaraugus, with or without you. And may God help you if you refuse this command."

"Peter, I had a nightmare—"

"Have you not discovered the—" Peter hesitated. "Nathan, I believe in you. Please let it be enough for you to know that we are together, and fighting a common enemy."

TWENTY-FOUR HOURS LATER, three boats nudged quietly onto the dark sandy shore several hundred yards west of the Cattaraugus Creek landing. Other than Jack Logan, the men with Peter and Nathan were unknown to them; unsuccessful farmers with muskets, they were militia whom General Meade had convinced, somehow, that it would profit them to remain at Erie and follow Perry's orders. They had rowed with a will and were exhausted now, even more fatigued than Nathan. Peter never seemed to tire.

"Quiet!" Nathan hissed. "You men stay with the boats, and don't make a sound. Logan, if one of us does not return within a half hour, send two men to look for us—but stand off the beach with the rest until sunrise. Do you understand?"

"Sir, don't you want us to—"

"No! You have your orders. Our mission is to prevent smuggling, not get everyone killed. With daylight, or the approach of a vessel, you will know which course of action is suitable."

"Yes, sir."

"The landing is just beyond those rocks there," Peter whispered. Wading and then climbing, he and Nathan reached the landing in a few minutes. Peter carried a rifle musket; Nathan had stuck two pistols in his belt and carried a cutlass like a corsair.

"No moon tonight—if it is tonight," said Peter. "A well planned operation, I suspect."

Skirting the undergrowth that surrounded the clearing, they slowly, carefully walked along the sandy path that lead to the main wagon trail. The dense growth of young trees seemed to make the night even blacker, though it was clear, and a few stars offered a dim light.

Suddenly, Peter held Nathan back, holding his finger to his lips. Nathan became aware of quiet footsteps ahead of them. Then there was a figure in the path just ahead of them. No, more.

"What a delightful encounter, gentlemen," spoke a calm, friendly voice. "No doubt we all carry loaded weapons. Our company bids you welcome. Captain Jeffries, again, I am at your service." Nathan recognized the voice, and Peter nodded as if he had known this would happen. Blocking their path, with four armed comrades to help, stood Death in the form of Phillip Thompson, Michael Fredericks' agent and good right arm aboard Nathan's beloved *Merlin*.

SIXTEEN

Off the New Jersey coast - *August 12, 1813*
Heavy seas in a short gale, afternoon aboard American brig Latona

WHAT WOULD NATHAN SAY? She thought drearily. Why and how did he, according to her sources, escape Halifax prison, only to disappear, along with a fellow *Chesapeake* prisoner? Catherine in her misery could only imagine that this silly man whom she could not lose lay injured, dying, alone—but unlike Taima, Catherine could not save her man. She could not save herself. It took a remarkable, dangerous plan by Taima to rescue her; except being saved felt infinitely worse than being prisoner of Michael Fredericks, the Charles and her other jailkeepers. Fredericks never did honor her with the nature of his plans for her. Catherine had prepared herself for the moment, and accepted the hopelessness of her position with the kind of courage Amy would have admired.

Instead of just thanking the gods for her delivery from Fredericks, she suddenly remembered the painful departure of Nathan Jeffries.

"Why do you keep evading my questions?" he had yelled at her, just before she left. "What secrets did Amy leave with you?"

"Your mother made me promise—"

"Yes! *My* mother, *my* mother! Damn it! Where is the big chest of priceless secrets she decided to leave with you?"

So much had happened since she left in anger for Havre de Grace on April 20. Would she ever see Nathan again? But how could the foolish boy feel betrayed by *her*, of all people, when she had given him everything, and had tried so desperately to save to Jeffries name—even giving up what was left of her own honor. Men are such fools. And Michael Fredericks—now that Catherine and Nathan were at large again, he would hunt to the ends of the earth to wreak his fury on both of them; and on Peter Hughes and Taima, too.

In spite of her misery, Catherine couldn't help but laugh. Not only had Fredericks been cheated of his final victory over Nathan, but his old nemesis, Captain William Jeffries, had rejoined the fray, albeit with the spectacular help of Doctor Anderson and the young women. She was desperate to know Nathan's whereabouts. Michael said he knew the "resilient bastard" had escaped Halifax with another man. Fredericks was unflappable; his frustration and impatience never erupted toward his own ruin.

But Nathan had his virtues. Catherine's love of him trumped any misgivings on Taima's part. She had left Peter in good hands in Buffalo and returned east to save Catherine from something much worse than deportation by the amiable and always pleasant Michael Fredericks. The war was not going particularly well for the British, either, on the Great Lakes or anywhere else. Hundreds of privateers ripped into merchant ships and convoys, and several dangerous naval ships, small predators, were still at large.

Napoleon fought on, and Catherine learned that their Lordships in London had hoped for better results from Michael Fredericks.

Catherine had been able to glance at the Admiralty letter when Michael briefly left the study, forgetting it in his fury over her resistance. It seemed that he was "requested" to rescue the matter and somehow produce significant British victory, or at least a moral triumph, and to help the beleaguered Tories stave off the Labour Party. Parliament was hopelessly tied to the war, and bitter debate over several possible actions before winter ended most activities for 1813.

To her amazed delight, she also read how unhappy Fredericks' London contacts were with the considerable sabotaging of his delicate operation both here and abroad. With so many secrets and counter-truths, she became convinced that he had learned all about her work—labors spanning more than a year—against the Austers, as well as himself. Catherine remembered Fredericks saying, after Nathan and another prisoner had already escaped, "I still can't believe that any political party would be so ignorantly arrogant, or crass, or in such need of a mercy killing as to sit in judgment on *my* operation. Next year may be better, but the economy at sea is ruinous."

Did he already know how the intelligence provided by Catherine and now Taima had outsmarted all of them, with resources Fredericks discovered too late?

Catherine was determined to save Nathan in spite of himself. She dreamed of Nathan's smile, plentiful wine and fare and wild nights, the soothing breeze; always safely over the reefs and battles, all financial accounts in order, damaged reputations restored, incriminating documents still securely in her possession. But she, Taima, Nathan, his father and Peter remained in danger as long as Fredericks and his minions were at large. Taima amazed her by traveling from Buffalo to Fell's Point, Baltimore, galvanizing old Captain William Jeffries and Doctor Anderson to find and save Catherine and Nathan, so that Taima could return to Peter in Buffalo. It was Doctor Anderson who found out where Catherine was, but there was still no news of Nathan.

Catherine knew Perth Amboy was closely blockaded now. British opinion was divided, but the weight of the government stubbornly continued the fight, sensing profitable concessions from America, and Detroit remained in British-Canadian hands. But Americans were not all the pusillanimous poltroons many in Europe took them to be. The British Pacific whaling fleet was being hunted down and decimated by American frigate *Essex*. An even smaller warship, *Argus*, was running amok off the coast of Ireland, near the Channel, and new warships would be launched, like the new *Wasp* in Newburyport.

Catherine had loved Amy like a good daughter loves her mother and accepted her hatred of war, but, like Nathan, Catherine was at heart a fighter, a powerful soul. And yet, while she despised weakness and defeat, she wondered now if her unexpected and spectacular survival at the hands of her dear friends—who must connive with the British to achieve this blessing—did not achieve a blessing at all. She had been told that the verdant hills of the New Jersey shore were a league to the west; the swells were very lumpy to leeward.

The "Swedish" *Margarette*, actually American brig *Latona*, rolled violently and threw both women to the deck. "Where are we going, if we are unfortunate enough to survive this storm?" Catherine shouted. "That British warship, *Boxer*—our 'escort'—why did they not just sink us or tow us in? How much are they paid for this 'service'?" Catherine wiped away the last of her supper, which had returned in a revolting form. "*Latona* is from Maine, you said? Is Maine still part of the United States?"

"We'll talk about it later!" gasped Taima, though not quite as sick, marveled at her companion's ability to talk at all.

"I am almost willing to return me to Michael Fredericks. Anything is better than this *torture*. Is that what our British friends had in mind, after all?"

The door had broken its latch and swung wildly back and forth in the gloom; light flickered nervously as a candle burning on brass gimbals over the desk cast bleak shadows around the small cabin.

Catherine and Taima, to escape the wet wrath above, had mistakenly plunged down below to the captain's cabin, supposedly the best place to be. Among the notables above them on the quarterdeck were *Latona* co-owner Rufus King, Doctor Anderson and Captain William Jeffries himself, leaning on Doctor Anderson as well as a heavy black walnut cane—a sober passenger trying his best not to take over the ship's management.

The vessel steadied.

"We must have made our offing; we're standing into Perth Amboy now," said Taima, no longer gasping.

The women began to recover, but were still alone as *Latona* began to show her true colors.

Catherine tried a new tack. "Do you think Doctor Anderson will ever forgive me for evading him like that?" Catherine's meeting in

Philadelphia had been a secret even from the Protectors. At first, she had been guarded. It was Taima who had planned the rescue and lead Anderson and William Jeffries to rescue Catherine from the Charles mansion, before Fredericks could remove her to a final destination. Taima had removed one of the guards, Doctor Anderson the other, in a blur that frightened William Jeffries, who was long unused to violent, quick action. It was Captain Jeffries who had known Rufus King and his brother in Maine.

"You do not want to know what the Doctor said to me in confidence—but he will never talk to you about it. He's . . . well—do not concern yourself on that score, Catherine. You're safe, and that is all that matters."

"Yes," she said absently.

Taima, who missed nothing, watched Catherine stare out the stern windows.

"And we will find Nathan," she said. "That is a hell of a man you got there, Catherine."

"Yes. However you mean it, yes. But if he is alive, why does he not—"

Then Catherine began to cry, and Taima hugged her tightly. "I know, dear Catherine," she said. "I am tied for life to another fool. At least I made him promise to stay away from any fighting. He is in a safe place, out of trouble, with friends."

For several minutes Catherine bawled into her still-clean left sleeve, and then she straightened up.

"I was such a fool," she said angrily, "to let this happen to me—after all this time! Just to stab deeper, Michael added that he happened to be drinking with Captain Reynolds and a few of his partners at Parishioner's Pub & Inn when he began to brag about *me*—described our relationship in such a manner that now everyone assumes an *affair*. He hates William Jeffries, you know. William, Michael and Auster, they all wanted Amy—so of course Michael wants to ruin Nathan, too. He destroyed Abraham Steward, you know, and—you know about Barbara. I love you for saving me, but Michael will never rest until he finds us both; and his punishment will be terrible. Taima, please, what will happen when we disembark?"

"Well," said her friend, smiling, "you are not going home yet, neither to Philadelphia nor Baltimore."

Seventeen

Cattaraugus Creek, Lake Erie - *August 20, 1813*

"YOU!" HISSED NATHAN. He clicked back the hammer of his first drawn, charged and loaded pistol. "Don't move!" In his other hand, the shining cutlass.

"Ah! Captain Jeffries, is it?" asked the steady voice. "Or rather, Lieutenant! Upon my word, this is a pleasure! But I would caution you against discharging your weapon, sir. It would alert my own force; also, I would have to kill you."

Thompson seemed preternaturally calm. "You have—what? A dozen men back there at the landing? 'Water, water everywhere'—but it is our loyalist friends on the other shore who starve like the Ancient Mariner, you understand. It does not look well for you, dear boy.

"But I wish you did not look on me as the enemy. This reminds me of one of your sentimental American novels. Have you read *Amelia*, or *The Faithless Briton*? Charles Brockden Brown almost rises to the level of mediocrity. Pity I cannot think of suitable lines by young Lord Byron for the occasion. Mister Fredericks would do so. And who is your companion? Is this—?"

"A government scout," said Peter quietly.

He is stalling, Nathan realized, and exchanged a significant glance with Peter in the moonlight.

"You're with Fredericks, so you are helping him betray people here, just as you did with me and the *Merlin*!"

"Precisely, Jeffries! You grasp the situation! We have cruised together from the West Indies to Northeast Florida to Chesapeake Bay to Lake Erie! And many thanks for the delightful hiatus you afforded me on Grenada—especially with Governor-General Halsop's wife, in her private estate on the other side of the island. Pity, Highgate and Reynolds will certainly want to kill you immediately. I am sorry I helped steal your money, Nathan. You are a fine seaman, Captain/Lieutenant, but on dry land people will always be stealing from you, friend and foe alike; on land, you are not quick." Thompson sighed. "Well, Towacuttaywah, go fetch—"

"Belay that!"

"Of course, you might object," said Thompson, "if I sent one of my native friends here to warn—"

"Most strenuously, Mister Thompson—or whatever your name is!"

"Thompson will do; I was born . . . but that doesn't matter, does it? Phillip Mark Thompson is a frequent appellation."

"Thompson, while you were aboard—"

"Yes, *Merlin*; a great loss in treasure—would have been a total loss, except for your brilliant meddling! You are slow on land but you are a master at sea, really admirable. And you saved my life so I have saved your life, in spite of your efforts—or tried to help you. Of course, we must discourage your warning anyone else of our presence. Towacuttaywah, light the lamp, then I doubt anyone will object."

They heard a grunt, and a lighted lantern and rifle appeared, held by a short, squat Indian with a tall beaver hat topped by a black feather. The other Indian was taller, with a long hooked nose, squinting under a feathered cap. Both had long earrings and beads, and colorful buckskin coats with long leather fringes. They carried muskets, with tomahawks in their belts. Thompson himself wore the blue wool and white nankeen uniform of an American naval captain, complete with half-moon, fore-and-aft cocked hat and gold epaulets. He also carried a brace of pistols. All three men leveled weapons at Nathan and Peter.

Thompson studied Nathan and Peter, pausing for a moment on the latter as his eyebrow flicked up.

"What happened to your able crew, Jack Logan and the others?"

"Most of them are dead, Thompson. Commodore Perry ordered Mister Logan aboard *Niagara*, but we will join them on the *Lawrence* soon." Actually, Nathan hoped that Logan would join him *here* soon.

"What a shame. As you can see, Mister Jeffries, I have been promoted, while you unfortunately stepped down in rank." He sounded jocular. "It is only right that the British army and marines and loyal Canadian militia should continue to humiliate you rebels ashore. But while your cowardly privateers and letters of marque even cut out ships from our Canadian and Caribbean harbors, we struggle to save not just England but the free world against Napoleon. When we defeat Napoleon, probably this year, the question of navigation will be settled: no trade except through Great Britain. You will be fortunate to preserve these God-forsaken states and territories of yours. Personally, I predict that New England will rejoin Old England. Perhaps these so-called United States will be completely dissolved, and a good thing, too. But the point—"

"The point is you are a traitor," said Nathan.

"I regret your foolishness. We could use you on our side. British dominion lies beyond *your* point, arching over turbulent waters. The passing storm of U.S. bumptiousness causes nothing more than ripples. Speaking of that, in the wake of *Shannon's* capture of the *Chesapeake*, this time an *equal* contest, have you heard the British riposte to your Yankee victory songs?"

Thompson sang out:

Brave Broke, he waved his sword,

And he cried, 'Now, lads, aboard;

And we'll stop their singing

Yankee Doodle Dandy, O!

Suddenly the tall, menacing Indian spat some words at Peter who shook his head. "I know this one," the man said to Thompson, gesturing at Peter with his musket.

"Yes," Thompson began, "he looked somehow familiar to me, too."

In a flashing blur of charging motion, Peter's arm and hand snaked out and a knife was suddenly protruding from Thompson's neck, sticking out between the front edges of his high collar. He collapsed sideways with a groan. Now Peter's tomahawk flashed, and the tall Indian's arm was suddenly missing a hand. The lantern crashed to the ground and flickered weakly as the tall, bleeding Indian leaped at Peter and they both fell over to struggle in the dirt. There was so little time to react. His own pistol was knocked from his hand by a quiver of arrows swung like a club. Nathan fell back, marveling at Peter's speed but wondering that no one had fired in the nightmarish moments since he began his attack.

Through the gloom, the other Indian rushed at Nathan, who just had time to pull his cutlass and parry a ringing blow from the man's tomahawk, powerfully and skillfully wielded. The man came on quickly, methodically, silently, slashing with the weapon and forcing Nathan back. Again and again he swung and metal clanged against metal. Nathan's arm felt numb, and he knew that his foe was ready to spring forward at the earliest opportunity. Hand-to-hand he stood no chance.

Just then the lantern died completely, and Nathan could see nothing. Fighting his terror, Nathan dived to the ground to the left of where he hoped the Indian was, rolled on his left shoulder, jumped to his feet and started desperately swinging the cutlass. He heard a muffled scream and felt the sickening sensation of his steel edge cutting through flesh and bone. He did not stop, however; he kept striking the helpless body with his cutlass, and then fell away, knowing the form would be forever still now. He started to catch his breath.

A light was struck, and he saw Peter's welcome face approach with the lantern; he was bleeding from a cut on the forehead.

"Are you all right?"

"Yes, and you?"

"The same."

They studied the hacked and bloody corpse at Nathan's feet.

"Quite dead, I should guess," said Peter brutally. "As is mine, from his own tomahawk. They're Seneca warriors; I did recognize the tall one, Mouhquatowacoh. We were fortunate; they were about to surprise us—unpleasantly. Shall we move east?"

INWARDLY FUMING, MICHAEL FREDERICKS paced impatiently in front of the small fire near the wagons. Damn that Castlereagh, damn those arrogant Admiralty idiots. Now he had to run the operation *personally*? Thompson and Highgate could not run it themselves? His sense of outrage nearly exploded. But it remained inside, fueling his plans, adding to the perverse pleasure.

Now that Catherine Charles and William Jeffries were properly dealt with, there was just one left to hurt and eliminate; Nathan. Fredericks was amazed that the young fool had proved more of a survivor and problem than ever seemed possible. The boy, Peter, he cared little about, one way or the other—unless that young fool got in the way again.

Just visible out of the darkness, the nearest few of nearly 400 head of cattle lowed and mooed, stamping their hoofs, while others lay sleeping in the grass.

A dozen men lounged in the clearing by the trail, guarding the animals, tending to their wagons or sleeping. Most wore red or black kerchiefs, tan, green or brown leather waistcoats, cotton or flannel shirts and rawhide pantaloons. Fredericks wore a dark silk suit coat and pale flaxen shirt, his only concessions to the wilderness being duck trousers, rawhide boots and a somewhat soiled broadbrim hat and scarf now draped over his scabbard.

"Keep those bullocks quiet!" he snapped. He stopped and turned to Highgate, leaning against the lead wagon.

"I don't like it," said Fredericks. "It has been over an hour. Even if no ship arrived, Thompson should have sent one of those savages back to report."

"Do you want me to take some men and look?" asked Highgate.

"You? Your huffing and puffing would alert anyone for miles around! No, we'll wait another fifteen minutes, and then—"

"Fredericks!" came a shout from the north, off the trailhead.

"Get your men out of the light!" Fredericks bellowed, dragging out a pistol and darting behind the wagon.

"Who are you?" he shouted back.

"Don't you recognize the voice?"

Fredericks laughed. "Jeffries! My word! The clown prince of Baltimore—come to heel at last!"

"You are my prisoner, Fredericks! Surrender, and no one will get hurt!"

Fredericks laughed genially again. "You are mad, truly! But let us discuss this as civilized men, if you have the courage! Show yourself, unarmed, and I will do the same!"

"Agreed!"

Fredericks was vaguely surprised, and amused. "Stay undercover, lads," he said, stepping back into the light, in front of the fire. No one else was visible.

Alone, Nathan walked out of the woods to his left; the trail ended near the shore about five hundred yards further in that direction. He approached the fire, stopping about fifty feet from Fredericks, near the edge of the light. In its flickers, he could see that Lieutenant Jeffries' normally tan, flat face was nearly black, the blue uniform torn and caked with dirt and blood; he carried a pistol and his cutlass at his side.

"I thought we agreed to meet unarmed," Fredericks sneered.

Nathan smiled and tossed both weapons aside. "I just wanted to make sure your men heard you."

They faced each other without moving.

"I must say you have finally succeeded in surprising me," said Fredericks. "Discovering our little operation here, then killing Thompson and his Indian scouts. They are dead, are they not? Very impressive. Not an easy man to kill, I fancy. But who helped you? Where are the rest of your men, Lieutenant?"

"Who is with *you* . . . Highgate?" asked Nathan. "After all, we must round them up."

Fredericks tilted back his head but then stifled another laugh. "That is rich, boy, rich. But let me offer you a counter proposal; would you like to live to see the sun rise?" He pointed disdainfully at Nathan.

"Then leave now, before—"

"Before your ship arrives, and your rear guard?" Nathan's eyes narrowed in hate, but he controlled the tone of his voice. "It will save a great deal of time if I disabuse you about them. You are a vain man, always sure you have the upper hand, Fredericks. Have you looked at the time lately? By now, I suspect, Conklin on *Tigress* and Holdup aboard *Trippe* have captured or chased back the barges and transports."

Fatuous smile now gone, Fredericks scowled, pulled out his timepiece and realized what Nathan meant. At last he had been delivered a truly unpleasant surprise: no Canadian buyers and reinforcements would arrive, and his ten men to the south with Captain Reynolds were not coming to his aid. He could see the shielded lantern now barely visible through the distant woods.

"So my rearguard is being guarded by yours. Well, what do we do now? You cannot win this war. And I am not the only man who knows where the profits lie. My God, young man, are you still blind? Most good Yankees would as soon trade with England as look at you."

"You may be right," said Nathan. "But I'll die happy if I send you to hell first!"

"Damn your eyes! Cock your locks, boys!"

From behind half a dozen trees and several wagons, Nathan saw the muzzles of muskets and rifles protrude, aimed at him. Heart pounding, he raised his arm.

"Killing me will do you no good," said Nathan, "*Lawrences!*"

A nearly equal number of muzzles were raised, mostly from behind trees and rocks behind and to the left of Nathan. Led by Jack Logan, the men from *Lawrence* came into the light. And their guns were pointed at Fredericks. In effect, he was surrounded.

"Bah!" snorted Fredericks, glancing around. He no longer smiled. "So we have a stand off. No doubt your commander would be impressed by a useless slaughter of Americans against each other, rather than Canadians."

"You're no American," said Nathan, "or British, or any thing else. You're a—"

"As long as we must play this out, let us enjoy ourselves, without the hypocrisy!"

"You're nothing but a—coward," said Nathan.

"Brave words," said Fredericks, regaining his good humor and unmoved by the insult. "And what do you think you are, you simpleton! Here, with plenty of men to back you up. Fools there! You fools! This man Jeffries is the coward! And I can prove it!"

Nathan knew that he or Fredericks or both would die on this sultry summer night. Nathan had somehow known it would come to this, the moment he had always dreaded. The final test of his courage and manhood would be the man who had directed or personally humiliated him and his father, and ruined Barbara, Abraham and Catherine. Catherine! The last farewell, the final betrayal, his lover. He remembered Catherine sobbing; she who had always been so composed. He had savored her lips, her scent, her smooth, firm skin against his. The pain of her betrayal would at least die with him. Even if he lost to Fredericks, there was some chance that death really did bring peace. He could only regret the broken promise to his mother and all the guilt, thanks to his disobedience, over fighting a duel again. But for a worthy cause? Suddenly, an insane idea began to germinate.

Eighteen

Cattaraugus Creek, Lake Erie

BUT BEFORE NATHAN COULD say anything, Fredericks shouted, "Bring her over here!"

Held up by two neatly uniformed militia men, a disheveled creature in dirty homespun, face dripping with water or sweat, Catherine Charles looked up, saw him and called out, "Nathan!"

He stared at her, catching his breath again at her raven-haired beauty, her thin, active lips, hating her for betraying him—to his enemy, no less, Peter's denials notwithstanding.

"I thought it would save time if I quickly disabused you of any silly notion you might have fighting me. This is not a stand-off, young man, although I must say you have proved considerably more resilient than I would have ever imagined."

"A chip off the old block," said Nathan.

"Yes, in some ways," Fredericks sighed. "All too true in some ways, since you will now follow your father's wake into oblivion."

Nathan saw the look on Catherine's battered face and realized that his father was dead.

"I was recaptured by Fredericks," she groaned, "and your brave father was—"

"The fool thought he was a hero. He tried to save her by offering me a duel—can you imagine?—in exchange for her freedom."

"Fredericks, damn you! I—"

"Now, *Captain* Jeffries, drop your guns, unbuckle your blades and order your men to—"

The explosion of Fredericks' pistol deafened Nathan as the blur of Peter's body crumpled at their feet.

"No!" screamed Nathan and Catherine. Both William and Peter —gone!

"Silence! Don't move!" A dozen cocked guns pointed at Nathan through the gunsmoke of Fredericks' discharged pistol. "Now, drop those weapons if you want this young woman to live through the night."

"Yes; damn it," said Nathan, unbuckling his cutlass and dropping his pistol. "Logan, men, that is an order."

Nathan's men, growling, threw down their weapons. Pistols, swords, knives, muskets, rifles, fell in a clatter of wood, metal, leather, dirt and powder.

"*Very* good," said a jovial Fredericks. "Now, sir, remove your hat, that cumbersome cocked affair you navy boys wear—so odd. Please, my good lad, remove it!"

Nathan snatched off his fore-and-aft and threw it on the ground.

"Do we see horns on his head? I have always heard that a cuck-old grows horns—or perhaps you did not know that your 'woman' has always favored me with her many charms? Even before Auster and long before you crept back."

"You lying . . . bastard!" Catherine screamed, and Fredericks back-handed her with a loud slap. A knife blade shone in the moonlight at her bare neck as Nathan lurched forward.

"Whoa, young man, if you want her to live. Perhaps now, you do not?"

Nathan froze, watching blood drip from her down-hung face.

Fredericks laughed. "You seem to carry death and loss of man-hood with you, Jeffries. You will get your turn, but first . . . well, surely while you were running away and chasing your tail and making a fool of yourself in general, you suspected that a man with more to offer than yourself," Fredericks interrupted himself with another mocking laugh, "would offer her the pleasure you are clearly unable to. After all, what do they say about half-breeds? 'Loyalty from the back of my hand'?"

Nathan heard some snickers and chuckles from Fredericks' men. He could only stare at Fredericks with hatred.

"Silence! Captain Fredericks, sir, I have a gentleman's agreement with this man—a matter of my personal honor." It was none other than Albert Highgate, the Baltimore bartender and gaming room manager, even more corpulent if less jolly. The one-time tavern keeper had his own score to settle with young Jeffries, from whom he and his part-ners had "won" so much money. Nathan could only smile at the bitter sense of it all. Hard not to generalize about these people: Highgate had helped ruin Nathan's life.

But Nathan was undaunted. "As a gentleman," he said to Freder-icks, "you will appreciate my desire to accept the honor and courtesy of a prior meeting with your lordship, and you alone, first. And after you have been kind enough to indulge me, and only then, gladly make ar-rangements with this man—"

"I am afraid—"

"Only a gentleman like yourself," Nathan yelled, "could hide be-hind a young woman of any rank, and abuse his hostage like a black-guard, or worse, and still consider himself a noble man of high rank—I salute your, sir. After you have finished with us, please do right by her—if she will let you."

Fredericks' smile was gone, and he stared back at Nathan in furious amazement.

"If you were a man and not cuckolded coward, I would accept with pleasure your challenge! But I must insist that you call on my friend. As the saying goes: 'to the victor belongs the spoils.'"

"What a novel solution! You would actual refuse a challenge from me, one on one, after this Highgate? You find me that unworthy?"

"Yes. And in the absence of Captain Reynolds, I will order these men to avoid any further bloodshed among the defeated, unless abso-lutely necessary."

A few men snickered. If Nathan survived his wound, and his fight with Highgate, Fredericks could hardly be surprised if one of his over-zealous militia reported that Nathan, a "badly wounded prisoner," had died from his wounds.

Fredericks smiled, pleasantly astonished that his plans had succeeded so smoothly and quickly, with the added anticipation of viewing Jeffries' butchered body. With the pusillanimous "patriots" already out of the way, he stood an excellent chance of delivering his bullocks and supplies, but it was actually too early. Dawn it must be, reaping an enormous profit in the process, in addition to the satisfaction of watching the demise of Nathan Jeffries. The trek up here in person had turned into pure gold. He would find a way to avenge himself against Castlereagh and those nautical bastards in London. He would make sure they regretted their insolent behavior. For now, Jeffries would do.

Fredericks knew that Jeffries would have one or more men posted at the shore to look out for his British trading partners on the lake. But they had arranged that she would try at dawn, after the moon rose. And even if Jeffries had sent word for reinforcements, or even less likely another vessel, Fredericks would still have time to get away—just as he always had a second pistol hidden in his coat, ready to quickly cock and fire. Of course, both sides had tried to be ready for any manner of double-cross.

"I will say this much for Catherine," Fredericks announced, eyeing the collapsed woman coldly. "She and her Protectors managed to—well, I felt compelled to repair the damage in Canada personally. Never let it be said that women are helpless creatures. Some can be dangerously clever! But I am happy to say her Protectors are being rounded up, while this half-breed squaw who fancied herself so clever, sprawls in disgrace.

"But to business. Delightful business," he repeated, forcing a chuckle. "Shall we say, then, pistols at twenty paces, one shot or more, until disabled. We shall start in five minutes. I would rather not wait any longer—certainly not 'til dawn! I shall be glad to provide my personal brace of Wogden dueling pistols. You there! Sergeant—?"

"Miller, sir," said the man.

"Sergeant Miller, my good man, there is a case of pistols in my saddle-bag; bring it over here for us, if you would be so kind. They have never been fired—of course."

When Miller returned with the case, Fredericks turned to Nathan, "Choose your second, Jeffries!"

Nathan nodded to Jack Logan, who took the case from the sergeant and, a few minutes later, offered it to his friend and captain, "Your choice of weapons, sir." Nathan took one from the ebony-inlaid pearl and ivory case. The wood felt smooth, cool, the barrel slick as ice. Would he live to hand it back to Logan after shots were fired? And would he be able, injured or uninjured, somehow to fight Fredericks, who had beaten his woman?

After returning the case to Miller, Jack Logan strode back and grabbed Nathan's arm. "Nathan, you're crazy," he said quietly, "to be playing their games. There must be a better way. Highgate is an experienced duelist. He will kill you."

"He may," Nathan said. "But at least Fredericks won't get away as quickly." If only he could be confident of that. In a blur he saw Logan talking to Fredericks. Two of the ten prisoners and two of Fredericks' men were ordered to corral the bullocks a few hundred yards closer to the lake, in case they started to stampede from the gunfire. The first shots fired might be the last. Even wounded, Nathan knew there would be no quarter. Sooner or later he would fall, and smugglers would continue their operation. Even if Highgate fell, Nathan would still die. Either way, Fredericks would win. But Nathan felt it was a worthy cause, to avoid even more bloodshed, even though he was sick and trembling. Logan as second for Nathan, and Fredericks himself as second for Highgate, had taken the pistols from the duellists and now carefully loaded, primed and checked each weapon. When Logan handed him the weapon again, he whispered, "Loaded and primed, Nathan."

This was it! Nathan could feel dozens of pairs of eyes fixed on him. I will not flinch, he said to himself. Was he shaking? Highgate and Fredericks stood silently, seeming at ease. Nathan heard the hoot of an owl, the screech of a bat, the cacophony of insects.

"Please position yourselves back to back, gentlemen," Sergeant

Miller announced.

"You will each advance ten paces, at the count of your seconds, turn, and fire at will. Ready, gentlemen?"

"Ready," they both said.

"One! Two! Three! Four! Five! Six! Seven! Eight! Nine! Ten!"

At twenty paces—lethal range, even for a pistol—the opponents were told to turn and fire.

Nathan felt his heart would burst, but he slowly turned. Highgate was equally measured; both pistols raised to the level almost simultaneously. Nathan, looking over the hammer and barrel of his pistol, saw the black hole of Highgate's pointed at his face, then lower, down to his ribs. Both weapons exploded loudly in acrid fire and smoke. Nathan stared through the gunsmoke of the discharge and saw his adversary standing, pistol at his side, with a wide eyed look of astonishment replacing his habitual gaze of fastidious disdain and cool self-confidence. Nathan heard no sound as the smell and powdery cloud dissipated.

Nineteen

Cattaraugus Creek

THE TWO MEN GAZED at each other for what seemed like eternity. Nothing had hit Nathan. He neither felt nor heard the whirring, windy passage of a lead ball next to his skin. Highgate was unharmed. But it seemed, incredibly, that the notorious Highgate had also missed. Both shots missed.

Highgate looked at Fredericks, who could not mask his surprise. Once again, Nathan Jeffries had eluded death. But Fredericks knew that he needed to focus on the more important business at hand. "A moment, please, gentlemen," he said, trying to appear calm.

"Mister Fredericks," said Highgate, "we have wasted enough time. Let's kill—"

"I have a better idea," said Nathan, hiding his desperation. "Yes, you can kill me—all of us, really—and you might get away with it. Michael Fredericks has won by hiding behind this woman with no honor but with the satisfaction of defeating a small group—"

"No!" Fredericks cried abruptly. "I do not need Catherine or any one else to crush you, Jeffries."

"No? Then why are you wasting time with this? Kill me now, you stinking coward!"

"Give me your pistol," said Highgate, turning to the nearest Canadian militiaman.

"Belay that!" shouted Fredericks.

Shaking his head, Nathan stepped forward, risking a shot in his already aching body.

"Hear me out, Michael," he said mockingly. "It is true that I am not significant—but eliminating the Jeffries in name and body has been significant to you. Why interrupt your triumph with questions of dishonor? We both know you will kill me, so why not make it more of a contest, for the sake of the final destruction of my father and I, the much-despised Jeffries?"

"Sir, I must insist that—" Highgate huffed, "I must protest this delay over some . . . gesture."

"Shut your mouth!" Fredericks growled.

"Sir, I agree with Mister Highgate, this is most irregular," said the sergeant diffidently. "Mister Highgate has had his chance, but now, thanks to you, we have them all! We have won this part of our mission! Why give the boy satisfaction? Surely we must not place the rest of this mission on the same footing as this . . . ruffian."

"Honor among fools, Lieutenant?" whispered Logan behind Nathan. "*Another* duel? And with Fredericks, the professional duelist? This is not the way!"

"This is the only way!" Nathan answered. "Fredericks will kill me; but it will delay him. You are a fine seaman and a good friend, Mister Logan. But do not interfere."

"Nathan, this is foolish, even for you. Please do not throw your life away."

"Enough!" Nathan hissed. "I am in command and you will obey my orders! Thank you, but it must be this way, my friend. Will you consent to act as my second—a second time?"

"Yes, of course," said Logan sadly.

"We kill them all now, I say—all the prisoners! This is absurd!" shouted Highgate, backed up by murmurs and grunts from the four remaining Canadians, who had handed him a loaded and cocked pistol and a half-sword.

Fredericks' eyes and stare in the lamplight were terrible to behold. There was silence.

"We don't know how many other hostiles maybe in the area," said Highgate, frightened, nervous, pleading now. "Sir, let the events—"

"Quiet! Or by God—!"

"I claim the right to specify weapons," Nathan said loudly, unintentionally saving Highgate from his own big mouth.

"Well?"

"We will fight with cudgels!"

"What?"

"Cudgels, staffs, staves, heavy sticks—you know. Oak or ironwood, cane-wood, hickory, usually." Nathan almost laughed in spite of himself.

Highgate did laugh. Nathan nodded to Logan, whose fleeting smile encouraged his friend in the hair-brained scheme.

"It will take but a few minutes to select the appropriate weapons," Logan said to Fredericks, who nodded slightly and smiled like a snake. "They can be quickly tested. I will help Mister Highgate, if you wish."

"This is ridiculous," said Highgate. "Why would you waste time with this boy? Fighting this . . . farce—and not even with swords, but primitive sticks and clubs? A boys' game?"

Fredericks had given brief instructions to Sergeant Miller, who now announced the rules.

"Any strokes and blows are legal. Once a man is down, or disarmed, fighting will cease until such time as he can fight again. The permanently fallen or disabled party forfeits the match. Jack Logan and Mister Highgate as seconds."

Highgate said, "This is insane!"

"Enough!" Fredericks said.

"Mister Fredericks, sir," Highgate still protested, "you must not—"

"Shut your mouth or I will shut it for you! It is agreed! Make the weapons."

Sergeant Miller and Jack Logan cut and trimmed stout green ironwood saplings, just the right resilience and length, five feet long and two inches in diameter. While most men watched the proceedings in ill-disguised disgust and amazement, an uneasy, suspicious silence reigned. The two opponents stood not ten feet apart. Nathan knew he would soon die, but maybe death was better than this gnawing pain of Catherine's betrayal. His sacrifice in this brutal slugging contest seemed the only chance of delaying and somehow defeating Fredericks' efforts to supply the starving British troops. And now he would discover that "undiscovered country" Peter had yammered so on and on about—that had been less than two years ago. The best mind he had ever encountered, until—

Even after all of his escapades, he shuddered at the thought of the painful, bloody and crippling fight minutes away—regardless of the immediate victor. Nathan outweighed his opponent and was two inches taller. He could take a punch and knew how to deliver one. He could only gamble that his short-term survival chances were higher if he did not fight Fredericks with pistol or blade, since Fredericks was known to be deadly with both weapons.

Nathan wondered what had happened to Fredericks' cattlemen, the two prisoners and Captain Reynolds' party. Probably ambushed by Indians. Elliott's men were too far away, and I have failed, thought Nathan. I will die a failure. My mother is dead, and my father. No one left who would object to this rank, self-pitying surrender. Defeat, final dismissal, humiliation. He feared his hands and voice shook. It was bizarre, macabre. Nathan had faced death on a number of occasions, commanded armed ships, fought brave, devious, dangerous men, and yet now, this night, he would surely face agony and death.

"Sir?" It was Logan and Miller again behind him, and his foe beyond. "Are you ready, Lieutenant—Captain?"

It was time. Nathan could afford to spare a glance at the few men near the campfires. They acted as if nothing much was happening.

"Mister Jack Logan," said Nathan, "your actions have been—"

"Ah! Stow it, Nathan! Kiss my cascabel, you sea fart," said Logan.

Oh my God, Nathan thought, he is crying. Neither dared speak. Was he actually—

But there was no choice, no choice. His friend handed him the staff, cool, heavy, nearly as smooth as a pistol grip. He raised it with one hand, hefting it, swinging it, getting the feel. Hatless, shirtsleeves rolled up, Fredericks, without Nathan's height or weight but lithe and quick, held his staff casually, horizontally with both hands in front of him, smiling.

The two advanced in the clearing, surrounded by a small circle of men. Would this be a legitimate combat showdown of strength, skill, agility and courage? Nathan soon found out. With a frightening blur, Fredericks' cudgel flashed out and cracked against his, again and again. Nathan could barely offer a defense, let alone attack. Constantly seeking an opening, Fredericks succeeded after just a few minutes; the searing pain drove into Nathan's side as the staff caught him below the ribs, then smashed immediately against his staff, barely missing his head. Nathan desperately whipped his staff towards Fredericks' head but it was easily parried. The smaller, lighter man laughed. He is much too fast, Nathan thought in panic, sickened with the conviction of an agonizing death. Too late he would avoid the man's powerful and deft wrists and arms, rapid, almost like a dance, as he circled Nathan and patiently probed and punched for weakness.

Wood banged against wood, smashing and echoing in the woods. He is wearing me down, Nathan thought, and knew that it was only a matter of time before a careless move, or mere exhaustion, gave his opponent the fatal opening he needed. Oh no! Fredericks' staff slashed against his forehead, and Nathan tasted blood. Another hit, almost paralyzing, struck his neck, nearly ripping his ear off in the process. One eye was blinded by blood as he limped away, a constant buzzing and grayness interfering with the terror that could sustain him. Fredericks jumped in again, Nathan barely managing to fend off the blows. A solid swipe in his belly all but brought Nathan down for good. Eventually the older man's relentless cudgel would slam into his side and break a rib, or thrust toward his belly again with enough force to rupture an organ. The left side of his face was covered in blood, and he thought he heard a groan from his tied-up men as another slash from Fredericks cracked against his temple. Stumbling back through the ringing in his head, though, Nathan realized that his torso and head had been the only targets; neither man had touched anyhting below the legs. It gave Nathan a desperate idea, his last chance. He knew that once he lost his footing and defensive capability, Fredericks would be instantly on top of him, working to finish him off before anyone could interfere.

"Most effective weapon, eh?" Nathan heard his enemy say with increasing confidence. "When one knows how to use it." Fredericks casually swung the stick, barely missing Nathan as he ducked.

Now! Nathan darted in low with the last of his clumsy strength and thrust the stick viciously at Fredericks' groin. It seemed to work. Fredericks screamed and leaned forward, dropping his weapon. Nathan stood up and brought down his cudgel with all the speed he could muster—too much. His aim was off and the glancing blow merely stunned the man. Nathan quickly grabbed Fredericks' staff, and stood over him, panting, swaying, but prepared to hammer anyone—or get shot. No one moved.

Highgate and Sergeant Miller and the four remaining young militiamen held their fire.

"Kill him!" Fredericks shrieked. "Shoot the bastard!"

Nathan started to groan; he stood over his enemy, sprawled in the late summer reeds, with a club, but feeling nothing, except pain from his wounds and weariness. Fredericks rolled a furious eye at his men, fully conscious now, and hateful to infinity.

"You cowards—I order you to fire! I dare you to kill me, Jeffries; you haven't the courage. I turned your incompetent father into a cripple, and I will yet destroy you, you ignorant—Do you hear me, Jeffries!"

"Let me kill him, then," said Highgate, jiggling with fear. Nathan heard the hammer cock as Highgate pointed his pistol at him. Somehow Nathan dashed towards him as he cocked, and before Highgate could take aim, hit him hard in the face. Highgate's piece exploded in his ears; the ball went wild and he stayed down.

"Nathan, by God!" It was Logan, approaching him. He heard other voices now, shouting, cheering, complaining; out of the corner of his eye he sensed gesticulations but no violent protest.

Then he heard a scream, drowning out the ringing insects. So much of what happened next seemed a blur. A black creature seemed to hop *over* the campfires—and another piercing cry came, not a woman's scream, more like a large raptor, a red-tailed hawk or eagle perhaps, some carnivore. A dark form appeared—the size of a small bear, standing on two legs.

Highgate screamed as a Bowie knife found its mark; a silver streak, and the handle protruded from Highgate's arm. His second pistol went off with a deafening crack, and Nathan felt a burning slice in the flesh of his own right arm. He whirled and went down on his knees, dropping the cudgel—first he felt numb, then the pain came, briefly blinding him. Gasping, Nathan saw two of his own men—the prisoners who had been taken away to help with the livestock—ambush two of the Canadians. Another man's throat was sliced by the apparition. Highgate crawled away from the circle of light struggling to pull out a third pistol.

Somehow Nathan arose and dashed towards him again as he cocked, and before Highgate could take aim, Nathan hit him hard in the face. Highgate's pistol exploded in his ears; the ball went wild, and the two men fell to the ground as the pistol skidded across the grass. Nathan slammed his fist into Highgate's fleshy face again, and struck bone. Stunned and bloody, Highgate stopped struggling. But before Nathan could climb over his body and search for a pistol or blade in the gloom, a blinding pain flooded his head. Fredericks had recovered enough to coldcock him with the butt of his pistol. Nathan collapsed on top of Sergeant Miller, who pushed him off and rose to his feet.

"You incompetent!" Fredericks shouted. "Where's your pistol?"

"Here it is," said Catherine, stepping into the light. It was pointed at Fredericks.

"Well, well! Another soul arises from the dead! And do you propose to shoot me, Catherine? What about my other gun?"

"Don't try it, Michael."

"How delightful! I'm pleased that you remembered my advice about a good offense."

In a blur his pocket gun appeared. She fired, but only harmless flash and smoke appeared—a misfire. Fredericks laughed, keeping his gun trained on her. He heard an enraged groan and turned to see Nathan behind him. Frdericks was knocked flat with a mighty blow, face up, sprawled on the grass, half in a diagonal slash of shadow.

Barely conscious through loss of blood and sleep, Nathan saw Catherine and Logan and other men untying the Americans and tying up the few surviving Canadian smugglers. The dark, deadly form had disappeared for good.

"And secure our weapons in the wagon," Logan bellowed at one of the men, then walked over to Nathan.

"Congratulations, Lieutenant!"

Logan's bright smile through his dark face seemed enormous, out of place. Nathan found by focusing on the pain he could maintain wakefulness.

"We can't stay here, Mister Logan—ah!"

"That's my neckerchief that Catherine wrapped round your arm; she dressed that wound like nobody's business."

The pain pounded and he had to fight to remain conscious, but Nathan could still concentrate.

"I have taken command of both groups," said Logan, "with Catherine's help," he said. "Until you are fit."

"I am fit now, you old barnacle bait." His voice sounded thin and shrill in his own ears.

"It's ugly, but only a flesh wound," Logan pronounced, looking at Nathan's right arm. Then his expression hardened.

"Nathan, Peter—or, Peter's body—has disappeared.

"What?"

"Gone—it is just gone."

Nathan shook his head, waved off Logan's help and struggled to his feet again, picking up Fredericks' pistol, its barrel still warm. He itched to wield the gun butt against the man. He could use it to pound Fredericks' face and head to bloody mush, just to hear his desperate breath bubbling through his own blood. No one would say anything. He fought the temptation.

"Don't kill him," said Catherine, now beside him.

Nathan left her and headed for the place where he had last seen Fredericks's body sprawled on the ground.

"No, I won't kill you, Fredericks," Nathan said, as he approached the shadows. "I will see you—"

He stopped. Fredericks was gone.

TWENTY

Presque Isle, Lake Erie - *August 22, 1813*

NEAR SUNSET, STRUGGLING against his illness and despair,
Perry sat at his desk re-reading those last, fatal words from his letter to
Secretary Jones.

"Under these circumstances, I beg most respectfully and most
earnestly that I may be immediately removed from this station. I am
willing to forego the reward that I have considered for two months
past almost within my grasp. If, sir, I have rendered my country any
service in the equipment of this squadron, I beg it may be considered
an inducement to grant my request. I shall proceed with the squadron
and whatever is in my power shall be done to promote the interest and
honor of the service."

Perry admired Secretary Jones—much more than the president
or the rest of his cabinet or his immediate superior Commodore Isaac
Chauncey in Sackett's Harbor.

"These Powers have no claims upon our impartiality," he read absently from the secretary's most recent letter to him. Our navy was vital
"as a means of annoying Great Britain ... by excluding our flag over ...
could more effectively annoy her commerce ..." Then, yes! Only small
war vessels, Jones and Perry both knew, could decisively deny England
food and supplies. Merchant commerce, on land or sea, could never be
adequately protected even by the mighty British navy.

But what is the use—after that Herculean labor of building and launching the 20-gun brigs *Lawrence* and *Niagara*, lifting and removing the guns, reloading guns and carriages, and by some miracle not getting attacked by Barclay's squadron during the most vulnerable moment of using the "camels" to float them over the sand bar—when there are not enough men to crew the vessels and the enemy can play cat-and-mouse until his food and supplies run out?

He had sailed in harm's way when the wind cooperated, searching for Barclay, attempting to engage the enemy. In their last sortie, Perry's small fleet had sailed west once more, running up to the Sandusky River, almost the westernmost extremity of Lake Erie, without finding any of the enemy out from their protected lair under the guns of Fort Malden. He had not heard again from the secretary or Chauncey, and debated penning a final resignation. Commodore Chauncey had been so regardless of my feelings and needs and accomplishments, Perry thought, that I have no choice in this matter. Perry's excessive pride, if nothing else, which had caused him to write the earlier letter in the first place, had also forbidden his abandoning his little flotilla until actually ordered to do so. He had told himself that he would not shirk his duty—could not. Barclay was out there, somewhere.

A great victory would have been within his grasp; he could almost smell it. A man less in command of his emotions would have burst into tears of frustration. He could have achieved so much! His wracked body yearned for sleep, as much as it yearned for action; it was nightmarish with the ever-present ravages of yellow fever, the "yellow jack." He looked over at his cot. The *Trippe* and *Tigress* had returned that morning to report a complete failure. They had chased one galley north, but had not sighted the enemy's barges or transports, nor had they found Jeffries' party at Cattaraugus Creek. For all he knew, the enemy had succeeded in obtaining their vitally needed food and supplies, and the men he had sent to Cattaraugus were lost. It appeared hopeless.

To Oliver Hazard Perry, at heart a fighter, it was extraordinarily painful to recognize that it was he who was now about ready to quit, to give up the ship, before the fight was even fairly joined.

Just then a pounding on the door startled him.

"Come," he said with slight irritation.

Out of breath from running, Midshipman Montgomery saluted at entrance. "Sir, *Ohio's* in the offing! The boats are returning—that is, they're being towed! It must be Mister—Lieutenant Jeffries, sir! They're loaded with supplies, looks like, and low in the water." Hannibal Collins mysteriously appeared and helped him as Perry struggled into his coat.

"Captain, you ain't well yet. You ain't ready for sea 'gain," said Hannibal.

"Oh, leave me be," said Perry peevishly. He had been trying to recuperate from the strain; sometimes chills and fever laid him up for days, as was the case with many of his men. But when he reached the shore, three boats were just pulling in sure enough, and his spirits soared when he saw Nathan, his right arm in a sling. Nathan wincing, looked pale, with dark blue-black patches on a face swollen, cut and bruised, but then he smiled at his commander. Jack Logan and a militiaman helped him out of the boat and he gingerly saluted Commodore Perry with his left hand.

"Mission accomplished, sir," said Nathan. "The British ships never appeared, but we caught the smugglers, twenty-two in all, and some 400 bullocks all right, led by Thompson and Fredericks himself. There are ninety-seven head of cattle aboard the *Ohio* and the barges; that took most of the day. She almost missed us, but saw our signal after dawn yesterday." Crew and onlookers cheered.

In that misty dawn, as Nathan tried to decide what to do with his prisoners and bullocks, the *Ohio* had been recognized, then someone had shouted that more distant sails, possibly the enemy, were in sight just over the horizon. But in the clear light of day, nothing was seen, and the two groups departed.

"Mister Logan, help the lieutenant to my cabin," said Perry. "Quiet there, you men, and light those lanterns. Oh, Captain Elliot, here you are; take charge here, will you?"

Elliot just stared silently at Nathan.

"Captain!" said Perry again. "Take charge here!"

"Aye, sir."

A few minutes later, the filthy and exhausted men sat across from Perry's desk, each with a cup of Madeira in his hand.

"The rest of the animals I sent with two of the militiamen—with Mister Cosby in command, since he requested it—escorting most of the prisoners and bullocks and eight supply wagons. Some settlers came up from the lake that Jack—Mister Logan—could vouch for, came up from the lake and agreed to help Cosby purchase the supplies and animals from the government in Jamestown or Meadville. If any un-friendly sails appear, they might easily make for another town, but they assured us that the turnpike is clear."

Nathan hesitated. "A woman, Miss Catherine Charles of Philadel-phia, she was . . . wounded, had been held hostage by Fredericks. I sent her with the others to Pittsburgh."

"No! The same beautiful woman I met at the Charles Ball? En-gaged to—"

"Yes, sir," said Nathan, whose face and tone discouraged further elaboration.

"Excellent, Mister Jeffries," said Perry, smiling for the first time in a long time. "What was the butcher's bill?"

"There were four deaths, sir, as well as Thompson. One of our men was killed and one missing and Corporal Ferrell has come down with lake fever. The enemy we engaged with various weapons, but exchanged no shots, after Fredericks' defeat." Even seated, Nathan weaved with exhaustion. Perry could see that he was almost sleeping as he described the bloody action that began after they left that little quay.

"Warm work on a summer's night, Mister Jeffries."

"Yes, sir. And I must commend the gallant behavior of my men, particularly Mister Logan here and Mister—Peter Hughes."

"Where is Hughes, by the way?"

"He is . . . missing, sir."

"Was he shot, cut down?"

"Yes. I . . . saw him lying there, in his own blood, and then—he was gone."

"You mean, he died."

"No, sir, I don't . . . know. His body was—gone. Missing. And there is something else—"

"You need rest, Lieutenant, and no wonder—"

"You must listen to me, please, Captain," Nathan coughed. "Not only Peter's body went missing. So did Fredericks'. And we only survived thanks to a . . . person, dressed all in black. A blur, sir. He took out their men, most of them. Some kind of—ask Mister Logan here."

Logan nodded. "It's all true, sir, everything Na—Lieutenant Jeffries—says. Can't explain it. No way we could've got the best of 'em, else. Our whole party was goners, sir."

Perry shook his head. "Well, I do not see how both of you could be seeing things. An apparition, a black savior. I felt God was on our side, but . . . that wound needs more care now, Lieutenant, and both of you are about to drop from fatigue. I order both of you to sleep! Write your report later." He stood, and waited as the other two struggled slowly to their feet.

"This is the very best of news—well done, Lieutenant, I am truly gratified," said Perry, taking Nathan's left hand in his right and grasping it strongly. "You have done the service proud." Perry wanted to say more, but his emotions were too strong.

"Thank you, sir," said Nathan, simply.

Perry knew that his bald report concealed much; and probably the written report would reveal little more. But such was the way of the navy, and his sincerity of praise for his subordinate shone through. It was a moment Nathan would never forget.

AFTER THE PRISONERS THEY had brought back on the *Ohio* were locked in the brig, Nathan and Logan celebrated at the rude officer's tavern. The ringing of the night insects competed with the dizziness in Nathan's head. Then came the painful ordeal of the surgeon's mate dressing—or rather butchering—the flesh wound in his right arm.

The next thing he knew, the bright morning sun forced him to cover his face and roll to the canvas side of the tent he lay in. After a few groans, Nathan managed to clamber into his only clean uniform and prepare to meet the morning coffee.

He left the tent and was greeted by the best sight of all, the loyal Mister Logan. "How much does the Commodore know about Fredericks, Auster, Thompson, all those bastards?" asked Logan. "Wait a minute—where are you going?"

"Where else? Coffee wasn't served in my tent, Jack."

"Yes, sir, only first we need to see the—"

"I'm perfectly shipshape, and mind your own business, Mister Logan."

But he knew it was hopeless. After a prolonged visit with the sawbones, some coffee and then the Erie version of grog, Nathan demanded that his friend explain the incredible disappearance of Peter, Fredericks and the apparition.

Logan shrugged, "Well, before you drink the rest of that jug, we had better prepare a report for the old man—he will want to see it in the morning."

"Nonsense, Jack!" Nathan grinned, three sheets to the wind. "I am an invalid, and shall return to my mansion to sleep 'til noon, in any case, and perhaps speak then to our commander."

But later in the morning, the two were reasonably sober again and touched their hats to Perry as they entered the rude cabin Perry shared as headquarters. Nathan and Logan had finished writing the fantastic, unbelievable account of the "incidents" at Cattaraugus Creek.

"Please, seat yourselves, gentlemen, and relax." Perry sat at the same desk, obviously exhausted himself.

"My report, sir," said Nathan, handing it to his superior, "written by my mate, here, Mister Logan, and myself."

"Oh, that is fine," said Perry. "Thank you. Actually, I first want to discuss your needs for the weeks ahead."

"My needs, sir?"

"Yes. Captain Elliot and I intend to send to Harrison with dispatches, while you recuperate here."

"But I must sail with you, sir, of course!"

"Lieutenant, you have suffered much, and you achieved much, but

I am sorry. We shall sail on the 31st, and unfortunately, you cannot join us with that arm, much as we need you with us. My dear Nathan, you have done enough. You have saved the course, and we have enough sick and wounded, God knows, without losing you too. Stay here, rest and recover. No doubt future opportunities will arise—"

"Sir, I do not intend to miss the most important action of the war. I really must insist!"

"Mister Jeffries, do not take that tone with me!"

"I am sorry, Commodore, but you must not leave me here. Have I not earned the right to serve with you in battle?"

"But your arm is wounded. And the eye is almost shut."

"Commodore, he is not handicapped, and anyway I can make up the difference," said Logan.

Nathan looked at him, his eyes wet. "Thank you, my friend, but—"

"Mister Logan? You will be responsible for Lieutenant Jeffries. You wish—"

"Between the lieutenant here and myself, you know there's more than one hand—beg pardon, sir."

"Still, I do not think—"

Nathan took the plunge. "Commodore, if you refuse to accept me on the *Lawrence*, I shall swim, or steal a boat. I will not remain behind, sir, for the last fight. I cannot! Please."

Logan and Nathan sat quietly and watched the gray-cheeked commander bow his head wearily. There was a moment of silence.

Then he looked up at them and smiled. "You win, gentlemen," he said, and stood up. His two subordinates followed as he walked to the door, and turned back in mock severity.

"I shall make up your action orders accordingly, Mister Jeffries. Mister Logan," he said, "the greenest possible recruit, watch out. And Mister Jeffries, I will see you at eight bells to discuss your report."

LATER THAT EVENING, NATHAN received an unexpected visitor, Captain Elliott, looking as spruce and fat-cheeked as ever.

"I wanted to congratulate you on your success at Cattaraugus,

Lieutenant," he said.

"Thank you," said Nathan, grudgingly.

"I trust you confirmed in your report that it was my information which resulted in that success, from my earlier layover there?"

Nathan stared at him, open-mouthed. The man's impudence was beyond belief.

"Sir, that report was for our commander, and it is not my intention to discuss it with you."

Elliott stiffened, but then relaxed again. "Of course, it was simply curiosity. I mostly wanted to offer you the position of first lieutenant on my *Niagara*. Now that we have lost Peter Hughes, I discussed the needs aboard my ship for you and Mister Logan with the Commodore. I understand you had requested to sail with him aboard *Lawrence*, but I convinced him it was best otherwise."

"You discussed with him—" Nathan's disgusted astonishment died of surfeit. This rudeness knew no bounds.

"Captain Elliott, I must say this," said Nathan, already short of breath. "I would never sail with you, even if it were the last vessel floating on the Lake. You will never earn my loyalty, and you're so wanting in the most base senses of a proper officer that I am surprised our commander has not stripped you of all rank. I have heard the way you and Chauncey have treated Perry, conspired against him in the most petty and vicious manner. There is even a rumor that he has sent a letter of resignation to Washington. In short, sir, nothing I've heard or seen about you would lead me to any conclusion but that you are a disgrace to gentlemen—"

"How dare you, Lieutenant! I am your—"

"Please *forgive* me, sir! But that is the way of it, bitter as the truth may seem; your talents in fighting, remain to be seen as far as I am concerned."

"This conversation is terminated, Lieutenant, and as I decide an appropriate course of action—"

"Yes, certainly, Captain Elliot! I am at your disposal!"

Elliott stormed out of the cabin and away into the late evening, brushing past Logan, who was just returning.

"My God, Nathan, I heard you two shouting! What was that all about?"

"I don't trust him, Jack, and I don't know when to shut my mouth."

At the final brief meeting of officers before sailing, Nathan and Elliott exchanged barely a glance, but before they were offered a final toast and dismissed, Nathan reluctantly spoke up.

"Sir, if I may make one suggestion?"

"What is it, Lieutenant?"

"If we do engage the enemy—"

"Thanks to your affair at Cattaraugus, Mister Jeffries, I believe they will now be forced to come out."

"Yes, sir, but . . . if you don't mind my respectfully pointing out; with their long guns, I urge most strongly that we press for immediate, close action at short range, and forgo your line of battle."

He heard some dissatisfied grunts and impatient, condescending sighs. Captain Elliott merely darted a dirty look at him.

"Mister Jeffries, when you are maneuvering a fleet, or even a small squadron like this—"

"Your pardon, sir, but the less maneuvering the better. We must all close with the enemy, sir. Our smashers must find their range in less than 100 yards as soon as possible. I . . . saw their effect on the *Guerriere*. If you don't mind—"

"Yes, thank you, Lieutenant. I will take it under advisement." Perry raised his glass of sherry. "Gentlemen, to the Goddess Victory, President Madison and the United States of America!"

TWENTY-ONE

Bass Islands, western Lake Erie - *August 29, 1813*

SOUTH BASS ISLAND WAS hot and humid and still, teeming with horseflies, wasps and remorseless clinging thistles in the sand dunes. Nathan was sick and tired of his daily duty as junior lieutenant to lead his gunners party ashore for water. He felt lightheaded from lack of sleep and boredom heightened by low morale of all the officers, who were on tenterhooks around Commodore Perry. Their leader had not resigned after all, but suffered his lieutenants—and Elliot—to hear *ad nauseum* the bitter, arbitrary treatment he suffered from the likes of Commodore Chauncey; building an enormous fleet of ships of the line with crew to burn. Elliott and Perry—though seldom together—had heard or made threats against various duelists who favored a Wogden & Barton, Durs Egg, Manton, even or a North pistol.

His only salvation was his staunch friend Jack Logan, who showed his unswerving, unquestioned loyalty—if limited intimacy—to Nathan and his priorities. The insect buzzing seemed unusually loud.

Logan came up now, sticking his thumb on his nose in mocking salute, to report on the water casks.

"We'll top off in half a glass," said Mister Logan, frowning at Nathan's silence.

"What did you say?"

"Nathan—look behind you."

There, in a ragged elkhide coat and feathered cap, was Peter

Hughes himself. Nathan stared at this apparition, then at Logan, who also stared at Peter.

"Jack, how are you, Mister Logan, sir?"

That mocking smile reminded Nathan of the other apparition.

Logan, his rifle on his shoulder, shrugged in amazement and looked to Nathan for guidance. And then all three were jumping and pounding each other's back like kids playing Skating the Fort. Nathan had never felt happier in his life.

"Where in hell have you been, Mister Hughes?" demanded Logan.

Nathan could only shake his head and laugh for joy, gazing at the red oak trees, now brown and wilting in the pale summer sky. *Quercus rubra*, as naturalist professor Peter would have pointed out.

"Peter has been with me—and I am not quite the devil," said another, less familiar voice from behind them.

They whirled around. Taima wore a man's dark cotton work shirt, filthy duck trousers and buffalo sandals. She looked heavenly. Before anyone else could speak, she walked up to Nathan and twisted her face into a hideous snarl. Nathan, startled, stepped back, staring at the sudden transformation.

"You—"

"Do you see me now, all painted black, a glimpse of—"

"Taima, or her—*creature*," Peter explained, "saved us all at Cattaraugus Creek, then rescued me to take me west and nurse me back to health."

"But—her *creature*—how could this little girl—" Logan started to ask.

After a sudden blur, Logan now saw his rifle appear in Taima's hands, pointed at him.

"It is a technique—dangerous, exhausting," Peter explained, "taught to few braves and even fewer squaws."

"Can anyone learn how to . . . release this—power/creature? Can you do it?"

"I had some training when I was very young, but Taima is much more advanced."

"I'll meet you back at shore, Lieutenant," said Logan gruffly, snatching his rifle back from the petite and deadly girl. "At least Peter and the woman are on our side." But they both smiled before he left.

"Taima, my God," said Nathan, as the three remaining people walked down Observation Hill towards the ships and boats in the Bay. "How can we ever return the favor?"

"How is Catherine?" asked Taima. "She was not shot?"

"Catherine was not shot, she was . . . beaten, Taima. And Fredericks—or his body—disappeared."

"Yes, I know."

"You *know?*"

"He is a powerful man, Nathan. You and Catherine were fortunate to survive."

"Yes, 'fortunate,'" Nathan agreed bitterly.

"Must I explain this to you, Nathan? Catherine fought Fredericks—and the Austers—in every way she knew, mostly for *you*. She loves you."

"She loves—" Nathan laughed in misery, looking at Taima's lovely face, only days earlier a devilish, black fright.

"Don't be a fool, Nathan. She would never betray you. She *saved* you, at risk to her own life. She is a hero, worth any ten of you, Nathan. She did not engage with Fredericks in any way."

"That's not what I've been told," said Nathan.

"Catherine does certainly love you," Peter chimed in.

"Love, we hear again," cried Nathan. "I have lost everything, Peter; I thought I had lost you! I have lost my mother, my father, my friends, my—"

The damn finally burst, and Nathan sobbed. He bent over, nearly collapsed in the grass, but Taima could hold him, and hold him up, even better than Peter could.

August 31

TAIMA REMAINED ON THE island as Perry's fleet sailed west again. They found the enemy still safe in Amherstburg, and decided to use the Bass Islands as their base. Put-in-Bay on the north side of South Bass Island suited admirably. With Elliott in command of one line of five ships and Perry in command of the other, battle drills were conducted every day. Fortunately for Peter, the weather was usually calm, though several squalls did hit. His friends' help—Logan's and Peter's—made all the difference to Nathan as he struggled to train the men at the smashers, the guns that would decide the battle everyone prayed for. Knowing Peter's discomfort on the water, Nathan was all the more indebted to his friend. But Peter waved away his friend's thanks.

"It is the least I could do, after letting you get shot," he would say, bravely hiding his nervousness when the *Lawrence* tacked.

There was a major conference with General Harrison, who loaned Perry 150 Kentucky sharpshooters. Later he received one hundred men from General McArthur. Gradually, his compliment reached almost 500—though over a hundred of these were usually incapacitated with bilious fever or other ailments. Incidents of lake fever were reduced when Peter Hughes and Surgeon's Assistant Usher "Pill" Parsons convinced Perry to boil all water before use.

And time and again they sailed off heavily fortified Fort Malden, where the tables were turned and Barclay's fleet was now effectively blockaded, playing the rabbit to Perry's fox—or the fox to Perry's hound. From reports they knew that Tecumseh had grown very impatient with the timidity of Barclay and General Procter, who had promised that British "Big Canoes" would control the Lake. Letters from Chauncey and Jones were conciliatory, refusing to accept Perry's resignation, but still filled with absurd and irritating comments.

The days dragged on; the enemy hungry, the wind sometimes blustery, sometimes nonexistent or useless. The waiting began to tell on everyone's nerves. They knew Barclay had to come out eventually, but when? Harrison had even suggested a combined land and sea invasion of Fort Malden, forcing the issue that way. Fortunately, Perry convinced him otherwise. No, Perry knew he must avoid giving the enemy any advantages, even drilling the men in case of a night attack, while they were at anchor. Once the lake was clear of enemy vessels, the Northwest belonged to Harrison.

Each vessel was assigned to one of the enemy's, contingent upon battle conditions. At close range, Perry's weight of metal was considerably greater than Barclay's. At long range, it was the other way around.

"You must close with them, one hundred yards or less, or their long guns will cut you to pieces," he said over and over again; ironically, this echoed the famous dictum of Admiral Nelson, under whom Barclay had served at Trafalgar.

It was still early September when the *Ohio* arrived, rejoining the fleet at the Bass Islands with news, messages, letters and official dispatches. The navy secretary's 18 August letter to Perry expressed surprise concerning Perry's complaints, saying that they were the "less to have been expected, as he selected you for the command . . . and has never ceased to speak of you in terms of the highest approbation and confidence . . . The indulgence of such feelings must terminate in the most serious injury to the service, and probably ruin to yourself. Avoid recrimination . . . and the result, I have no doubt, will enhance the fame . . . A Change of Commander, under existing circumstances, is equally inadmissible, as it respects the interest of the service and your own reputation. It is right that you should reap the harvest which you have sown . . . It is the duty of an Officer . . . to sacrifice all personal motives and feelings when in collision with the public good . . . I calculate, with confidence . . . your . . . carrying into effect, the great objects of your enterprize."

They also learned that, on Chesapeake Bay, the development of an armed gunboat and barge flotilla by Captain Joshua Barney and the successful defense of the frigate *Constellation* against British attack at the south end of the Bay had been offset by British atrocities at the north end. Admiral Cockburn had attacked other towns after burning Havre de Grace, Fredericktown and Georgetown. On Lake Ontario, minor and inconclusive actions between the fleets of Yeo and Chauncey had resulted in galling American setbacks—two armed schooners captured by the British and two others, the *Hamilton* and *Scourge*, capsized in a storm with heartbreaking losses.

The Massachusetts, New York and Pennsylvania papers carried stories about the exploits of privateer Captain Boyle and others, now leaving *Comet* for the *Chasseur* and a run at the waters near Great Britain. Other privateers had captured supply ships bound for the Duke of Wellington's army fighting Napoleon's army in Portugal—the very same destination still for many ostensibly American ships, like Fredericks', with false papers or British licenses, eager to sell to anyone. But the American navy had finally been authorized to treat these ships as enemies. The once-mighty American overseas trade had virtually ceased to exist; $100 million in annual exports had shrunk to $10 million. Even in Boston, only a few fortunate or ruthless merchants, letters of marque and privateers, had thus far escaped ruin. With harbors blockaded, ships rotted and grass grew at silent, empty docks. Yet Nathan felt sure Michael Fredericks' ships still operated somewhere—according the *Providence Journal* the British 20-gun *Boxer*, captured by *Enterprize* off the Maine coast, had an understanding—or other illegal arrangement—with Fredericks.

The *Ohio* been sent back to Erie in early September for more supplies; she was so slow as to be almost useless, anyway, in a fleet action. The *Trippe*, rigged as a sloop rather than a schooner, was almost as bad; she and the *Caledonia* and *Somers* had begun life as merchant vessels. But in fact, all of the vessels, except *Lawrence* and *Niagara*, were gunboats, a mere 50 to 80 tons each. In the next few days, escaped American prisoners told Perry that Barclay was finally ready to sail, and take him on. That would mean nine American sail opposed to six British. The enemy had more men and more guns—roughly 60 to 50—but Perry was now convinced that in close action his strength, the greater weight of metal thrown, would prove decisive. If he could just get close enough.

September 9

AT DUSK, NATHAN WAS bringing *Lawrence* to her mooring near the islet, jokingly called Gibraltar, in Put-in-Bay, with its perch called Observation Hill, or Perry's Lookout.

"Keep alert there!" Nathan shouted up at the man at the main royal mast head truck. "Look lively, you men at the sheets! Clew up! Haul down!"

"A quarter less eight, and gravel," intoned the man with the lead line, sounding from the mainchains.

"Stand easy, Mister Jeffries," said Yarnall, the first lieutenant. "Forrest has the cable secured."

"Aye, sir, but we could use a few petty officers, that's certain."

"Even the old man seems relaxed tonight, somber," mused Yarnall, in an odd non sequitor, drifting off. "I see you will enjoy some handsome new scars, Mister Jeffries."

Forrest ran up to Nathan as Yarnall quit the quarterdeck. "Mooring secured, sir," he said breathlessly.

"Very good, Mister Forrest," said Nathan, and meant it. Twenty-year-old Dulaney Forrest, acting third lieutenant, had attached himself to Nathan for some reason; it wasn't just the fact that Nathan was now his immediate superior. Forrest had been a busy midshipman aboard the *Constitution* when she captured the *Guerriere* and liberated Nathan. Perhaps it was because Nathan was willing to fill in some of the gaps in Forrest's knowledge of seamanship. In the stern-heavy preponderance of officers aboard, Perry had decided to award Forrest his new acting rank more because of his eagerness and helpfulness than because of his technical knowledge or skill. Fresh-faced, plain and pleasant, short of homely, with his brave attempt at sideburns, he was energetic, desperate to please, impossible not to like. But as time wore on and the strain of frustration, delays and waiting began to tell on officers and crew, few had the patience for his mistakes. Nathan took the time, sometimes explaining a brace or buntline to Peter and Forrest at the same time.

That evening, the commodore delivered another one of his lectures on the line of battle, the importance of close support and close range. Doctor Parsons recited his doleful sick list again. Elliott, a bold seaman, still demonstrated his irritating lack of cooperation, constantly complaining and disputing with everyone, including his superior. Nathan avoided him as much as possible. At 10 PM, the commanders returned to their ships, and Nathan, finally off-duty, turned in for some welcome sleep—and perhaps some respite from the concerns and frustrations of the long months.

September 10

BUT JUST AFTER DAWN, a pounding on the door of his tiny cabin shattered his fitful dream.

"Sails sighted to the north, sir!" yelled Forrester. At long last, the waiting was over.

TWENTY-TWO

Battle of Lake Erie - *September 10, 1813*

OUT OF THE DAWN mist, now lit by the rising sun, Nathan could see the masts appearing to the northwest; Barclay's ships reaching from the northwest—no more delays! It had finally worked; they had cut off his supplies, starving the British and forcing the British fleet to attack. Now the Americans would sail west for a showdown, close action at short range against the British. Barclay fooled at Presque Isle, running from unarmed *Lawrence* and four 50-ton gunboats in early August; then Barclay ran again, with more reason, when he had only *Queen Charlotte* against two powerful American brigs. But now, the wait was over: Barclay had his new ship, the full-rigged, 300-ton *Detroit*, larger and perhaps more than a match for at least one of Perry's brigs. They knew that the enemy suffered from want of men and cannons—*Detroit's* odd composite battery had to be fired with pistols, in lieu of the defective quills and flintlocks for the heavy guns.

"Signal for the fleet to up anchor!" roared Perry through his speaking trumpet. "All plain sail!" The crew had already been called. As men sprang aloft, manned the capstan or ran aft to haul the braces, Nathan and Peter hurried to the quarterdeck.

"Six sails northwest of Rattlesnake Island, sir—maybe five miles from West Sister," he heard Yarnall say amidst the shouting of orders.

"We'll never reach a windward position with these damned westerly airs," grumbled Perry. "Jeffries, you make sure your starboard battery is ready." His tone suggested nothing more than another gunnery practice drill—except for the omission of the word "Mister."

"Aye, aye," shouted Nathan, rushing to his station as the topsails were sheeted home and the *Lawrence*, followed in formation by the other eight vessels, got under way. Rounding the entrance to Put-in-Bay, they could see Barclay's tight line of six sail, still hull down on the horizon to the west, showed clearly above the mist of a rapidly clearing day. Rain showers before dawn had made for blue skies this morning, and there was a final brief shower before the hot, humid sun returned. By 9 AM it glistened blindingly on the smooth water. But the light, baffling southeast airs past Green Island barely filled the sails, and they were falling behind; to approach the enemy on the weather gauge would require hours of tacking, or they might never beat to windward of Green and Rattlesnake Islands. Nathan could see Perry arguing with Sailing Master Taylor. He knew what they were discussing. If they gave up on the channel and ran to leeward of the islands, they would have to approach the enemy from leeward. But Perry would not delay.

"He will fight me today!" said Perry. "I will have at him now, from the lee or from the weather! Good God!" Everyone looked at the starboard quarterdeck in surprise. Perry never cursed. Even getting away from the islands was proving to be a frustration.

But before 10 AM, the wind backed to southeast and freshened, though it stayed very light. Perry signaled the squadron to put helm down again and bear away from the wind and the islands; at last they stood off towards the enemy under full sail.

"Nathan, look," said Peter, pulling on his sleeve. Above the masts, a lone eagle flapped its wings fitfully in the faint breeze. It seemed to be guarding over the *Lawrence*. When Nathan looked back at his friend to make a comment, he noticed a strange, faraway look in Peter's eyes.

"I am no longer afraid," he mumbled, and that was all he would say. Perry saw the eagle, smiled and nodded.

The fickle breeze died again, then rose, struggling toward four knots. Perry must be losing his mind, Nathan thought. Was everyone aboard so eager to die? Barclay had given up the weather gauge to Perry, heaving to and waiting in light of battle, heading southwest on the larboard tack, about nine miles west of Put-in-Bay; but Barclay could rake him with his long guns as they approached.

Perry had assumed that *Queen Charlotte* would be at the head of the British line, so *Niagara* was in front of the American line, to lead against her, then *Lawrence* and the *Detroit*, a good match. But as they approached it became clear that the British had ordered their battle line thusly: *Chippeway, Detroit, General Hunter, Queen Charlotte, Lady Prevost* and *Little Belt*. Perry wanted Elliott and the *Niagara* to fight the *Queen Charlotte*, so at 10 AM, with the fleets still about five miles apart, Perry changed his own battle order. He signalled *Niagara* to heave to, and then called over to Elliott to let him pass, so that *Niagara* could drop back behind the small brig *Caledonia*. *Scorpion* and *Ariel* were ordered to move ahead to support the flagship. Now behind *Lawrence* were the *Caledonia, Niagara, Somers, Porcupine, Tigress* and a distant *Trippe*. The long guns of the *Ariel, Scorpion* and *Caledonia* could help support *Lawrence* until the brig's carronades found the range.

Lieutenant Yarnall staring through the glass gave a brief summation and estimation for both sides. "It's like this—as we knew, Commodore—*Detroit* is a somewhat larger ship than ours, and full-rigged; it has mostly long guns, about twenty. The others are mostly brigs and schooners like ours: *Queen Charlotte* a few less, mostly 24-pound carronades; *Lady Prevost* about 100 tons, ten or fifteen guns, bigger and heavier than the *General Hunter*, with less than ten guns, lighter guns. The other two smaller vessels, *Little Belt* and *Chippeway*, the smallest and weakest, have just a few little guns each. They have more pivot guns, but they have no 32-pounders; they have more—many more— long guns. More carronades too, in fact. But we should have more long and short-range *weight*, since they use a lot of 12-pounders and even smaller guns. I figure we can throw almost double their broadside metal, per gun and overall, about 1,200 pounds to their 700. We have a larger crew, thanks to the blacks and Indians." The lieutenant avoided eye contact with Peter.

Almost all of the punch was in the *Niagara* and *Lawrence*. Even though the smaller vessels in aggregate could throw a considerable weight of metal, could they work effectively in conjunction with one another? The fleets crawled toward each other, the straggling gunboats using sweeps to try to maintain position in the light, baffling breeze.

"Tecumseh is not with him," Peter said. Nathan and several others stared at him, but the face remained inscrutable.

"Pass the word," ordered Perry. "All hands assemble aft."

Then he disappeared below and returned with a roll of blue fabric that he unrolled, standing on a gun truck to display the crudely made motto, "DONT GIVE UP THE SHIP."

"Lads!" he called. "My brave boys, this flag has Captain Lawrence's dying words—my friend's last defiance. Shall we hoist this flag?"

The entire crew cheered loudly. Lieutenant Forrest and Perry himself raised the flag; it was not yet 11 AM. As the flag reached the top of the halyard, the fitful breeze briefly gusted and the flag flew out proudly, the white words plainly readable. Three cheers erupted from the flagship, and then more cheers rose from the other ships, echoed up and down the line. Nathan's throat constricted in the warm, hazy air.

"Beat to quarters, Mister Yarnall," said Perry. "And then early lunch, make it a good meal, and splice the main brace—a double ration." There would be no time for food, grog or whisky at noon, and a good commander always made sure his crews had full bellies before a battle. More shouting of orders erupted as breechings were cast loose and the guns run out. Perry, Yarnall and Nathan checked every man, every touch-hole, every lit match, every shot in the rack and netting, every sand bucket. Sand was scattered on the wetted deck so that men would not slip in fresh blood. Sixteen volunteers came up from the sick bay to help serve the cannon. Kentucky riflemen climbed into the fighting tops.

"Marines ready for inspection, Commodore," he heard from Lieutenant Brooks.

Ahead of the *Lawrence* were the fastest and most powerful schooners, *Ariel* and *Scorpion*. Astern were the small brig *Caledonia*, the largest gunboat, then the *Niagara*, and the rest of the schooners, *Somers, Porcupine, Tigress* and the slow sloop *Trippe*, falling further and further behind. Only the two big sister brigs could throw a substantial broad-side; the other seven vessels carried but one or a few guns each—some heavy guns to be sure, 24-pounders and 32-pounders, mostly. With some adjustments, the line of battle had placed the largest, strongest ships nearer the middle than the van or rear on both sides.

With the men at quarters, Perry inspected the squat 32-pounders, smiling at the men from Newport and the gunners from Old Ironsides herself. Buzzing silence filled the air again as they crept down toward the enemy line, obliquely, making less than three knots. The tension mount-ed as the sun approached its zenith. When the two fleets were five miles apart, Perry inspected the men for the last time, exchanging lighthearted remarks with those he knew best, encouraging those he did not.

"You have most of the 'Ironsides' here, I see, Mister Jeffries," he said. A few of the gunners laughed. Some of the crew were too nervous to speak, and Nathan saw comrades exchange notes, hastily scrawled in pencil; names, addresses, makeshift wills and farewells to loved ones.

"The old frigate herself carries these guns," he said to the gun crew nearest him. "I have no fear of the outcome with you men to fire them."

"These bully boys yonder is goin' to join the *Guerriere*, sir!" shouted a young man, bare to the waist with a red bandanna. His mates laughed as he hastily saluted.

Perry walked over and clapped him on the shoulder. "Well said, lad! I know you men will do your duty today! Send that signal to the fleet, Mister Forrest! Barclay heard something like that from Nelson at Trafalgar—lost his arm there—well, we'll see who knows best how to close with the enemy."

They would come within extreme range of Barclay's guns when the distance was about a mile. The British ships were newly painted, their hulls black, white and yellow, and red plainly visible on the inner bulwarks.

As it dragged toward that time, Perry, who had gone below again, called Nathan to his cabin.

"Yes, sir?" said Nathan. He noticed Perry had been tearing up let-ters and placing some in a wax-covered packet.

"From my wife Betsy," said Perry hoarsely, olive eyes wet. "The enemy will not read them." He quickly regained control of his voice. "Lieutenant, I have already told this to Mister Yarnall, Forrest and Usher Parsons, and I gave the lead box to Sam—I mean, the purser, Mister Hambleton, and—"

"Yes, sir?"

"Lieutenant, it goes without saying that I am proud of you, proud of these officers and crew. But I just want you to know . . . What I am trying to say is, in case I should fall, it has been an honor and a privilege serving with you, Mister Jeffries."

He offered his hand, and Nathan took it.

"I feel the same way, Commodore."

"Now you had better return to your station."

As Nathan reached the deck again, about 11:45, the quiet was shattered by a distant bugle call aboard Barclay's flagship, the *Detroit*. It sounded clearly over the water. Then they heard a band playing "Rule, Britannia," followed by the singing and cheers of the British crews. The ships sailed, or drifted, closer; the British got underway, heading south-southwest. In the bright sun Nathan watched the British line lengthen and grow ominously in size in front of them. The band music from *Detroit* suddenly ceased with another bugle sounding over the water. At about a mile, the Americans heard the bang of a gun, and a column of water shot up from the splash, a half-cable's length ahead of them, nearly abreast of the *Scorpion*. Behind him, Nathan could see *Trippe* now lagged two miles astern.

"When will they—That is, how long before—"

"A 24-pounder, a ranging shot," said Yarnall judiciously. "They may try a few more; the next one may not be so short."

The flatness of the water made their approach seem eerie. Sure enough, they saw another puff of smoke from the British flagship, followed by the crash of the explosion and a geyser of water near the *Lawrence*. The British cheered again. Then another gun went off, and then another. There was a crash forward, where the shot plowed through both bulwarks. A man fell on the deck and remained still.

About noon, the *Lawrence* started firing her few forward guns; but her bowchasers were answered by devastating broadsides from the enemy ships, sweeping and tearing and punching the length of the ship. Soon, the sides of the *Detroit* and the *General Hunter*, roughly equidistant from the *Lawrence*, were obscured by the smoke and flame of guns firing—and they were firing mostly at the *Lawrence*. Were shots from the *Queen Charlotte* or *Chippeway* hitting them? Nathan could see the few guns from the *Ariel* banging away at the enemy, and even occasionally a shot from the *Scorpion*. There was something wrong there; now she was silent again. Periodically one of the *Lawrences* would scream in agony as he was hit by round iron or wood splinters. The sound of cracking wood and snapping lines was somewhat less sickening. Nathan fought against the urge to duck, hide or run below; no one could possibly display such a common sense reaction. These were brave men. He feared ghastly injury, dismemberment, grotesque deformity, excruciating pain and other things worse than sudden death, but he tried to put it out of his mind.

Perry, even more oblivious than most, shouted at Yarnall.

"See if you can get the *Scorpion* to fire!"

"Aye, sir!" And Yarnall jumped into the forechains with his speaking trumpet. Sure enough, the schooner's guns began to belch back at the enemy. But for the *Lawrence* the range was still too great for carronades, and the punishment had to continue. It was still a thousand yards to the enemy's van; equally worrisome, Perry's rear ships were about the same distance behind. Once he could concentrate the firepower of his two brigs, however, it would be a different story.

Soon round shot were hitting them regularly, even simultaneously; Nathan heard the crunch of wood and a scream below. The bulwarks offered no protection; cannonballs could easily penetrate any timbers aboard. The gunboats were falling behind, almost out of range, as *Lawrence* crawled along at three knots, shaking with impact of British hits. There! A shot from *Scorpion* fell close aboard the *Detroit*, partially concealed in her own gun smoke. Nathan felt smothered in his own sweat, and prayed for a decent breeze.

The men aboard the *Lawrence* were being crushed under rigging and spars and overturned guns, ripping and tearing ship and men apart. Perry at the speaking trumpet warned the crews not to overload cannon, which could burst or get blown off their mounts. One carronade had already been knocked off its slide by enemy shot, crushing a man.

The ship continued to receive the brunt of the battle as men fell. Cut rigging waved and hung uselessly and splinters flew high in the air. Peter yelled at Nathan and pointed: on the deck, covered with with woodchips, blood and sand, Nathan saw the red bandanna of one of his men, still wrapped around a severed head. He fought the urge to vomit. This was growing even worse than the scene he had witnessed aboard the *Guerriere*. He saw Perry signaling him, and hurried to his side, fearful every moment of suffering the same horrible fate as the gunner. At least he died quickly, thought Nathan. He felt a sudden attack of nausea, a panic. This is too appalling, he thought. I cannot do this.

"We're well within musket range, Mister Jeffries," said Perry. "Yarnall is wounded; he's below with Parsons, but I hope he shall return. We'll luff up to give our broadside a chance, then bear for the *Detroit* again. You take command of the starboard guns, and make sure every man aims true."

"Aye, sir!"

Nathan ran along the deck, checking the guns, hearing the ominous whir and whistle of incoming death.

"You're too high, number six! Lower your elevation! Ready, men! Fire!"

At about 12:20, after several tries at ranging parallel—still too distant—*Lawrence* had finally taken up station opposite *General Hunter*, now at 250 yards. The rear three schooners and *Trippe* had begun firing at the rear of the British line, at over 1,000 yards distance where carronades were ineffective. *Niagara* stayed out of carronade range, about a thousand yards, close behind *Caledonia*. Only a few long guns were fired.

In a satisfying broadside, the double-shotted carronades finally roared their deafening reply, and the men cheered. Coughing through the smoke, Nathan could see *Detroit*'s masts tremble as the shot pummeled her hull. But he knew Perry wanted to get closer, to truly lethal carronade range—pistol range—about fifty yards. He heard Perry shout "Helm down!" The bow of the brig slowly pointed back toward the *Detroit* amidships. As she crawled toward the enemy again, only a few bow guns could bear; and the punishment continued. Partially shielded on *Lawrence*'s larboard, the *Ariel* and *Scorpion* fired at *Chippeway* and *Detroit*. But *Caledonia* and *Niagara* were still far behind, and Nathan could see, down the British line, *Queen Charlotte* was moving to support the *Detroit*. Almost every British gun bore on the *Lawrence*. Even if we don't sink or surrender, Nathan thought, the battle is lost. There's another gun out of action: number four, "Yellow Sal," has only three men working her!

At least Peter was still there, helping Logan at the bowchaser. If Nathan kept his mind focused on the business at hand, he could almost forget about the fact that he might soon be dead, or a prisoner, or . . . worse. The afternoon sun beat down, and the acrid stench of powder, blood and death would not be blown away.

He heard Perry call for more sail. Yarnall had returned, face smoke-blackened, and taken over command of the starboard battery. More broadsides; the battle was becoming general as *Lawrence* closed with the *Detroit*. A musket ball smacked into the rail near; their own Kentucky riflemen in the tops must be making life miserable for the enemy.

From the still-distant *Niagara*, only the one long gun was firing.

"Mister Jeffries!" Perry bellowed. "Signal the *Niagara* to make sail and close with *Queen Charlotte*!"

But Elliott continued to lag behind.

"Damn him!" shouted Nathan. "Your pardon, sir, but he wanted the command, and this is his—"

"Enough of that, Mister Jeffries! See how Parsons is doing below and report back to me—quickly! We need more men!"

This horror could not continue—he would go mad! But Nathan followed orders and tried to ignore Usher Parsons' mangled patients.

Two men returned to help him work the guns. He could see *Queen Charlotte* crowd on sail and maneuver ahead of *General Hunter* to join *Detroit* in the brutal pounding match with *Lawrence*.

AT 1 PM, IN the second hour, both principal ships were being shredded and many men had been killed or wounded. Men were falling every few minutes, and more guns were out of action. The three ships were now roughly parallel, exchanging broadsides that regularly ripped through wood and canvas. Most of the rigging on the *Lawrence* was cut away and the ship could not be maneuvered. Before he had gone below, Nathan had looked at Peter, who stared back at him expressionless. The *Lawrence* was doomed. Where was Logan?

Shot from more than thirty guns peppered the *Lawrence* regularly now. With all sail set, she still seemed reluctant to close, and every minute brought more horror on deck. Rigging was ripped apart, men cut down. The *Caledonia* was helping with her three long guns. But where was the *Niagara*? The two long 12-pounders forward were firing again as Perry luffed to try the range, roughly parallel to the punishing vessels; the bow slowly swung away.

"Ready for a broadside, Mister Jeffries!"

"Point and elevate your guns!" Nathan shouted to his gun crews at the carronades. The angle was adjusted as the slow match was brought to the breech of each cannon left to man.

"Fire!" Lighted matches reached the touchholes and the deck exploded in the deafening roar of the seven great guns still in operation.

"Sponge your guns! Load! Ram home! Run out!" Nathan screamed over the deafening roar.

"Still out of range!" he heard Perry shouting above the yelling nearby. "Bear away!"

Several more times this occurred in the nightmare of destruction, until they were at less than canister range and his men could fire at will. But he could tell from the forced calm, the mechanical denial on Perry's face glancing through the acrid smoke, that things were falling apart.

"That damned Elliott is hanging back, sir!" he heard Yarnall yelling at the commodore.

When Nathan turned to look, he could see it was true: instead of closing with the *Queen Charlotte*, *Niagara* had brailed her jib, furled her topgallants and backed her main topsail. Hovering to the north and to windward, firing an occasional long shot, she was inexplicably laying off, more a spectator than a participant as the *Lawrence* suffered unspeakable horror.

If I survive this battle, he thought to himself, there will be a reckoning! But he put his hate and anger for Elliott into the task of firing at the enemy, not thinking about iron or wood surely about to enter his hide. Peter would appear and disappear, shouting encouragement, helping bring shot up from below, carrying down the shredded and mutilated bodies of the dead so the crowded decks could remain clear. Round shot buzzed right through the ship and the top hamper hung tattered and useless; but the *Lawrence* did not need to maneuver now, anyway, only to continue firing.

They were hurting the enemy, Nathan could see that. But soon the wounded and dead aboard the *Lawrence* outnumbered the living. One by one, the big guns were silenced, out of action because of damage or lack of crews. At this range, even sharpshooters with rifles could be effective.

The action was on the starboard side, but Yarnall and Nathan would change sides in their working and tending the guns, begging for more men from Perry, as Forrest divided his time between them. Soon the larboard side was utterly deserted. It didn't seem to matter. The bulwarks were smashed flat, and yet Perry was everywhere, and so was Yarnall, encouraging and exhorting, miraculously uninjured, seemingly charmed with invincibility. Then Yarnall disappeared, and Nathan saw Peter lying against the mainmast. Their eyes locked; Peter shook his head, and smiled. He was not bleeding, that Nathan could see. Perhaps he was merely exhausted.

The rear American schooners began catching up and having their effect on the *Lady Prevost* and *General Hunter*; the former began drifting to starboard out of line, almost hiding between and behind *Hunter* and the unscathed *Little Belt*, which was also back in the line from the larger British ships. The cannonade became less regular as the smoke-filled arena headed slowly southwest, canister and grape too, sweeping the decks of men and guns. *Lawrence* fell back away from *Detroit*, guns remanned and remounted and dismounted again and again, all in ruins, almost out of the fight, helpless, more casualties than not in a crew of 103. Perry continued to be everywhere, as if there were a prayer of saving battle or ship. Nathan knew that he was losing his grasp of reality. Men were buried under falling spars and overturned guns, the clang of metal striking metal, while *Niagara* backed its main topsail.

"I will kill Elliott!" Nathan swore. Visible off their larboard stern, the *Niagara* was virtually out of the battle.

Then there was Logan at his side again.

"It's almost 2 PM," he said to Nathan. "How much longer—"

A shot glanced off the deck a yard away, and Logan shook and twisted around in shock. Nathan saw that he was impaled in the side by a foot-long splinter. Blood spurted as he collapsed on the deck. Nathan carried him below, sensing that Logan had known this would happen, and hating himself for wanting both of his friends aboard—now they would all die.

It was even more frightening below deck. The wardroom, still above the waterline, had become the cockpit, since the *Lawrence* drew only ten feet, so there was no safe place below deck, either. Round shot had punched holes through the side, killing men already wounded, as Parsons and his men, surrounded by delirious, shouting men, death and agony, worked their gruesome trade under the skylight with primitive tools and no more laudanum to relieve the pain. Nathan saw the rough sutures, gaping wounds, primitive splints and tourniquets, exposed bones, scissors and knives to slice through flesh and then saw for amputation. Men less severely injured promptly and matter-of-factly returned to duty.

Nathan began to wonder if he deserved to survive this madness, while at the same time fiercely tempted to jump over the side or run down to the bilge, anywhere to escape. As wounded Midshipman Laub was leaving Parsons, the surgeon's hand still on his arm, a cannonball dashed him against the other side of the room. A seaman limping back to duty aft was torn in half by a cannon ball as he began to climb the ladder. A shot passing right through the hull hit and killed another wounded man, smashed in both his shoulders and cut him down as he descended the forward companionway. It was a scene from hell. The screams of agony were continuous from the wounded, from amputees, as blood dripped down through the deck seams above and the surgeon and his assistants tended the remains of men as best they could. Fighting nausea, Nathan grabbed his arm and laid an unconscious Logan down on the bloody deck in front of him.

"He may be bleeding to death, sir!"

"I'll do what I can for him," yelled Doctor Parsons.

They could hear through the din the growling and howling of Perry's terrified spaniel, locked in a cabin. They heard another crash, then louder barking, and looked over to see where the dog, thrusting its head through the hole punched in the door by the British shot, yelped at all the world. Almost every man nearby, including Nathan, began to laugh, some more insanely than others. Caught up by the madness and hilarity, even Parsons laughed uproariously before returning to his grim task.

But everyone laughed again as Yarnall approached, his face a grotesque, bloody mask, puffy and bandaged with a handkerchief. His huge, swollen nose had been sliced by a sliver of wood, like an enormous beak; evidently feathers and lint from a ruptured hammock stuffing had stuck like a surrounding mantle to the bloody cuts on his face and head, turning him into comically gory creature, a mockery of an evil owl.

"The Devil has come for us!" yelled one wounded man.

"The Devil is among us!" cackled another man in pain.

"He has come for his own!" echoed others, laughing near the wardroom/cockpit.

"Hambleton was hit by a round shot," Yarnall said to Nathan. "He's begging Perry to shoot him and end his pain. Come help me with him, and then help Perry man gun number seven. All the gun captains are smashed and shattered. He's got marines laying the aft carronade. I'll see to Mister Logan here."

Nathan hurried on deck again after one last look at Yarnall, just in time to see more horror. Lieutenant Brooks was talking with Perry when a 24-pound cannon ball hit his leg and tossed him to the other side of the ship. Brooks' hip joint was crushed by the ball, and he was carried below, screaming in agony; clearly not much could be done, and Nathan doubted he would live through the battle.

But it seemed no more dangerous on deck than below—less horrible, any way. Nathan's arm was causing him agony, bleeding again from the tear from that pistol ball, but he had thus far miraculously escaped from any further injury. He could not see Peter. Perry was everywhere, amazingly unscathed; Nathan saw another man cut down next to him as they were talking. The commodore went up and down the ladder, asking for more help from the sickbay, hands to man the pumps or the guns, to help in any way they could; but by then few men needed his cajoling or could heed him. Nathan remembered the eagle flying along with the flagship before the battle, when Perry said "We will fight today, come what may." Peter had said, yes, it was an omen, the eagle; surely he would know. But there were few guns left to fire; though uninjured, Perry's luck had failed him. His arm burned horribly, but Nathan seemed to share Perry's immunity to further injury. He helped Yarnall and Forrest with one of the last guns. The important thing was not to lose sight of the objective—what was that? To kill, to die? A curious detachment seemed to wash over him, as he saw Perry consulting with Taylor. They pointed furious fingers toward the *Niagara*. The firing throughout the battle had become noticeably more desultory.

"Well, this is not the Battle of Salamis," he muttered, "and we are not the Greeks."

TWENTY-THREE

Battle of Lake Erie

"SIR?" ASKED FORREST, NEARBY. Several spent grape shot and canister balls rattled into the side of the ship, partially imbedded, looking like gray pustules. "What makes the commodore go on?"

Nathan wondered, ignoring the boy, his curiosity beyond duty, or honor, or country; the cohesion of the survivors refused to disintegrate, the bombardment had not broken down the training, somehow. He suspected that the most primal needs of trusting one's companions was the driving force now; that compassion, or determination that led each of them to refuse to let his brothers down, in spite of the fear and hardship, the fatigue and the regular perforating of the hull. This force was strong enough to endure even a sinking hulk, but it would not save them from defeat when the British sent boats to board the helpless *Lawrence*.

Lieutenant Forrest was talking to a man from the *Constitution* when he was suddenly knocked down by a musket round. As Nathan rushed over to him, he opened his eyes, stunned, then looked down to where the slightly flattened ball had ended up after hitting a button on his waistcoat. Nathan handed him the musket ball and helped him to his feet. "This must have been spent."

"'Tis mine now," Forrest said, calmly pocketed the misshapen lead ball as a souvenir. Nathan thought he had given up all hope of life or fear; yet he could still be startled. He jumped and jerked around when he heard the last powder monkey scream. The boy spun around and fell, but rose again a moment later, his face a strange, ghastly white, a reddish splotch showing where he had been hit in the face. He approached Nathan, screaming again, and then collapsed. Nathan somehow stifled the need to retch. Piles of human wreckage lay near the skylight that opened to the wardroom/cockpit, where more gruesome business persisted under Parsons.

"Oh, my God!" Nathan yelled in despair. "When will this end?"

"Lieutenant!" It was Perry, signaling him to join his personal aide, Handy, and Chaplain Breeze at the one remaining carronade that could fire.

"Help us man this gun, if you please!"

It seemed pointless, but Nathan was too tired to protest. As if in a dream, he carried a 32-pound shot to the gun. Even the invalids were gone. Of the 103 men aboard, perhaps two dozen hands remained unscathed. A few others crawled about, tattered, limping wraiths. They blasted another round at the enemy.

Nathan felt the breath knocked out of him as he landed flat on the deck.

"Are you hurt, sir?" said Perry himself, pulling him up. "The air of that shot caught you."

"The *Lawrence* is lost, sir, and that hurts more than—" The blinding pain in his arm now numb again, Nathan bit back a sardonic ending.

Perry shook his head. Still in a daze, Nathan returned to help fire the gun again.

An uncanny, ominous silence seemed to be taking over the ships that lay mostly hove to on the idle sea. It seemed as if the battle were over. But Perry fought on, blindly, mechanically. He did not appear to accept defeat.

"Run out!" he cried, just as an angry boom foretold at least one more incoming shot from the British.

Then the heavy carronade bucked and squealed as Nathan felt a searing rupture in his left calf. Lying on the deck again, he passed out.

"It is almost 2:30, Lieutenant," Nathan heard as he came to. But no one was talking to *him*. He was lying amid the shrieks of man and groans of suffering in the cockpit.

"Only twenty men aboard are fit for duty," the voice continued remorselessly to someone else. "The butcher's bill stands at twenty-two dead, sixty-one wounded; last gun silenced."

Wounded again, Nathan thought, bleeding to death in the ward-room; he heard British cheers as another shot pierced *Lawrence* through and through with a nasty crunch. Where was Peter? It was agonizing; where was his friend? Was Logan still alive? But he must return to the deck and not let the ship be given up, except in his own mind. Some how Perry inspired that nonsensical loyalty. He had written himself off and did not know if the battle was lost; but he knew their ship was crushed, floating lifeless with no weigh on, and still flying "DON'T GIVE UP THE SHIP." They must do just that. He could imagine the flag lowered, the beaten vessel almost abandoned with a few left walking on deck like somnambulists. How many were hoping as he was that Perry had finally surrendered the remains of *Lawrence*? He tried to hate the British but knew their decks were just as covered with torn and screaming men, bloody body parts, agony and terror. He tried to hate Perry. As he tried to rise, stabs of pain shot up from his thigh that made him cry out. Then he recognized the faces of Doc Parsons, the chaplain and Yarnall.

"You just lie easy, son," Parsons said. "The captain and Mister Yarnall have things in order; he, well, it has been decided to—"

"Excuse me, Doctor," said Perry, his face appearing and leaning over Nathan. "Lieutenant, I am going to scuttle the ship."

He hesitated as Nathan simply stared at him.

"Do you understand, Mister Jeffries? I have asked the men who will stay with me here to put the suffering to rest; the wounded and those who can't swim will be put in the two boats that survive and the rest lashed to spars, gratings, anything that will float. I believe the gig or cutter and the bow of the longboat remain serviceable, as well. A very few of us will remain aboard to—"

"No, sir!"

"I know, Mister Jeffries, but I wanted you to know how glad I am that you are still with us. I'm sorry!" He tried to hold Nathan's arm, but Nathan pulled away. He noticed that Perry was carrying his blue and white battle flag rolled up under his arm.

The commodore stood up, "Well, sir, I would be deeply gratified if you would take this flag for personal—"

"The *Lawrence* is lost, sir," Nathan said, nearly screaming, "but not the battle!" Of course he knew it was, everything was lost, but it did not seem to matter. There were tears in his eyes as he turned away, rolling painfully so that he could peer out the jagged, gaping hole near him in the side of the ship. Head buzzing, yearning to rest, he heard Perry leaving, then Nathan said abruptly, "It is time for *you* to leave the *Lawrence*, sir."

Everyone stopped and turned to Nathan silently.

"Give up my flag?" asked Perry. "No, I cannot . . . give up *this* ship."

"You must transfer your command, sir—to the *Niagara*; by boat, if possible." Nathan's voice sounded tinny, unreal to his own ears. But he saw Yarnall start, and then nod, a gleam of approval in his one barely open eye.

"I respectfully agree with Mister Jeffries, sir," said the chaplain. "It is the only hope left. We helped you fire the last shot from the starboard carronade."

"But perhaps we can turn the ship around, a fresh battery—"

"No, sir!" Yarnall almost shook him, but the commodore quickly realized it was their only chance, albeit a slim one.

Eyes glazed, Perry nodded slowly, looking to one side of the wardroom and the other; then he shook hands with Nathan and climbed the ladder.

"Good luck, sir," Nathan called out; it was more of a lifeless croak. But a few minutes later, struggling to remain conscious as Parsons busied himself with Lieutenant Brooks, Nathan turned to look at him.

"How goes the battle?" the handsome, dying Brooks asked Nathan calmly, then turned away. It was quiet now, as quiet as a tomb, except for the agony of the wounded—moans, heartbreaking groans, and then a scream punctuating the air as Usher Parsons and his assistants, looking like butchers, cut meat.

"Where is Peter Hughes?" Nathan asked no one in particular. One of the loblolly boys heard him, shrugged and shook his head. Someone on this deck would know where his friend was.

"Where are you going, Lieutenant? You're in no condition to—"

"I must return to the deck," Nathan croaked.

Using a broken pike as a cane, he limped aft in time to see that Perry was about to give up the ship, after all. Gazing over the side, he saw Perry leap down into the gig, which had been towed behind ship and had somehow survived the carnage, shot-damaged but floating. As Perry ordered the gig to pull away from larboard side, with his "DONT GIVE UP THE SHIP" battle-flag with him, Nathan could see that Perry had ordered his broad pennant hauled down as well, and had changed to his uniform coat from the plain sailor's jacket. Perry's 12-year-old brother James was also with him, and four oarsmen.

Standing in the gig, looking up at the floating hulk of the *Lawrence*, Perry called out for the last time. "Nathan, you have saved me— my brave men! Mister Yarnall will continue to fly the colors as long as possible, to honor our flag as you have all done, and surrender at his discretion. Sir, I am transferring to the *Niagara*!"

As if in comical relief, Nathan, leaning and weak-headed, could see the oarsmen gesticulating while Perry, who, absurdly remained standing, made himself a perfect target. Sure enough, columns of water suddenly erupted several yards from the small craft. Was that the boat being struck? Smaller flicks showed the splash of musket balls as the men complained, and he still stood up in the boat.

"Sit down sir, or we don't row!" he thought he heard. It all seems so ridiculous, Nathan thought, wondering if he was losing his sanity. Their guns silent, four seamen, a midshipman and a madman with two flags, pulling away from the *Lawrence*. He could see the commodore, now seated but with his precious blue battle flag actually wrapped around him, the oarsmen rowing him madly toward the *Niagara*, topsails barely filled, about a thousand yards off the larboard quarter, looking fresh and perfect against the blue sky. Suddenly the boat disappeared again in spray and splinters from an enemy salvo. But it reappeared again, even as *Niagara* began to bear away and close behind *Lawrence*. Yarnall sighed.

"It is time, gentlemen," said Yarnall. Nathan, Taylor and Forrest nodded sadly. "Lower our flag, Mister Forrest," said Yarnall. They could hear the British cheer. Perry had given up the ship!

Would the British send a boat for capture? Could they? The Americans' poor, unmanageable wreck of a flagship, flag lowered . . . But perhaps no British were in a position to take possession. And yet, with defeat imminent, it was conceivable that Barclay would release one of his convoy to destroy *Lawrence,* and Commodore Perry, at last. The nightmare continued. They heard some wounded below chanting, "Sink the ship, sink the ship!"

Nathan felt burning tears and saw glistening streaks on the grime- and gunpowder-blackened faces of the other men. Meanwhile, they watched *Caledonia* bear up and move closer to the British line to let *Niagara* sail around her stern and toward *Lawrence*. But *Niagara* sailed not toward *Detroit* in front of *Lawrence* to relieve her, but behind *Lawrence,* passing to windward of her, so that their ship was between the British and the *Niagara*.

"Those cowards!" Yarnall hissed. Even before Perry arrived at *Niagara,* she set more canvas and began to close on *Lawrence.*

But at least the fresh *Niagara* had set more canvas, and was closing with the gig, on an interception course. But too late. They could see splinters fly from the little craft from small arms fire, and geysers of water all around the boat as the guns from the British ships sought the range; another near-miss, right alongside, then the gig disappeared in more splashes. Perry was finally visible again; but how could the enemy fire miss now? One solid round shot would sink them.

With the breeze freshening, the *Lawrence,* sails and rigging shred-ded, began to fall behind most of the ships. The smaller American vessels in the rear began to pass her to starboard, sweeping in a fairly orderly line. From time to time the men on the deck of the *Lawrence* lost track of the gig. But fifteen minutes later the boat somehow appeared again beside the *Niagara*, and they could make out the figure of Perry climbing her side, followed by his brother. Perry's miraculous luck again, thought Nathan; the eagle. He yearned to search the ship for Peter, but he must watch!

"Is that Elliott," said Yarnall, "almost three hours into battle?" One man climbed down into the boat.

"That looks like Elliott, the bastard," said Nathan.

"Good!" said Yarnall. "Heading for the gunboats, maybe, trying to get *Scorpion, Porcupine* and *Tigress* and to join the battle proper! There! *Niagara*'s squaring her yards, now steering towards what's left of the enemy line, instead of away from it! The commodore is in command! But one ship against two or three? He hasn't a chance! There! Pennant and blue battle flag rise—they're flutterin' the breeze."

A weak cheer went up from the few men on deck, echoed by the other American vessels. Few guns were firing anywhere now.

Yarnall studied the action with a trembling glass.

"*Niagara* is bearing down on the British," he said, "heading to cross *Detroit*'s bow! The *Queen Charlotte* is sailing under the lee of the *Detroit*, trying to pass her stern. The British seem gathered up together, ready to rake her. 'Tis suicide for Perry! The *General Hunter, Little Belt* and *Lady Prevost* are all almost directly to the lee of the *Queen Charlotte* and *Detroit*; their line is gone, but *Chippeway* remains in the van. Is that *Little Belt* coming up to pass her? *Niagara* stands no chance against all those guns!"

"Lieutenant, careful there!" The wounded sailing master caught Nathan as he blacked out again and fell, cushioning his fall to the deck. That man is strong, thought Nathan, stronger than—where is my friend?

As Nathan slipped into unconsciousness, he thought bitterly of how victory, so well deserved, was slipping from their grasp.

TWENTY-FOUR

Annapolis - *October 4, 1813*

Banquet in honor of Senator Mordecai Denton, William Paca House

IN A PERFECT INDIAN summer afternoon, on the small veranda overlooking the garden, Catherine Charles stood with two esteemed gentlemen: portly Captain Isaac Hull and William Jeffries' old friend, Captain Joshua Barney.

"There is no doubt, Captain?" asked Catherine quietly, gazing out at the famous gardens of the Paca home. It was a bright day. But she wore a dark gown somehow glistening in the afternoon sun. It was the first time Hull had visited Maryland since William Jeffries was lost—one of the few times, in fact, he had ventured south to New England since taking over command of the Portsmouth Naval Station, New Hampshire.

"No doubt, my dear," said Hull. "Your Lieutenant Nathan Jeffries and Jack Logan sailed with Perry in late August, not long after capturing British supplies run by your friend Fredericks near a place called Cattaraugus Creek. But from these reports, the scout Peter Hughes has disappeared."

Catherine shivered, though it was still warm enough, this early in October.

"We need a victory on Lake Erie," said Barney. "They say the British have 10,000 savages as allies. We could lose the war there."

"Instead of compromising with the native peoples of our land,"

Catherine said, "we exterminate them. Do settlers have the right to force all of the tribes from their own land?"

She spoke sadly, not really expecting an answer; and she received none. The jovially fat, red-faced, blue-eyed Hull, who had removed his navy uniform coat at Catherine's insistence, sipped his brandy and looked at Barney.

"There is no doubt, in any case," Barney said, "that we must wrest control of the lakes from the British. It is the key to the war. We are losing this conflict, and at sea we're squandering our—Captain Lawrence, a great leader was a brave man, but disobeyed orders. Then *Pelican* captured our *Argus*. Our commander did the same, after burning 20 British merchantmen; insisted on a slug-out, and lost everything."

"And poor Burrows," said Hull, "at least lucky little *Enterprize*— my first naval command, you know—captured *Boxer*, but Commander Blakeley still waits for his sloop-of-war *Wasp*. Most every port is bottled up now. Privateers and small commerce raiders are about all we have now—just like you and William Jeffries always advised. I don't believe the British will choose to attack our Portsmouth Yard; the harbor is well defended. But they could invade almost anyplace they care to; the northern frontier border and most of the coast invite raids at least."

"I know," Catherine sighed. She and William had run supplies down the Chesapeake Bay, where thousands were suffering from the British blockade. And now British troops occupied Kent Island.

"I was sorry to hear that you lost the Jeffries house," said Barney.

"We will manage," said Catherine, once again calm and composed, turning back to Hull.

"And how is Ann, Captain?" she asked. Catherine liked this good-natured seaman.

"She is feeling rightly enough, sound and rigged taut. Thank you, ma'am," said Hull with a little more of his old humor. "She is sailing main well through Portsmouth society. After a few storms in the beginning, I—"

Hull could see that Catherine was no longer listening, but was gazing out at the garden again. She had caught a movement in the corner of her eye; a chaise had pulled up right outside the other side of the garden on Seaman's Square, near to the freshly painted white picket fence in front of the gazebo. There was some delay, as its passengers apparently were having difficulty exiting the carriage, opening the gate and negotiating the floral maze.

"What is it, Miss Catherine?" asked Barney. "Are you all right?"

At first she did not quite recognize the first man, dressed in a stylish brown suit with his left arm in sling, as he carefully lowered himself down to the ground and looked back inside the carriage. Then she remembered: Mister Jack Logan. The second man was evidently injured in the right arm, as their clumsy efforts made progress getting down from the chaise, but . . . the other man! No!

Did she scream or faint? Her pounding heart seemed to take flight as the other figure, a large man wearing a dark blue and gold uniform, helped by the first, eased himself out of the chaise and hobbled with a sturdy wooden cane, sometimes leaning on Jack Logan's good shoulder.

"Catherine, is something wrong?"

She ran outside.

"By God, Joshua—look!" Hull turned to Barney, and laughed, patting his beaming friend's shoulder.

Catherine ran up to Nathan as he slowly made his way through the fence, his friend Jack Logan right behind. Without a word, she threw her arms around Nathan; he tried to maintain his balance.

"You listen to me! I will hold you!" she cried, smothering his pale, gaunt, battered face with kisses.

His eyes were as wet as hers as he weakly tried to pull away, tried to smile. She noted a scattering of gray hairs already, like the early touch of frost, in his long sideburns, his face still flat, but now harder, stonier. Logan looked remarkably the same as ever.

Catherine whispered to Nathan, "I did not engage with that man Frederick," she said. "But I would have, to save *you*. Neither one of us has—"

"Never mind, Catherine. You are—I hated you for what I thought was your betrayal . . . but I hated sending you away even more. After

Fredericks disappeared—we know he is not buried among the dead at Cattaraugus—"

"I know, my love, I know. Here, Captain, would you mind helping us?"

As the two captains, Hull and Barney, helped Nathan, exhausted and shaking, to the Chippendale sofa, Catherine noticed that Jack Logan had disappeared.

Nathan, now lying down, saw Catherine looking around.

"Mister Logan has gone to deliver the news to the State House."

"What news, Nathan?"

"Captain Hull," said Nathan, "would you mind? This is a copy—please read it aloud."

Nathan awkwardly pulled out a dispatch letter and crumpled envelope from his leather waistcoat and gave them to Hull. The corpulent captain saw it was addressed to the Secretary of the Navy William Jones.

"My God!" Hull shouted, bringing people from the banquet to the door of the parlor. The captain read loudly and slowly, almost giddy with happiness.

"It has pleased the Almighty to give to the arms of the United States a signal victory over their enemies on this lake. The British squadron has at this moment surrendered to the force under my command, after a sharp conflict. Thanks be to God."

There was a stunned silence as Hull looked at Nathan, and Barney, then studied the envelope; the front was illegible, but a few words were scrawled on the back. Hull read out loud again:

Dear General Harrison.

We have met the enemy and they are ours:

Two Ships, two Brigs, one

Schooner & one Sloop.

Yours, with great respect and esteem

O H Perry.

"Huzzah!" someone shouted. Others took up the cheer. They heard the bells ringing in St. Anne's Church, and cheering outside the house and beyond.

Sturdy Hull waved at Barney and shook Nathan's left hand in an iron grip, then made his way to the door as Catherine noted Nathan's white face with alarm.

"If you would join me, Joshua. We'll ask the surgeon to visit them here," said Hull.

"Certainly, Isaac," Barney said. And the two no-nonsense captains quickly shoved everyone out of the room so that Nathan and Catherine would be undisturbed.

"He'll be fine, ma'am; you'll see," said Hull, as he shut the door and left them alone.

"Thank you, gentlemen. Do not sit up, Nathan, please," said Catherine. "Let me fetch you some brandy."

Much as he would deny it, Nathan would always treasure the look of Joshua Barney, his father's dearest friend, beaming; the look on Hull's face, of pride and relief; and Catherine's look, almost transfixed—that dark, entrancing face, flickering like those lips—as she bent down as best she could.

"I cannot speak," she suddenly cried, then grasped his good arm. "Nathan, what happened to—"

"Peter's left a letter for me," said Nathan, handing her a bulky envelope. "Would you please read *this* one aloud?"

She looked alluring in black and brown. Her gently curving smile warmed the room as she took the letter. Even on the verge of losing consciousness, Nathan could hardly take his eyes of that black hair, commanding face and bare arms.

September 10,

My dearest friend,

After Perry left you and Yarnall on the lifeless *Lawrence,* I found myself on that gig with Perry—you did not see me. Less impressed than angered by his show of courage, Perry's men forced him to sit down in the boat and present less of a target. By another miracle, we reached the side of the *Niagara* and I was not crushed in the bottom of the gig. Perry himself helped me write about the end of this battle, as I am no maritime adept. Perry wanted you to know that this victory was largely your doing."

Catherine looked up a Nathan. "My darling hero," she said.

"Bah!" said Nathan.

"You are!" she insisted, then continued reading:

When Perry climbed over the side of his new command we could hear cheers from the *Lawrence*, but then Perry saw the *Lawrence* strike her colors, and wept as the colors dropped. We heard cheers from the British, the cries of our own wounded on board the abandoned brig, and wondered if the British would take possession of her. Nervous, safe, Elliott took the gig to fetch up the lagging gunboats as Perry, now in command of *Niagara*, ordered the helm brought up so the trysail could be brailed and the yards squared. When Perry's flag was hoisted, and the crew saw that the *Niagara* would bear down on the disorganized enemy with double-shotted guns, they give three mighty cheers. The *Lady Prevost* had passed the *Detroit* near the Chippeway; the *Little Belt* heading west, near the *Lady Prevost and* at 2:50, the *Chippeway* to the lee of *Queen Charlotte* and *Detroit*. The *Niagara* steered for *Detroit*'s bow in the freshening breeze, then made for the center of the British line; *Detroit, Queen Charlotte* and *General Hunter* to starboard, *Lady Prevost, Chippeway* and *Little Belt* to larboard. Barclay's flagship fired its few undamaged larboard guns at us, but Perry remained steady. Suddenly the *Detroit* tried to tack, to present her fresh broadside to the oncoming brig. Leeward of the *Detroit*, the *Queen Charlotte*, trying to get closer, found the flagship backing into her larboard side, and her bowsprit ran into the mizzen rigging of the *Detroit*. Both ships had already suffered greatly a low and aloft, and now they were now fouled together, help-less, unmaneuverable, with virtually no guns able to bear.

That was our moment! With clewed up courses and topgallants, braces eased, helm to starboard as sweetly as an exercise, the *Niagara* slowed and rounded to under the hapless British ships at pistol range and fired lethal broadsides, raking the two main British ships from stem to stern. They could hear the screams as 640 pounds of solid iron hurtled across the narrow gap of water, ripping into the guts of the enemy. Rigging and life on deck was swept clear from side to side. The scuppers ran with blood. The larboard side fired at the smaller vessels, which now caught the hell of *Niagara's* other broadside.

We had broken the line! Backing the main topsail, the *Niagara* paused and then belched fire again as the gunners reloaded even more quickly. There were more shrieks from the enemy as the torturous storm of death erupted for a third time, and then again. The *Lady Prevost* was as silent as the dead, guns overturned, crew deserted below with one lone officer who, hanging over the rail and staring at them, maddened by his painful wound, screamed in torment. As if in a trance, Perry ordered the larboard guns to cease fire.

Then it came, a white cloth from the battered *Queen Charlotte.* The crew of *Niagara* cheered. The Union Jack still flew from the flagship, but Lieutenant Inglis hailed from the *Detroit,* pleading that Captain Barclay was below, badly hurt, but lucid enough to agree that the British flagship must strike. A British tar waved a white cloth on a boarding pike. The Royal Ensign was torn down from where it had been nailed to the mast.

When Perry ordered a general cease-fire, the pall of yellow-gray smoke gradually drifted away from the crippled ships. The final signal of surrender came from the brig *General Hunter;* she hauled down her colors moments later. Some aboard who had been pressed earlier into British service wanted to continue firing. But the guns remained silent. It was over.

Of the surviving officers on the British vessels, only one commander had escaped injury, the commander of the *Little Belt.* That was at 3 PM—fifteen minutes since Perry had taken command of the *Niagara.* Meanwhile, in and out of consciousness, I had recovered sufficiently on a cot that night to look over and roll into the scuppers like so much debris. No one could find me. But Parsons had stopped the blood by then; my injuries were minor compared to some.

I know that we will all remember wounds opening, bleeding to death in the wardroom, enemy cheers, shot piercing poor *Lawrence* through and through. And how you saved us, raised the flag again after getting Perry to give up the ship and take the *Niagara* into the battle, with the rising breeze to rake both sides with fresh broadsides in close action, guns trained by you. And surrounded by smoke and death, how the enemy had quickly struck, and the squadron cheered, amid the screams and groans from vanquished British.

A bizarre scene greeted us on the slippery red deck of the defeated *Detroit.* It will haunt me for the rest of my life. Barclay's mascot, a black bear, had been uninjured and was wandering among the strewn bodies, mute and dead; it slipped, covered in lifeless gore, and began licking blood from human remains.

Perry converted *Lawrence* into a hospital ship, discovering after the storm that *Detroit* and *Queen Charlotte*, had rolled their shattered masts overboard.

I must conclude my dear friend. You have been left in good hands—the very best—and I must return to Canada with Taima. Her magical abilities finally exhausted her, and now I am the one nursing her back to health. We are safe, following Perry and Harrison, at a more leisurely pace. I hope to see you and in the spring.

Most obediently yours,

Peter Hughes.

Catherine looked up at Nathan, her dark eyes burning into his.

Nathan tried not to look at Catherine's wet eyes. He had seen carnage before, but this had been different, and a hungry compassion had begun to replace the implacable enmity that had driven him.

He shuddered, thinking of Fell's Point, the oval rug with its anchor motif, the sword over the mantel—and a wood splinter entering Jack Logan's side. He remembered his fears aboard the *Lawrence*, feeling useless and helpless, not knowing whether Peter or Jack had survived. His father was gone, murdered by Fredericks while trying to save Catherine. She had been unable to give Nathan any more details concerning William's death, or what had happened to Barbara Steward, for that matter. He must find Fredericks and get some answers before killing him.

Catherine, sitting beside him, holding his hand, her eyes swimming and her gaze caressing, nodded slightly.

"You have changed," she said quietly, almost in a whisper.

"I am the same man, more or less," he croaked.

But she had seen the look of infinite sadness and guilt that would pass like a cloud before his eyes.

"What will you do now, Nathan?"

"I suppose I'll go where ordered, serve where needed," he said. "Maybe Blakeley needs another lieutenant for *Wasp*."

"What if you are needed here?" asked Catherine, with a sly look. "I have new orders for you now, sir!" she exclaimed, her dark eyes twinkling.

"Yes, ma'am?"

"Kiss me!"